MW01076276

SIMON FAYTER
AND THE EYES OF STONE

Austin J. Bailey

Copyright © 2020 by Austin J. Bailey

All rights reserved. No part of this publication may be reproduced, distributed or transmitted in any form or by any means, including photocopying, recording, or other electronic or mechanical methods, without the prior written permission of the publisher, except in the case of brief quotations embodied in critical reviews and certain other noncommercial uses permitted by copyright law. For permission requests, write to the publisher at the address below. Please contact by email.

Austin Bailey
www.austinjbailey.com
Email address: austin@austinjbailey.com

Note: This is a work of fiction. All characters, places, and incidents are a product of the author's imagination. Any resemblance to actual people, living or dead, or to businesses, companies, events, institutions, or locales is entirely coincidental.

Editing and interior book design by:
Crystal Watanabe
www.pikkoshouse.com

Printed in the United States of America

To Dad,

For all the books we read together, and still will. Also, in remembrance of Tolkien, who, like Gandalf himself on Bilbo's doorstep, began all our fantastic journeys together on that fateful day at Costco in 2001 when The Lord of the Rings Omnibus *was on sale for $11.99. I remember it like it was yesterday. Thanks, Pops.*

P.S. I still owe you twelve dollars...

Turncoat

Left

	1	2	3	4	5
A	Fish	Whisper	Curse	Forecast	Nap
B	Leap	Silver-tongue	Poet	Ninja	Hair
C	Chameleon	Breath Stink	Sponge	Headlight	Jig
D	Copy	Distraction	Summonator	Giggle	Sidestep
E	Clone	Pause	Daze	Size	Thoughts

Diagram

Right

6   7   8   9   10

S.P. Transport   ~~Epiphany Stroke~~ *Epiphany*   Transportaion   Do-Over   Bouquet

6   7   8   9   10

Strength   For Diving   Enemy   Luck   Sight

6   7   8   9   10

Juvenille   Gravity   Unfathomable   Mass   Inflation

6   7   8   9   10

Lightning   Disarm   Lie   Slick   The Strangeness

6   7   8   9   10

Travel   Path   Stash

TABLE OF CONTENTS

PROLOGUE[1]

THE SHADOWS COME

Without a family, man, alone in the world, trembles with the cold.

—Andre Maurois[2]

The sea roared in the night, its windy voice echoing through the dark cave like a monster in the throes of death.

Flint clutched the precious package to his chest as though it were a shield against the darkness. "He's late, Dad."

"Hush, Flint. He'll be here."

"But what if he *doesn't* come? What if this was all for nothing?"

"Shh! Listen."

By the light of their small candle, Flint saw his father's brows knit together in concentration. The flame danced in the sea air, sending wild lights and shadows sliding across the green walls of the cave. "What?"

---

1 Hey! I finally wrote a prologue that isn't completely pointless!
2 A lesser-known (in this country) French author who wrote many books. Among them is a 1930s middle-grade fantasy novel called *Fattypuffs and Thinifers.*

"There. Footsteps…" Flint's father took his son's small head in his hands and turned it toward the mouth of the cave. Sure enough, Flint heard the soft sound of wet boots on stone.

"Dad," Flint hissed. "Aren't his boots magic? They don't make any noise. Everyone knows that. We shouldn't hear him coming."

The old man's face paled. He snuffed out the candle, blanketing them in darkness. Flint didn't dare breathe. He strained to hear, but the soft sounds were gone.

"Kylanthus," a voice said sharply, not ten feet away, and a line of bright-red fire ripped through the dark, revealing a glowing sword. A large man held it. He was hooded and cloaked, but the flames showed a strong face beneath the cowl. He had black curly hair that framed a square jaw and dark eyes set above a nose with a chunk missing from the left side. "Maudrik?" His voice was low and raspy, like rocks sliding around the bottom of a bucket.

"Yes," Flint's father said. He was nervous. "The night is dark," he said, giving the code phrase they had agreed upon.

The man cocked his head thoughtfully. "And what will you do if I don't know the correct response to your code, Maudrik? What if I am an impostor—a member of the Shadow, come to slaughter you and your child for trying to aid me? What then?"

Maudrik took a step backward, hand flying to the hilt of his dagger. "The night is dark," he repeated.

The man sighed. "But the sun will rise."

Flint felt his father's body relax beside him. The big man's sword vanished, and the fire that had wreathed it hung in midair for a second before flicking toward the ground and settling down at their feet in a merry circle. Flint edged toward it unconsciously, extending his hands to the warmth.

The man sat back into an invisible chair of air and began warming his own fingers. He lowered his hood.

"Yes, it is me. I'm not going to hurt you. Though I do suggest that if you plan any more dangerous secret nighttime meetings in the future, you make the *other* party sit and wait in the darkness, rather than telling them to come to you. Much safer that way. Particularly if you plan to bring your children along."

His dark eyes studied Flint, then he clicked the toes of his boots together. "You're a quick thinker, lad, to notice these boots made sound where they should not. I lent my boots to a friend who needed them more than I did tonight." He glanced back at Maudrik. "You are old to have a son so young."

Maudrik wiped a strand of gray hair out of his eyes and laid a hand on the boy's shoulder. "Flint was a surprise, but a pleasant one. We lost his mother, so now he goes everywhere with me. I hope it's not a problem."

The big man studied Flint again, then noticed what the child was carrying. "Is that it?"

"Yes, Mister, uh, *Rellik*…sir." The name felt heavy in his mouth, like a word he knew he shouldn't be saying. He passed the package to his father.

Maudrik held the package out at arm's length, offering it to Rellik. It was wrapped in brown paper and bound with cord.

Rellik started to reach for the package, then stopped and folded his hands in his lap. "What is it?"

Maudrik glanced sideways at Flint, unsure of how to proceed.

"You are, among other things, a noted maker of wizard cloaks," Rellik continued. "But I already have a cloak, Maudrik. And I think you know that. I came to you because your offer intrigued me, and I'll admit, because I'm desperate for whatever aid I can get. Yet I am wary of those who act so mysteriously as you have done."

Maudrik shuffled his feet uneasily. "It's not a cloak, sir. Not exactly…"

Flint was bouncing up and down on his heels with excitement. "It's a coat! Go on, open it!"

Rellik cocked an eyebrow. "A coat?"

"A *turncoat,*" Flint corrected.

Maudrik thumped him softly on the back of the head. "Hush. What have I told you about naming things that aren't yours to name?"

Maudrik looked apologetically at Rellik. "He calls it that because of the pockets. It is a leather jacket, you see, with small pockets on the inside. The pockets have little brass turn-lock closures, hence his nickname."

"And why did you feel it was so important to give this to me?" Rellik said. "I was told that you are a serious man, Maudrik. I risked much coming to meet you here. I was

hoping you had crafted me something useful. A weapon or—"

"There are *fifty* pockets," Flint blurted, earning another cuff from his father.

Rellik, who had been massaging his temples, froze. He looked up sharply. "What?"

Maudrik nodded. "I made it years ago, sir. Decades ago, when I was a young man. It came in the old way. Premonition. Spontaneous creation. I never knew who it was for. It's powerful. Very powerful, but strange. Unlike anything I've made before or since."

The words were pouring out of Maudrik with the cathartic energy of a man who had held a secret for far too long. "I've hidden it all these years. Never guessing that—well, but then I heard of you, of what…happened. I heard the rumors, the one stone that became many. *Fifty*, they said. And then I knew. I knew that it must be for you. To help you, in some way."

Rellik was staring at the package, but whether it was wariness or hunger in his eyes, Flint could not tell. He made no move to open it. "Is my brother aware of this? Has he touched this coat, or even seen it?"

Maudrik shook his head. "No. No, of course not."

"You know what he is capable of, I presume," Rellik said. "How he can gain control over a person's mind? This is how he does it, often. He gives a gift, a harmless object. And just by touching it, you become his." His dark eyes snapped back up to meet Maudrik's. "Tell me no lies tonight, Maudrik, if you value your life. Who has seen or

touched this coat? Name everyone you can think of."

Maudrik shook his head. "No one. I mean, just me and Flint." He was sweating now, despite the chill of the cave. "I made it in a day. A single day. When I was apprenticed, long ago. I never showed it to my master. I knew what it was—a frathenoid object—a creation of pure magic. And I knew that it was for someone in particular. It frightened me, you know. I hid it and never showed it to anyone. Not even my wife." He put a hand on his son's shoulder again. "But Flint is my apprentice now. I tell him everything."

Rellik still held the older man in his gaze. Finally, he nodded, looking down. He flicked a finger, and the cord fell away in pieces. Then he tore off the paper and unfolded a dark-brown leather coat. He inspected it slowly, running his hands along the sleeves and then the lining. He closed his eyes as if listening. Then he let out a long, slow sigh of awe. "I've never seen anything like this. You spoke truly, Maudrik. Rone could not use this as a hook even if he tried. The magic in it would defy his power. What does it do?"

"I do not know," Maudrik said. "I could guess. But then, so could you."

"Yes," Rellik said. "So I could." He rose to his feet, suddenly towering over them, and removed his cloak. Then he threw the coat on. It fit him perfectly. He drew a small reddish-gold translucent stone from the pocket of his pants and slipped it into one of the small pockets sewn into the jacket's inner lining.

"Is that—" Flint began, but his father stepped on his foot, silencing him.

Rellik closed the little flap covering the top of the pocket, slipping the brass clasp over the rectangular knob. "If this does what I think it does, Maudrik, if it allows me to unite the stones, and perhaps use them together as if they were one again, then you may have just changed the fate of the universe."

Maudrik gulped. "Sir, what will happen if *he* finds them first?" His face went pale. "Forgive me. It is not my place to ask."

"And is it true that you still wield the six?" Flint chimed in. "And that you don't feel the pain?"

Maudrik hushed his son again but looked up eagerly, hoping Rellik would answer the impetuous question.

Rellik gave them a pitying look. "No," he said. "I do not feel the pain, for truly I can still touch the six branches of magic."

He held a hand palm up. From the center of his hand, a small tree sprouted as if from a seed. Flint shouted in surprise, for from his perspective, the tree was not a small thing in Rellik's hand, but life size and right in front of him. He shuffled back, but not quickly enough, and when the tree's leaves brushed the top of his head, he remembered the sound of his mother's voice on the day she died.

A sudden, unwanted rush of emotion came over him. The tree grew, then burst into flames, first blue, then red, then white. The tree began to smoke then, and when Flint

smelled it, he felt strong, as if waking from a deep and restful sleep. The next second, the tree flashed, turning to gold. It spun, ratcheting and clinking, until it was a tree no longer, but a shining tower.

As Flint stared into its mesmerizing, reflective surface, he thought he saw himself there. Yes, it was him, older, and more tired and ragged looking, but definitely him. Deep down, some part of him knew that this was no trick, but a real glimpse into the future.

A second later, the tower collapsed into a coin. Flint nearly fell forward, staring at his feet, where, to him, the tower had seemed to shrink away. He blinked, then looked up to see the coin sitting in Rellik's hand. He gasped as the coin melted back into Rellik's skin.

"That..." Maudrik whispered, gripping his son's shoulders, "is a thing I had never thought to see again."

Flint looked up and was surprised to see a tear glistening on his father's cheek.

"Listen well, son. That is the sign of mastery I once spoke to you of. The Golden Oak Tree. You felt them all, didn't you, as I did? The effects of all six branches?" Maudrik's voice was desperate, hoping beyond hope that he was not going crazy. "Name them, son."

"Physical," Flint recited automatically, "spatial, mental, dimensional, emotional, mechanical. Strong, quick, bright, seer, muse, clink."

Maudrik was crying more tears now, looking at Rellik with an expression that Flint had never seen on his father's

face before. "There is hope, then," he said. "You can bring it back to us?"

Rellik sighed. "Sit down, old man." He waved an arm, and two more invisible chairs swooped forward out of the air behind Flint and his father, buckling their knees.

"Maybe," Rellik said heavily. "Maybe is the best I can do. I'll not lie to you and tell you otherwise. My brother broke the bindings that held you to the six, and I will try to undo what he has done, but I can promise nothing. As to your other question, what will he do if he finds the stones before I do?" His face contorted, as if the prospect caused him physical pain. "We must never find out..."

Rellik stooped forward then and clapped Maudrik on the shoulder. "Thank you, my friend." He leaned in closer, so that Flint could not hear. "And be careful. The Shadows come. I will try to get you out of here safely, but after that, I cannot protect you. They will know that we have met. Even now, they are tracking you."

Maudrik paled. "B-but—" he stammered. "I took precautions."

"They will know," Rellik repeated, stepping away. "They always know."

He glanced down at the jacket then, with a curious expression, and turned the knob on the pocket he had previously placed the bloodstone in, locking the flap shut.

As the knob clicked into place, Rellik flickered and then vanished.

Flint gasped. "Where did he go?"

"I don't know," his father said.

"Did you know that would happen?"

"No. I thought…" Maudrik scratched his head. "No, I didn't know."

Flint edged closer to his father as the magical fire that Rellik left behind faded away in his absence. Presently, they were left in the dark once more.

And then the sounds came. The same *thwap thwap* of boots and stone, but this time much louder. There were more than one pair of feet coming toward them in the cave.

"Is he back already?" Flint asked, confused.

"No, son," Maudrik hissed, and he shoved Flint toward the back of the cave. He pushed him into a fissure in the rear wall of the cave, hiding him from view, and pressed something into his hands—a small white orb.

"Watch quietly," his father instructed. "If it goes badly, leave. Do not try to help me. Go home and lock down the moon. You know how. Let no one in but Rellik. Fren will guard you."

Maudrik stepped quickly away from the crack as red fire erupted through the darkness, illuminating seven black figures. The foremost figure, in whose hand the fire glowed, spoke loudly. "Maudrik, my good man. Where *has* my brother gone? I know he was here."

Maudrik straightened his back, forcing himself to stand tall despite the fear he felt. The man's voice had a horrid, inhuman quality to it that made Maudrik's stomach turn over. "I don't know. He left. Disappeared."

"So you admit to meeting him?" the man said with a

sneer. "How stupid of you." He raised his hand, and the six men behind him scattered, searching the corners of the cave. Luckily, none of them went directly for Flint's hiding place.

The man stepped closer, grabbing Maudrik's chin in a vise-like grip. "What did you give him?"

His voice echoed from the distant corners of the cave now, and Maudrik realized that he was speaking out of the mouth of each man at the same time, as though their bodies were slaves to his will.

"What did you give him? A weapon? A stone? Tell me, and I will spare your life. Where was he going? Has he found any of the bloodstones yet?"

The old man felt something then, like a block shifting into place deep within his mind. He knew that he would die. Rone would not let him go, whatever he said. He began to laugh. It rolled out of him in deep, chuckling waves, so that Rone released him with a gesture of disgust.

Rone removed the jackal's mask, revealing a soft, careworn face some years younger than his brother's, though with an unmistakable familial resemblance. He bent down to where Maudrik had fallen to the ground. Maudrik was still laughing, and Rone inspected him with a curious expression, holding the fire up to see. When he spoke, his voice came only from his own lips.

"What is it, old man? What have you seen? Are you crazy?"

"You need him so badly," Maudrik said between laughs. He was crying now too, partly from the intensity

of the laughter, and partly because he sensed the violence that was coming. "You're so desperate. You can't use them, can you? The bloodstones. You were cut off from the six, just like the rest of us, so you can't use them. You need *him* to do it for you, don't you? How do you plan on doing that?" He laughed again. "Not a very good plan. He's already won."

Then, with great speed for a man his age, Maudrik slipped a knife from his belt and lunged forward on his knees, thrusting it toward Rone's chest. Before the knife could reach its mark, however, Maudrik froze. His expression went rigid, as if he were suddenly experiencing a great internal struggle, and the knife quivered in the air, two inches from Rone's breastbone.

"Yes," Rone said with a sigh, getting to his feet again as if he was entirely untroubled by the fact that he had nearly been stabbed. "I admit that I need big brother's help. Very vexing, that. I'm not in the best position. Still, as you are learning, I can be quite...*influential* when it comes to the actions of other people." He hissed the last two words like a snake.

Maudrik was sweating. His whole body was shaking, but beyond that, he seemed entirely unable to move.

"I will find those stones," Rone said, almost to himself. "And I *will* force my brother to use them as I see fit. I will not be dependent upon his power for long. Of course, he is not so easily controlled as you are, but there are ways..."

He bent down until his face was level with the kneeling man. "You're not going to tell me what I want to know, are

you?" He bent in closer, whispering, "I can take it from you, you know."

He set the tip of his finger on the center of Maudrik's forehead, and the man's laughter halted, replaced suddenly with a howl of pain.

"Father!" Flint called from the back of the cave, slipping out of his hiding place. Two of the six men grabbed him, hauling him toward the spot where Maudrik knelt before Rone.

"How lovely!" Rone exclaimed. "A child! You brought your child with you, man? Tsk-tsk. You should have known better. What uses I could put him to! What lovely uses." He knelt down next to Maudrik's quivering form and whispered in his ear. "You know, the only thing better than torturing someone for information is making their children do it for you. Would you like to see? Go on. Speak, dog. I give you leave."

"No..." Maudrik breathed. "Please, no... He's just a boy."

"Give me what I want to know, then!" He placed his finger on Maudrik's forehead once again. This time, the old man didn't scream. His body went rigid, then limp.

"A coat," Rone said, his voice shaking with rage. "A tool to unite the stones? This is what you have given him?"

Maudrik's eyes rolled, and he would have toppled over with exhaustion, but Rone's eyes flashed, and the old man's body went rigid once more. "You look tired, my friend," he said gently.

The sound of that voice made Flint's heart sink.

"It must have been a great deal of work to make such a powerful tool for my brother. Here, eat something." He held up the handful of fire.

"No!" Flint cried, writhing in the arms of his captors.

"Open your mouth," Rone commanded, and the old man's mouth dropped open.

Rone shoved the fire in, and the old man slumped to the ground, shaking and smoking.

"No!" Flint screamed again. He jumped and kicked, and one of the men holding him let go. He ran toward where his father lay but stopped when Rone stood and turned toward him.

Rone considered the child for a moment without speaking, then sighed and slowly replaced his mask. "It is a terrible tragedy for a boy to grow up fatherless. I could never let that happen." He opened his hand, and the fire appeared again. He took a step toward Flint.

"No!" Flint said. He looked from Rone to his father and back again, then reached into his pocket and withdrew the small white orb.

"Stop!" Rone shouted.

Three of the men grabbed Flint, hauling him into the air between them. Beyond that, Flint suddenly lost control of his body, his mind, seeing only the dark eyes of Rone, full of malice.

But Flint had already activated the sphere. The *safe house* as his father called it—one of their secret inventions. A perfect sphere of white fire erupted around him, severing everything it touched, including several inches

of the cave's stone floor and the arms of his would-be captors. They screamed and fell back, and Flint stared at Rone through the white dome of fire. The malice was still there, but the control was gone. A second later, the sphere shrank to the size of a fist, and Flint shrank along with it. Then the white ball exploded, and the child was gone.

Rone walked slowly from the cave with his two surviving followers in tow. His mind was elsewhere, searching out the thoughts and intentions of his brother, pondering what this new coat might mean for his plans.

He did not hear the low groans of the fallen wizards as he left them to be swallowed by the rising tide. Nor did he think much again of Maudrik's child, or the hate in the boy's eyes, or the things his father might have taught him, or the fact that children, when injured very deeply, often grow up to become quite dangerous.

1

ICE MOON

*Heroes need monsters to establish their heroic credentials. You
need something scary to overcome.*

—Margaret Atwood

I stared into the glowing red eyes of a lion and felt a fear
that I had never known. The lion was made of stone,
yet the eyes held a living menace. I tore my gaze away and
glanced down to discover that I was floating in the air. I
drifted back to the stone floor and looked around.

Above me, the lion's eyes lit the cave, and the pool of
water that filled it, with a mean red light. The arch stood
on two pillars that rose out of the water. The only other
item of note in the cave hung suspended in the air below
the arch. It was a sword. *My* sword. Kylanthus. It hung
there, tip down, as if waiting for me. As I watched it, the
blade burst into flame, and the water over which it hung
began to bubble.

"Wake up, genius. It's morning."

Tessa's soft hands shook me awake, and I stared up
into her eyes. They glistened like the radiant dawn,
reminding me at once of childhood, and sunshine, and
popsicles, and—

"I said, wake up!" Tessa said, slapping me across the face.

"Ouch! I'm up! I'm up! See how my eyes are open?"

"Oh, sorry," she said, without the slightest hint of contrition. "Thought you were still dreaming. You were all glazed over. Anyway, I'm off to relieve Hawk. You're on breakfast duty. *Don't* mess up my eggs again, or I *will* kill you, fate of the universe notwithstanding." With that, Tessa sauntered out of our igloo.

The dome of ice that we had come to call home since landing on the mysterious snow-covered moon was just large enough to sleep the five of us.[3] We could have made it even bigger with the help of Hawk's magic, but I insisted that a smaller igloo would be easier to heat, and more stable, and since I (being the only member of our intrepid crew who had ever read the special Eskimo edition of *National Geographic*) was the reigning expert on igloo architecture—not to mention the most important and powerful wizard in the world (allegedly)—the others deferred to me.

I rose and stretched, noting the hulking, hairy form of Drake across from me. As usual, he sat hunched on the edge of his bed, staring into the empty eyes of Rone's golden jackal mask. He had managed to hold on to it

---

3 Technically there were six of us. I have a super powerful dragon who lives in my boot, but being one of the last remaining members of a strange and ancient race with a mysterious relationship to magic, *and* being the standoffish frustration of a friend that he is, we usually don't count him, or count *on* him. He is really useful in a pinch, but only if he is in the mood to save my life, which isn't very often.

since the arena, and now, since he had long since lost his backpack and the mini library he kept inside it, he was reduced to staring at the mask for inspiration.

I cleared my throat. Ever since Drake experienced his kulraka and transformed from the puny, prepubescent minotaur wimp that we all loved into a massive, hulking beast, he had been a bit moody; I didn't like interrupting his train of thought without a bit of preamble. "Morning, buddy," I said brightly, moving to stoke the small cook fire in the center of the igloo. "Have you thought of a way out of our predicament yet?"

"No," he said. His voice was deeper now. Parts of him were the same old Drake. Some parts…

"Well," I said, propping up the long flat stone that we used as a griddle, "I wouldn't worry. Probably not a challenge that we can think our way out of."

Drake snorted. "Thinking certainly had nothing to do with getting *into* it."

"Hey," I said, brandishing a spotted purple egg at him before cracking it over the stone. "That hurts, man. I'm a genius, remember? I knew exactly what I was doing bringing us here to this, uh…"

"Deserted, uninhabitable, brutal, frozen wasteland?"

"Well." I cleared my throat. "It's not uninhabitable. *We're* inhabiting it, aren't we?"

"Yeah, yeah," he said, adjusting himself on the too-small bunk. "For now. But you have to admit, you were flying by the seat of your pants when you brought us here."

I cracked another egg. "Yeah, but *you* have to admit, that usually works for me."

He grunted. "Usually." He reached around to scratch his hairy back, and his bunk collapsed beneath him with a sound like a tripping rhinoceros. "Ah, fish scales!" he swore, climbing to his feet and kicking the broken bunk. He had to duck to avoid the low ceiling.

"Why don't you just ask Hawk to magic you up a bigger bed?" I asked.

Drake generally broke his bunk within a matter of hours. Actually, the fact that it had survived through the night might have been some kind of record.

"We barely fit in this dinky snow shack as it is." Drake growled. "Plus, you know as well as I do that Hawk can only recreate things he has seen in real life. Obviously he's never seen a minotaur bed."

It was true, and of course, I did know this. Our little igloo was, in all respects, lavishly furnished, considering that we landed in this frozen wasteland with nothing but the clothes on our backs. Hawk was a powerful wizard, but he was a Quick, not a Bright or a Muse, so his magical fabrications weren't the best in the world, nor did they last very long. He had to recreate most of them every day or so—work that was draining for him. Doing magic took energy, and we weren't exactly eating like kings.

"Do minotaurs *have* beds?" I asked, cracking the last egg.

Drake blinked at me. "Of course we have beds. Simon, we're not barbarians." As he said this, he opened

a large wooden box that Hawk had fashioned for him and scooped out a handful of dirt, then mixed about half of it with bulbous white spiders. He deposited the whole thing in his mouth and licked his lips.

"Right," I said. "Forgot. Are you sure those things aren't, you know...poisonous?"

Drake shrugged his massive shoulders beneath his deep-blue sleeveless cloak, which he had recently adjusted to fit his newly enlarged body. "Don't know. Tastes good enough, and I haven't died yet, have I? Say, you want me to chop some of these up and throw them in with the eggs? I can spare some."

"Nah, thanks, Drake. Tessa's on a rampage. Might not appreciate the gesture."

"She did sound angry," Drake said. "Probably hasn't forgiven you for chopping her legs off without her permission, destroying an ancient civilization, and killing a bunch of our friends."

I shook my head and began to scramble the eggs. "Girls..."

"Yeah," he echoed, gazing off into some memory. "Girls..."

I stopped scrambling, lost in my own memories of the recent horror. That dragon coming down from the sky like the nightmare of some angry god. The fire. The screams. The city burning. "I *am* sorry, Drake. Really sorry. You know that, right?" As soon as the words were out of my mouth, the codex around my neck flushed

with warmth.[4] We had not talked about it yet, he and I. My adventure in the ancient city of Tarinea had led not only to the destruction of the greatest wealth of magical knowledge and culture in history, but also to the death of a girl Drake had taken a liking to. Even if she had survived the destruction of the city, we left her a thousand years in the past when I brought Drake back to the present, so she was still just as dead today. I had basically killed her either way, simply by leaving.[5]

He snapped out of his memory, glancing at me in surprise. "I know that, Simon. I mean, it's not your fault. We all knew Tarinea was destroyed. Technically, we had already done it long before we even got there, so we didn't really have a choice."

I pondered the weirdly circular logic of his words. Several arguments came to mind about why he might be wrong, but I kept them to myself.

"Are you burning breakfast again, Simon Fayter?" Hawk's voice barked the accusation from the doorway. The silver bird that was his namesake flew from his shoulder and landed on Drake's splintered bed, picking up a piece of egg from the stone mid-flight.

"Ahh," Hawk said, following her movements. "I see

---

4 Remember the codex? It has my code inscribed on it (I will be my best self. I will honor my word. I will help those I can. I will never give up.), and it stores up magical extra energy from the Zohar when I keep my code. In this particular case, I was being my best self by apologizing.
5 Worst friend ever.

you've finished breaking in your new bed. Shall I make you another one, or should I fashion you a big sturdy rock to sleep on this time?"

Drake chuckled. "Not a bad idea."

"Probably suits the new you better," I added.

"Oh!" Hawk said, glancing back and forth between us. "Are you two speaking again? Drake, did Simon finally apologize for killing your girlfriend?"

"She wasn't my girlfriend," Drake said.

"Technically, we don't know if I killed her," I said.

"Splendid!" Hawk said, leaning in to take the wooden cooking stick from me. "Speaking of your penchant[6] for destroying things, why don't you back away from breakfast, eh? Nice and slow. That's it. Give me that stick. Ah…" He prodded the eggs sadly. "You had better get out of here before Tessa sees these."

"Scouting again?" I asked.

He nodded. "I scouted another two hours to the southwest this morning and found nothing. You two should pick up where you left off yesterday. Be careful on the ice floes, and don't be gone past noon."

"You ready?" I asked Drake, scooping up a handful of scrambled eggs. I threw the whole lot in my mouth, buttoned my turncoat up, and turned the collar up to guard against the cold that was waiting. "I'm feeling lucky today."

---

6 Penchant (pronounced just like it looks, or, if you want to sound smart and Frenchy, *paw-shaw*, with nasally sounds after the w's) means a tendency toward certain behavior.

"You've said that every day." Drake sighed. "Don't you keep yourself lucky all the time now that you found the knob that controls it?"

"Sure," I said. "But just think, we've been here for eight days, and so far we've nearly died of exposure, starvation, and drowning."

"Your point?" Drake said, pulling aside the door flap and unleashing the cold. Kestra flew onto his shoulder as he left. On Hawk's orders, she accompanied us whenever we went out, in case she had to go quickly and fetch help for us.

"My point is," I said, clapping his big hairy back, "just think about how bad off we'd be if I were unlucky!"

Drake and I stared out over yet another frozen ice floe. As usual, we didn't see much. "Is that a ridge on the other side?" I asked, squinting.

"Maybe," Drake grunted. "I suspect we will find out tomorrow."

"Nah, let's go have a look right now."

"No way! It'll take us an hour to cross that floe. Hawk said to be back at noon."

"Do you see that?"

"See what?" Drake said, following my gaze.

"That tall thing, there, in the middle of the ice."

"Tree?"

I shook my head. "I think it's a man."

"What? Nah… Wait! Come back, Simon!"

But I was already sliding down the bank toward the ice. I hit it and slid out, getting to my feet slowly. Walking on ice still didn't feel natural. Hawk had showed us how to do it—short, smooth steps, like you weren't really trying to get anywhere at all. It took forever to walk like that, but there was nothing else for it.

I heard a thud behind me as Drake struck the ice. "Atta boy, Drake," I said without turning around. "Try not to fall too much this time." There was a muffled thud behind me, and I grinned, still moving forward.

"It's these boots," he complained.

Thud.

"It's not my fault!" he said, getting to his feet again. Then he began grumbling to himself. "*Untrippable*, Burgess said. *Won't fall down*, Burgess said.[7] Apparently that doesn't apply to ice."

Thud.

I sighed, turning slowly, careful not to shift my balance and slip. "Drake, maybe you should just wait there while I investigate the frozen man."

"It's a *tree*!" he insisted, gesturing wildly.

Thud.

"Gah! Just try A8 again, will you? Maybe we'll get lucky."

The turncoat knob he was referring to summoned a

---

7 Burgess was the magical shoemaker at Skelligard, in case you forgot.

mode of transportation out of thin air. Trouble was, it wasn't always applicable to the situation. On one day, it had actually conjured up a pair of ice-climbing crampons, but Tessa had confiscated those almost immediately. On our subsequent excursions, the knob had failed us completely, producing a unicycle (with a flat tire), a Formula One car (with no fuel), and a rope swing. And that was just a sampling.

I shrugged but did as he said, gripping the A8 knob with my mind and giving it a turn. A bright-pink pogo stick appeared, complete with glittering streamers.

"Perfect!" I said, tossing it to Drake. "Here you go."

"What is it?" he asked eagerly, reaching out to catch it. *Thud.*

"Simon, wait! How does this work? Simon! Wait for me!"

Drake quickly discovered that if he sat down, he could use the pogo stick to push himself along. It reminded me of a Venetian gondolier, using his pole to push his little boat of tourists around a canal, except there was no little Italian guy, or pole, or canal, just my big hairy half-human friend, a pink pogo stick, and his now frozen keister.

"Holy halibut," Drake said,[8] coasting to a stop beside me. "It's *not* a tree."

"I told you." We were within several yards of the frozen figure now, and it was clearly a man of some sort, except…

"He's huge!" Drake said, and he was right. Easily nine

---

8 You know it's serious when Drake takes the name of a fish in vain.

feet tall—just a bit taller than Drake if he were standing up. Not only that, but he didn't really have the lines of a human man. His body was thick but graceful, like some futuristic concept-car version of a human body.

"He doesn't have any clothes on!" Drake said suddenly. "No wonder he froze to death!"

"How can you tell?" I said. "The ice is so thick."

"I don't think that's ice, Simon…"

I cocked my head. He was right. What I had initially taken for a thick layer of ice, hiding a body somewhere inside, didn't seem to be hiding anything. It was transparent all the way through. What's more, the man wasn't necessarily a man at all. More of an androgynous[9] form. The only detailed part of the body was the face, which was oval in shape and had two almond-shaped eyes, closed, as if in sleep.

"It's just a sculpture," I said, relaxing. "But who could have made it?"

"Someone!" Drake crowed. "Someone made it! We're not alone on this frozen moon after all!"

I glanced around, half expecting to see the mysterious sculptor pop out of the ice floe and present himself.

"Huh," Drake said, walking around behind the sculpture and running his muscled hand over the sculpture's head. "It's so smooth. Ice would be really beautiful if it wasn't so cold and slippery."

"It tastes good too," I said.

---

9 Not specifically masculine or feminine.

"Really?" Drake, of course, had never so much as seen ice in the outdoors before, being from a much warmer climate.

"Sure. Go ahead. Give it a lick."

Drake extended his tongue and leaned in toward the sculpture's elbow cautiously. Before he could make contact, however, the ice man's eyes snapped open, and his torso rotated 180 degrees, smooth and machinelike, to face Drake.

"Go away," it said. Its voice was deep and slow.

"Wa—WAHAAHAA!" Drake screeched, flinging the pogo stick into the air. "I don't think it's a sculpture, Simon!"

The pogo stick landed point down on the ice several feet away and bounced back into the air. The ice man shot it a cold look. By which I mean, little bullet-shaped ice cubes shot out of his creepy black eyes at like 900 miles per hour and blasted the pogo stick out of the air.

"Dang!" I said, impressed. "If looks could kill, eh, Drake?"

But Drake had fallen down again and was scrabbling[10] away across the ice. Kestra the hawk left my shoulder and darted away toward her master.

It would be a couple minutes before he arrived.

The ice man, satisfied that Drake was not a threat,

---

10 To scratch or grope around with your fingers to find or hold onto something. Not to be confused with *scrambling*, which means to move with urgency or panic, or to move over steep terrain with the help of your hands.

turned his creepy eyes on me. They looked empty. Lifeless. "Go away," he repeated.

"Nah," I said, spreading my hands wide. "I'm in the mood to chat. Marooned on an ice moon and all that… Who are you?"

"I am Fren. Guardian of the House of Grievs. There is nothing here for you to find. Go away."

I cocked an eyebrow, circling around the ice man so that we were facing each other diagonally rather than straight on. "Really? If there's nothing here, then what are you protecting, Fren, Guardian of the House of Grievs?"

The ice man's eyes narrowed in displeasure.

"Ah," I said. "I see you are unused to sparring with a wit as keen as mine. Don't feel bad. Perhaps we could—"

The ice man's chest sprouted a foot-long ice spike, which rocketed toward me like a surface-to-air missile.[11]

Of course, I had been expecting something like this and turned D5 (*Sidestep*) just in time to avoid catastrophic[12] exenteration.[13] I reappeared three strides to the left and turned B4 (*Ninja*) just as ice man turned toward me and raised an arm. I darted inside his reach with a series of lightning-fast blows: right forearm strike to the bicep,

---

11 Yeah, I know. I wasn't in the air, so it was really more like a shoulder-launched, antitank rocket-propelled grenade. You nerd, you. Stop playing so many video games!

12 Really bad.

13 To disembowel or eviscerate. In medicine, to surgically remove an entire organ. I know what you're thinking: when would disembowelment *not* be catastrophic?

elbow to solar plexus, fist to groin and nose. Side thrust kick to the hip, creating distance.

The ice man remained completely unmoved. Then he slapped me across the back with an open palm, and I went flying like a slice of bad salami from Tessa's sandwich. He lunged toward me with a skull-crushing stomp, but I rolled smoothly away and flipped onto my feet.

Then my five seconds of magical fighting skills wore off, and I squealed, nursing my right forearm, fist, and elbow. Dang! Ice is really hard. Forgot about that…

He reached for me, seizing me by the throat in a vise-like grip.

"Wow, dude!" I rasped. "You put the ice in *vise*." Then I turned D6 (*Lightning*), and a lightning bolt flashed down from the sky and struck his head (which was a mere two feet from *my* head, by the way),[14] blowing it clean off.

Of course, another head melted out of the ice man's torso a second later, hardening into shape.

"Figures," I muttered. I turned D7 (*Disarm*), and his arms dropped off, releasing my throat and shattering against the ground.

"Ha!" I crowed. "Get it? I dis*armed* you! Grow *those* back, you big— Oh, squid farts…"

His arms had already grown back. I bounded away, sliding to my knees on the ice, and he followed with slow, steady steps.

I spun around at the end of my slide, leaping to my

---

14 PROFESSIONAL WIZARD. DO NOT TRY THIS AT HOME.

feet once more. He came at me, then stopped as a small rock bounced off the back of his head. He looked around curiously to where Drake was standing, sling raised. Another rock struck him dead center[15] in the nose. He took a half step backward, felt at his nose, then sneezed in Drake's direction, spraying the air with a thousand razor-sharp shards of ice.

"Gah!" Drake said, falling down again and shielding his face. "That was close."

"Thanks, buddy," I called. "But I think you'll need some bigger rocks to hurt this guy."

"Bigger?" Drake said, sitting up. "That's it! Simon, get bigger!"

The ice man turned back toward me and raised both fists, which were transforming into spikes.

"Huh," I said. It wasn't a bad idea. I turned E4 (*Size*) and rocketed upward. Twenty feet tall now, I looked down on the ice man, who barely came up to my waist. I kicked him and subsequently grabbed my toe, hopping on one foot like a giant wounded toddler.[16]

---

15 Drake was deadly with that sling now, as he could control the trajectory of the stones with his mind. Philistines beware.

16 In case you were wondering, this is where the "fantasy" bit comes into the story. While *most* of this autobiography is very honest and trustworthy, I do have to add in little fake moments like this to make myself appear more flawed and loveable. If I presented you with a 100% accurate picture of my cold, calculated genius, you average people just wouldn't relate to me. It's embarrassing, but my editor insists on this. Therefore, I bring you the giant silly hopping wizard boy—*Simon Fayter on Ice.*

The ice man tilted his head back, looking up at me curiously. I turned C9 (*Mass*) and felt my body become exponentially denser. I kicked the ice man again, and he sailed away from me like Barbie from a baseball bat,[17] his whole body cracking down the middle in several places.

"Ha!" I shouted, my thunderous voice shaking the air.

"Nice!" Drake shouted up. "Just be careful of—"

I took a step forward, and the ice cracked beneath me.

"—that," Drake finished.

"Rats," I said, sinking down to my waist. "EEEYOWZERS, that's cold!"

"Watch out!" Drake cried.

I glanced up to see Ice Man sprinting back toward me, and I hopped out of the water to meet him. The ice must have been thicker here, because it didn't break again.

As he neared, Ice Man grew, sucking ice out of the glacier into his legs, his arms doubling in size so that we were evenly matched again. He raised his right arm, and a twenty-foot-long sword burst forward into his hand, sharp edge glistening.

"Watch out!" Drake shouted. "He's got a sword!"

"Yes, thank you. I can see that." In a last-ditch effort to avoid a duel, I turned E1 (*Clone*) and took my giant dumb clone by both hands, swinging him around in a wide arc like a club. Ice Man however, was *not* bowled over by the impact of my dumb clone hitting him. Rather,

---

17 If you just gasped in horror, you are probably a nine-year-old girl. Relax! It's just an expression.

he cut through Dumb Me with an expert stroke, dividing the giant body in two and spraying the ice with several gallons of pink, sparkly insides (which, oddly enough, smelled like bubble gum). Giant Dumb Me's legs sailed away, and I dropped the top half in surprise.

"Ouch," he rumbled, before his eyes closed for good.

"Yuck!" Drake shouted, raising two sparkly pink-stained arms in disgust several yards away. "What were you thinking? I can't believe you just did that! Nobody likes unexpected gore and violence! That was COMPLETELY inappro—"

"Sorry!" I said. "Little busy here." As the words came out of my mouth, I spun sideways, avoiding a sudden thrust from the giant ice blade.

I drew Kylanthus from my back. "I was trying to avoid this, Popsicle Boy!" I said coldly. "I was *trying* to keep you alive so that we could talk…"

Ice Man scowled, then lashed out at me with a series of quick blows that I barely parried. He was quick. Deadly quick. He growled, and I growled too—the name of my sword. Kylanthus erupted into magical fire. I lashed out, severing Ice Man's left arm, which hit the ground and shattered as before.

This time, it did not grow back.

"Magic fire," I said. "And you're made of *ice*." I raised an eyebrow. "See the problem?"

He froze.[18]

---

18 I mean, more than usual…

"Can we talk *now*?" I said.

Ice Man was still staring at Kylanthus. His expression looked thoughtful, and he turned it on me, scanning my face as if he had only just noticed that I had one.

At that moment, there was a giant boom from across the glacier. I turned to see Hawk barreling over the frozen ridge, rocketing through the air with blue fire streaming out of his boots. He was moving faster than seemed possible, as he often did, and a split second later he landed on the ice beside me, the fire from his boots springing out like a giant spinning lasso, encircling me and Ice Man in a flaming vortex. Kestra dropped down into the fire circle from above. She was magically enlarged, as I had seen her once before, and Tessa was riding on her shoulders, the Tike holding on to her talons as if hang gliding. They both dropped onto the ice.

The Tike drew her knives but seemed unsure what she should do with them against a giant ice man. Tessa landed and rolled toward him. She had what looked like a silver pen in her hand—her cram cudgel—which became a four-foot-long silver bat when she flicked it. She swung it four times in quick succession, utilizing her magically enhanced strength as she summersaulted around Ice Man, cracking the ice in a circle at his feet. The circle of ice upon which he stood teetered, and he lurched, trying to balance.

"Surrender, sir," Hawk said.

I flicked Kylanthus, cutting Ice Man's sword in half, then held my blade to his throat.

He glanced down at the blade, then back up at me. The corners of his mouth broke into a wide grin, and then he closed his eyes.

And melted.

It didn't take long. One second he was there, the next he was splashing down, down, and gone.

"Where did he go?" Tessa shrieked, turning around and kicking water off of her boots. "Get him, Simon!"

"Sure," I said. "I'll just scoop up the puddle and stab it…" I turned the appropriate knobs again and returned to my normal size to find Tessa glaring at me.

"What?" I said. "We had him. I made sure the fight lasted long enough for you to get here so we could take him together and all that, just like we discussed, in the *event that we meet a dangerous creature while exploring.* It's not my fault that he can turn into a puddle."

Tessa was about to launch into a criticism of my actions, but Hawk held up a hand. "Enough, you two. Simon, you fought well. Tessa, we did what we could. This…*thing,* if I am not mistaken, is a bit of very old, very powerful magic. A Lathspell. Guardian spirit, from the old days. Bad news for us. Few now remain, and they are very dangerous when awakened. Invulnerable to most types of magic, you know…"

"Most types," I said, looking down at Kylanthus, which was still wreathed in flames.

"Indeed," Hawk said, following my gaze. "It is good to know that we have a weapon to use on it. Though I fear it is a much more competent foe than it made itself out to be

just now. It left by choice, and will surely return."

"Return?" Drake said, sliding up beside us.

"Oh, yes," Hawk said. "You have simply *awakened* it. It perceives us as a threat now, and it will not rest until we are destroyed. Or its master calls it off."

"So it does have a master?" Tessa said. "You don't think it—he—whatever—was just marooned here or something?"

Hawk rolled his shoulders, and Kestra alighted on the left one, restored to her normal size. He reached up and petted the bird unconsciously. "I think not. Such a beast is too great a treasure to lightly leave behind. It is more probable that this moon serves as the secret hideout of some powerful old wizard family, and the Lathspell guards it. Still…" His brows knit together, as if in deep memory. "It has been long since I knew of a family that still owned a Lathspell. Very long ago. Whose could this be, I wonder?" He glanced back up at the group, then straightened his cloak. "It's possible that we have stumbled into some danger here, friends."

"I'm shocked," Drake said dryly.

"Hmm, yes. Come on. Let's get back to base. The night will tell us our future, to be sure. I have eggs roasting on the fire, and some of those spiders, and some rather delicious-looking dirt besides. We might as well enjoy our supper."

"Especially if it might be our last," I said brightly.

The Tike shot me a dark glance as she sheathed her knives. "Black luck to draw blades without using them,"

she said, spitting on the ice. "And I do not like this new foe. Give me something with flesh that I can slay with skill and iron."

I patted her well-muscled back. "There, there, Tike. We'll find you something to kill later on."

"I'm just glad we're not alone on this giant ice cube," Tessa said.

"Even if our only company is a magical beast that wants to kill us?" I said.

She shrugged and flashed a grin that made me, against my better judgment, go slightly weak at the knees. "Beggars can't be choosers."

2
PREMONITIONS

Your vision will become clear only when you can look into your own heart. Who looks outside, dreams; who looks inside, awakes.

—Carl Jung[19]

I stared into the glowing red eyes of a lion and felt a fear that I had never known. The lion was made of stone, yet the eyes held a living menace. It looked down from its place in the top of a stone arch, casting a pale red light across the water of an otherwise dark cave. Beneath the arch, Kylanthus hung in the air, tip down and wreathed in red fire, beckoning me to pick it up.

A light flashed, and the scene changed. Tessa laughed down at me from far above, her voice wrong—evil. "We'll leave you here to consider," she said. "There are worms in the walls, I am told. If you dig a little. Just in case you get hungry."

The light flashed again. I held the Tike in my arms. Her black jacket was slick with blood. "Don't die," I said. "You can't."

---

19 A famous Swiss psychoanalyst and one of the principal influencers of modern psychology.

"Don't worry," she replied, smiling sadly. "This isn't what it looks like. He'll have to kill me more than once to keep me from protecting you." And then she breathed her last in a soft, inhuman rattle, and her eyes went still.

Flash.

I saw the Tike, alive once more, engaged in hand-to-hand combat with a dozen young wizards, throwing fire. They stood on a turreted stone wall suspended high above a dark abyss.

Flash.

The boy with coal-black eyes, dying to save me.

Flash.

Skelligard in flames.

"Simon, pass the poker, would you?"

I gesticulated wildly, startled as my mind lurched back into reality. In so doing, I threw the pointy stick— which we used as a poker—directly at Hawk's face. The Tike reached through the flickering flames of our small campfire and snatched it out of the air just before it impaled him. My mentor did not even blink. "Are you all right, Simon?"

"Need a nap?" Tessa said.

"I'm fine."

"You were standing there staring into space, dude," Drake said.

"I'm fine."

"Was this the first time, or have there been others?" Hawk asked. All eyes turned toward him. Nobody knew

what he was talking about—except me, of course. I tried to pretend I didn't, though.

"Huh?"

"Do you remember why I became your sponsor when you first came to Skelligard?" Hawk asked.

"Because no one else would?" Drake said.

"Because you're a sucker for punishment?" Tessa said.

"Because you had a momentary lapse in judgment?" the Tike asked.

"Thanks, guys," I said.

Hawk cleared his throat. "Because I am the foremost authority on the history of Rellik the Seer. The *Seer*, Simon." He raised an eyebrow and continued in a tone of measured patience. "The look that just crossed your face is one I have seen before on Gladstone's face, for he, too, is a Seer. What did *you* see, Simon? And how long has it been going on? You are not a Seer exclusively, but you can touch that branch of magic, and it appears to be revealing itself."

"Fine!" I said, getting to my feet. There wasn't much space inside the igloo with all of us, but I paced back and forth in front of the little fire. "It's the second time. Last time, I was asleep. I see things. Some of it has already happened, some of it hasn't yet, but I think it will. Maybe. Or it might just be random. I don't know what's going on."

"It is not random," Hawk said. "That much is for certain. If it is like other Seers, than you are seeing possible, or probable futures, as well as their seed points in the past."

"I don't get it," Tessa said. "Why is Hero Boy having visions *now*?"

"That's *Mr.* Hero Boy," I corrected.

She winked at me.

If the others had noticed our awkward and not-so-subtle flirting over the last few days, they had been kind enough not to let on (except for the Tike, who inevitably rolled her eyes). The fact was, something had shifted between Tessa and me after our day together in the turncoat. *She* wasn't ready to admit it, of course, but I could tell she was feeling it too.

During the past week on the ice cube, her usual brusque sarcasm had been punctuated by periods of downright *pleasantness*. We were both trying to come to grips with the change. The two of us had by now, of course, recounted the tale of our adventure to the others. I left out a couple of the more personal things that Xerith had said to me, but I gave them the gist of it, and we were careful to inform them of the things we had learned about the turncoat.

"Fine, then," Tessa went on. "I don't get why *Mr.* Hero Boy is having visions now."

Hawk held up a finger. "Remember, our Simon, being unbroken, can touch all six branches of magic, and therefore may manifest the powers of any of them. Did you do it on purpose, Simon, or…"

"By accident, as usual," I said.

Hawk tried his best not to look disappointed but failed. My lessons with him had continued, of course. Rain or

shine, ice moon or no ice moon, full stomachs or empty, he spent a couple hours each day attempting to teach me how to touch my powers the way normal wizards did, but to no avail. He insisted that a wizard's connection to magic flowed from his seat of power—which was somewhere in the gut—and that to "open the door" for power to flow, all you had to do was focus your attention there. Same old shpeel,[20] and totally unhelpful.

In my defense, I *was* now highly adept at using the turncoat. I could turn the knobs with my mind almost effortlessly now—which really sped up my reaction time in difficult situations—and I did often feel a little tug in my gut when I touched magic through the turncoat. However, I remained unable to repeat what I had done all those long days ago when I had touched the magic and called the Midnight Blue (magic megafire) without the help of the turncoat.

The others insisted upon hearing about my vision, and so I told them. Mind you, I left out the part about Tessa being an evil prison warden. And the stuff about the Tike dying, obviously. Vision or no vision, that's just not polite campfire conversation. The part about Skelligard going up

---

20 This is an incorrect spelling of the word, "spiel" which means "a long thing you say which other people don't really want to hear (like this footnote)." In case you were wondering, I have spelled it incorrectly just to mess with you. Also to see how many angry letters I get from readers, accusing me of not knowing how to spell. This way I can write them angry replies about how they don't know how to read footnotes. Childish? Perhaps. But it's the only way I get fan mail...

in flames seemed to bother Hawk the most.

"What?" I asked as he shifted uncomfortably.

He gave a deep sigh. "Gladstone has often maintained that Rone will someday attack the school. To that effect, great precautions have been taken to guard the children there. However, hearing you confirm his visions with your own makes it feel…"

"Inevitable?" Drake offered.

I shivered at the memory of the school burning. What a horrible place for a battle, if that was indeed what the vision meant. All those children…

"Well," the Tike said, snapping us out of our dark thoughts. She was leaning against the door, keeping watch over the night. "Are we going to set a trap for this Lathspell or wait for him to kill us in our sleep?"

Hawk was about to respond but stopped short. His hand went to his chest.

"What?" I asked, and then I began to feel it too. My chest was vibrating, buzzing. My *codex*, I realized. "What's going on?"

"Festering fish spit!" Hawk swore. "Close your eyes, Simon! Whatever you do, don't—"

Of *course* I didn't hear him finish that sentence. There was a flash of light, and he was gone. My codex was vibrating more strongly now. I gripped it under my shirt, and it went suddenly hot. There was a sound like thunder, and, not for the first time in my life, I felt myself being pulled through space and time, squished into the size of a pancake.

With a blinding blast of light, I emerged on the other side. I was sitting on the floor, leaning against something hard. The air smelled like mothballs. I blinked and blinked, but the light from a moment before had blinded me. All I could see were twirling pinpricks of color.

"Hello?" I said hoarsely, feeling through the empty air. "Hawk? Is anyone there?"

"Great," Hawk whispered somewhere beside me. "He's been blinded."

"You didn't tell him to close his eyes?" The voice was panicked, if you can tell that from a whisper.

"Of course I did. He doesn't listen."

"Hey, Hawk. And, uh…whoever else is here, how long am I going to see these sparkly lights?"

"Two or three minutes," Hawk said.

"At *least*," the other voice said. "Sorry. I didn't know it would be you who came when I called. I just saw him and panicked."

"Tinnay?" I said. Though I had only met her a couple times, I thought I recognized the voice of Hawk's former pupil. She was a member of the Circle of Eight. "Is that you? How did you bring us here?"

"Yeah, it's— What do you mean how did I bring you here? Hawk, didn't you tell him how the codexes work?"

"Of course not," Hawk said. "I didn't want him panicking in a tight situation and summoning the entire Circle of Eight to his side, to the detriment of the world elsewhere."

"*What* are you talking about?" I demanded.

"Shh!" Tinnay hissed. I imagined her youthful, pretty face twisted with fear for reasons that I still didn't understand.

"The codexes connect us," Hawk rattled off briskly, clearly annoyed at being forced to give me information before he was ready. "Members of the Circle. Because we all carry bloodstones, we can call on each other for help. No doubt you've heard stories about how we appear when needed."

"Well, that's nice to know," I said, trying to make my voice drip with disdain. Hawk had some nerve keeping *that* from me. Who did he think I was? Some *kid*?

"Shh!" Tinnay repeated, barely loud enough for me to hear. "He's *here*." I felt her small hand clamp shut over my mouth then, and she whispered again. "Don't even breathe. He's coming up the stairs."

Sure enough, as I watched the sparkling swirls of light dance before me, I heard the faint squeaking of stairs on the other side of the wall against which I was leaning. After it had come and gone, she released me.

"Tinnay," Hawk asked, voice flat. "Is Rone in this house?"

She must have nodded, because Hawk cursed again. "What are we doing hiding in a closet?"

"I thought it would be better for two or three knights of the Circle to pop out and take him by surprise than one to die before him alone." She sounded defensive.

Hawk grunted, and I heard the closet door creak open. "Where are we?"

"Alabama," Tinnay said. "Home of Charles Simpson. Skelligard candidate, turns thirteen tomorrow. We were successful in keeping him off the map until this afternoon. Kid had an episode that made the local news, and someone must have seen it. Bloodhounds arrived in town a couple hours later and sniffed him out."

As she spoke, I remembered my own "episodes" as a child. Moments of magical growing pains or some such, when my powers would flare. Of course, mine happened pretty much every day, so I figured this kid had it easy. Still…I thought of him sleeping peacefully in his bed with Rone bearing down on him and shivered.

"Backup?" Hawk asked.

"No. Safe house was attacked simultaneously."

Hawk pulled me to my feet. "See anything yet?"

"Depends. Are you wearing a revolving pink sparkler hat?"

"Hmm… You stay behind in the closet."

"What? You don't think I can take on the most powerful wizard in the world blindfolded? Tie my hands behind my back, and he might have a fair chance."

"Yeah," Hawk said, pushing me back through the door.

"Wait." I did a mental inventory of the turncoat knobs and turned B10 (*Sight*). I'd never tried that one before, but sight was what I needed right now, so it seemed like the perfect time for experimentation. I turned it, and the hallway flashed into view. "Huh."

"What?"

"Hawk, his eyes are glowing."

"Yeah…" I said. "I…did something. Anyway, I can see again. Everything's just blue, and—holy shin splints, Batman! I can see *through* stuff! I've got x-ray vision or something!"

"Where is Rone?" Hawk said, taking my new powers in stride.

"Next floor up, other side of the of the house, approaching a bedroom."

"Go."

I paced quickly down the hallway, drawing Kylanthus. The light of its flames distorted my x-ray vision, so that I had to hold the blade off to one side. Behind me, I felt my fellow knights drawing their swords as well. We were on the second-floor landing now. The hallway was empty.

"He must be in the room," Hawk whispered.

"Confirmed," I said. I could see him, three steps from poor Charles Simpson's bed. I broke into a run. We weren't going to make it. Rone was reaching for the kid.

"Go, Hawk!" I shouted.

Instantly, Hawk was gone. He was a Quick, after all, and he could move very fast when needed. The room blazed with light, obscuring my vision. Then Tinnay and I were there. Hawk was locked blade to blade with a tall, dark-cloaked figure. It wasn't Rone, though. I recognized this being. The way his black clothes ate the night. Its ridiculously tall, broad-chested frame. It was a shade—one of Rone's elite, super-scary magical creatures/henchmen. It had not drawn the huge, seven-foot-long sword at its

hip, instead opting for a pair of green daggers—more maneuverable in the confined space of a child's bedroom. They glowed with a sickly green light against the gold of Hawk's blade. Beyond the two figures, Charles Simpson had yet to wake up. He wouldn't have heard any of this. Not yet...

The shade's head twitched in our direction.

"Is that fear I see in your beady black slimeball eyes?" I taunted. "*Three* knights of the Circle a bit much for you?"

Tinnay and I attacked in unison. She went low, I went high. The shade pushed Hawk back and pivoted, catching my blade in the air and dancing over Tinnay's attack.

"Halt," he commanded. "This is not your fight."

My blade went heavy, tip dropping to the carpet with the weight of a boat anchor. Tinnay's did the same, but Hawk was still moving. He struck twice, beating the shade back a pace and placing himself between it and the bed. "Yes, it is," Hawk said through gritted teeth.

"Right," Tinnay said, steeling herself. "*Yes*, it is." With an effort, her blade began to move again, and she rejoined the fight.

I followed suit, and the shade spun across the room, deflecting the combined surge of our blades. He looked rather put out. On my previous encounter with a shade, it had been sent to kill (me, of course), and as such could only fight me. Anyone else that tried to engage it was subject to incredible magical mayhem. Here, however, I guessed that the shade had been sent to collect this kid, not to kill anyone, and one of our purposes as knights of

the Circle of Eight was to protect kids like him.

"Hawk, you're one smart cookie," I mumbled, ducking as the shade threw a dresser at my head. It crashed into the opposite wall and fell to the floor in splinters.

"I don't like cookies," Tinnay grunted. She trapped one of the shade's blades, and her sword doubled in size. "More of a brownie girl." She screamed and lunged forward, ramming the shade's dagger through the wall.

It stuck there, and his eyes widened. No doubt he had never been overpowered by a human being before, let alone a slender young woman. Shades were incredibly strong and accustomed to having the upper hand in combat situations. His hood fell from his face then, and the shadows parted for a moment, revealing a scaled head, covered in slime, and three vertical nostrils. His black eyes went wide, and he screamed with rage as Hawk relieved him of his other dagger (and his hand). We lowered our swords, aiming all three points at his chest, and then... something very bad happened.

He went completely dark—shades are called that for a reason. They suck in light like a black hole, but for a moment, he went even further. He completely vanished, leaving behind only a cloud of darkness. The darkness sucked in more than light. My very thoughts were pulled from me, so that I found myself standing there in a stupor, unable to recall what I had been about to do.

The shade reappeared then, his huge sword drawn and already midswing. I reacted on instinct, which is to say that although I didn't do the smartest thing I could have,

I at least did *something*, which almost certainly saved my life. My sword was hanging at my side, as I had lowered it in my confusion. Hawk and Tinnay had theirs raised still, and were ready to catch his blow on their blades, but I would have been toast[21] for sure if not for the turncoat.

I turned C7 (*Gravity*) at the speed of thought and fell upward, the shade's sword passing just beneath my belly as I rose. Hawk and Tinnay caught the blow on their raised swords, but the shade had put his back into it, and, unprepared, they were hurled backward to slam into the wall. Tinnay crumpled to the ground, and Hawk went right through, disappearing from view.

Meanwhile, I was standing on the ceiling now, having reversed gravity for myself, so I swung at the monster's head. Lucky I did too, because the shade chose that moment to hurl his seven-foot sword at me like a spear. As it happened, my swing deflected the mammoth blade just in time. However, when I had regained my bearings, the shade was looming over the boy in the bed. He wrapped his huge remaining hand around the kid's chest and picked him up as if he were a gallon of milk. Then he turned one black eye on me and grinned. There was an explosion of darkness, silent and cold, that sent me tumbling backward. When I opened my eyes again, the shade was gone.

---

21 I'm not sure why broiled bread is a euphemism for doom. Pretty random. Can you imagine if it were something else? "Hey, what happened to Steve?" "Oh, he's chips, man. He's totally soup. He's pretzel!"

Tinnay groaned and rolled over, looking up at me where I crouched at the corner of the ceiling. "He's gone?"

I nodded.

"Poor kid."

Hawk pulled himself back through the wall, looking half dead, half crazy with rage. "Yes," he said. "Little Simpson is going to have a very bad day."

"Charlie," Tinnay said, burying her face in her hands. "He went by Charlie. I failed him."

"How?" I said, flipping C7 again and returning to the ground. "How did that happen? Three on one? We should have had him!"

"Shades are very unpredictable," Hawk said. "I have fought a few, which is more than most can say, and I've never seen one do *that* before."

"The vanishing part, or the part where he apparently transported magically out of here?"

"Both," Hawk admitted. "Both acts would require immense magical power. Especially the vanishing at the end. One-way transportation to a designated location *is* possible, but at a price. The transportation powers of the bloodstones, on the other hand, are completely impossible with simple magic. I'm guessing that wherever Rone is, *that* cost him a great deal. He will be weak now. Tired. It would be a good time to attack him, if we knew his location. More's the pity."

"What's going to happen to the kid?" I asked.

But I knew the answer to the question already, and the others didn't respond. He would become one of the Fallen,

a wizard enslaved to Rone, bound by magical mind control to do his bidding. *If* he survived the process of breaking and enslavement—apparently some kids didn't. I thought of Jake Solomonson, a Fallen boy I had met previously, and how he said his friend had died.

I shivered. The thought of Rone gathering a private army of enslaved wizard kids made my skin crawl. What was he doing with them? No one knew for sure.[22]

Just then, my codex began to vibrate again. "You've got to be kidding," I mumbled.

Tinnay glanced up at us, and I saw tears on her cheeks.

"Don't be too hard on yourself, Tin," Hawk said, touching her shoulder gently. "Sometimes we just lose on—"

Before he finished his sentence, the room vanished. My body compressed and decompressed once more, and I found myself standing in our little igloo, worlds away.

"They're back!" Drake shouted.

The Tike, who had drawn her knives at our sudden appearance, sheathed them immediately. "Where did you go?" she said, glancing from me to Hawk. "What happened?"

I stared at her, dumbfounded, reeling from the unexpected battle I had just been ripped from. I could

---

22 Taking over the world, duh. Why else does a super-powerful, evil megalomaniac build a horde of zombie wizard slaves? I'd even seen him do it already. Remember Mistress Zee, aka McKenzie, whom he planted on a foreign planet to literally take over that world? It was only a matter of time before he let loose his battle on all wizardkind.

still see the shade, picking up Charlie Simpson like a jug of milk.

"You explain it," I told Hawk, then left the room and stepped into the night.

My friends were wise enough to leave me alone while Hawk explained what happened inside. When he was through, Tessa came out to find me. She put her arm around me and kissed my cheek. The gesture stopped my brain in its tracks, shade battle and kidnapping notwithstanding.

"What?" I said stupidly.

She gave me a little grin. "I didn't say anything, doofus."

"Right." I felt my face flush with embarrassment. These were *not* the circumstances under which I would have liked something like that to happen. Not that I had thought about it at all. Ever. Not even in my sleep. Especially not in my sleep. Or late at night when I was bored and listening to Tessa snore. Not at all. Still…beggars can't be choosers and all that. If she was trying to distract me from the pain and shock of my previous experience, she had succeeded.

"Um," I said. "Thanks…"

Someone cleared their throat behind us, and I spun around, automatically turning D5 (*Sidestep*) so that I was instantaneously transported three feet to the left, putting all kinds of space between me and Tessa.

"I didn't mean to interrupt," the Tike said innocently. She grinned, her eyes alight with pure joy.

"What? Noooo…interrupt what?" I fidgeted with the

lapel on the turncoat, as if I had been standing out there adjusting my wardrobe.

"You being a doofus, I expect." Her grin was growing, if that was possible. "Hawk says it's time to practice."

"Practice?" I said. "You've got to be kidding! Aren't we going to set a trap for the Lathspell or something?"

"No need for a trap, I think," Hawk said, coming to the door. Lathspells have very direct dispositions. When he is ready to attack, he will in all likelihood simply walk up to our camp. Possibly in broad daylight. Keeping an eye out for him will be a sufficient security measure. We have seen that he is vulnerable to the blades of the Circle of Eight, so if it comes to fighting"—he flicked his hand, and a gently curving sword appeared there, wreathed in yellow fire that matched the color of his one remaining eye—"we will give him two blades to deal with this time."

"Hopefully two is enough," I mumbled, thinking dark thoughts about how I had just seen *three* fail.

"Of course, it shouldn't come to that," Drake said. He had followed Hawk out of the igloo.

We all looked at him. Hawk grunted. "Has our resident Bright thought of something the rest of us have missed?"

Drake shifted uncomfortably on his broken bed. "Maybe. There are fifty bloodstones, right? When all this started, there were thirty-seven in safekeeping in Gladstone's office at Skelligard. The Circle had eight, minus Bartholomew's stone, which was stolen by Rone when he was killed. One stone was found in the turncoat. This left four unaccounted for. The four missing bloodstones

that Rellik commissioned Simon to find. Simon, with the bloodstone in the E6 pocket, turned that knob, and we were transported to Daru, where we found the first bloodstone. He turned that knob, and we were transported back to Skelligard—where there are bloodstones, by the way. After that, we traveled to the tomb of Rone, where the second bloodstone was hidden…"

Drake's voice went cold, no doubt remembering the horror of losing Captain Bast. "Rone got that one," he said. "He turned it again, and we were transported to Tarinea, where we found a bloodstone. And then"—he gestured around us—"Simon turned the knob, and we ended up here. Every time he turns a knob, it takes us to a bloodstone. Almost as if that is the function of the pocket…to take you to objects similar to what you place inside it."

"What's your point, Drake?" Tessa pressed. Most of what he said we had already guessed.

"My point is, the last bloodstone must be here. Somewhere on this moon. And if this Lathspell is some wizard's watchdog like Hawk says, then that wizard probably has the stone. We don't need to kill the watchdog. We need to meet his master."

We all stared at Drake in silence.

"What?" he said, pulling his cloak tighter around his massive shoulders.

"Drake is right," I said.

"I agree," Hawk said.

"So what are supposed to do when the Lathspell comes

back?" Tessa said. "Ask him to take us home for dinner?"

"Very politely," Hawk said. "Though I don't think we should use those words exactly. Might give him the wrong idea."

The Tike sighed. "If we're not going to fight him, you should all get some rest. If he shows up, I'll try to wake you before he kills you all."

"Very kind of you, Tike," Hawk said, "but Simon and I still need to train. Every day, you know. Practice, practice, practice. No excuses. Not even impromptu battles with a shade. We'll take the first watch."[23]

Hawk and I spun across the white frozen ground, swords dancing in dizzying circles of fire beneath the starlight. He caught my blade and sent it flying, throwing me off balance. I turned B4 (*Ninja*) and engaged my five seconds of extreme fighting skills. I caught my balance and pressed him back, but he actually *did* have extreme fighting skills of his own, so the advantage didn't win the bout for me.

"Too soon," Hawk chided, a hint of a smile spreading across his face. "When facing an opponent more powerful than you are, you should save that particular knob for a moment when you need it most."

He caught my sword and twisted, pinning our blades

---

23 My teacher, as you may have noticed, is a level 10 nutjob. Seriously! Give a guy a break already! "Practice, practice, practice." The man's possessed...

together in midair, the tip of his snagging against my crossguard. He grabbed the collar of my coat, meaning to grapple, but I turned D9 (*Slick*), and his hand slipped off as if I were covered in oil. Then I turned C6 (*Juvenile*), which, I admit, I did not know the function of.

Water squirted out of the tip of my finger. "Huh," I said, raising my finger and pointing it at him. I squeezed my fist, and the water squirted out again, as if my hand had become a child's squirt gun.

"Blagh!" He disengaged his sword from mine and stepped back, wiping his eyes.

I turned C9 (*Mass*), and leaped forward. When my sword struck his, it arrived with about 4,000 pounds of force behind it, and Hawk flew several yards back.

I chuckled, but not for long. Even before he hit the ground, Hawk's body spun in the air, turning over and over like a giant twirling, bearded taquito.[24]

I panicked and tried a new knob. B8 (*Enemy*). Immediately the sound of a dark, familiar voice filled my head.

"—came out of nowhere!" it shouted. "Nowhere, Fidget! Blasted Fayters. I hate you all! Came out of nowhere and nearly killed a shade that was collecting for me. Can you believe that? But I beat him. I beat him, just like I beat you, and I'll destroy him, just as I have destroyed you…"

The voice faded, and I knew for certain that it had been

---

24 Also known as a *Hawkito*. Sorry for the random metaphor. I'm hungry…

Rone's. My mind spun with the implications. Meanwhile, as I stood there stupidly, Hawk had not stopped fighting. His spinning form became a kaleidoscope of flashing light bright as the sun, assaulting my senses. I stumbled and dropped my sword but maintained just enough wits to turn B10 (*Sight*) in time to see through the illusion he had created and roll aside before his sword slashed me open. It was a close call, a little too close for comfort,[25] and I decided to end the fight. I turned E2 (*Pause*) before he could attack again, and time stopped.

I walked around the older wizard, taking in his frumpy appearance, his flyaway beard, his bedraggled, too-short cloak and frayed, mismatched socks. He certainly didn't look like one of the eight most powerful wizards in the universe. Then again, neither did I. I pulled off his boots while he remained frozen in time, then turned the knob again while standing behind him. He swung his sword, then looked around in confusion.

I brandished his boots. "You're dead," I said. "I win."

He glanced down at his stockinged feet and wiggled a big toe, which poked out of a hole. "So I see."

I tossed him his boots, and he put them on, scowling. "I don't think you *want* to learn, Simon. We have these fights, and it's the same thing over and over. Are you even trying to use magic on your own?"

---

25 If you must know, his blade neatly trimmed all three of my chest hairs.

"Uh..." I said, feeling somewhat guilty. "What gave me away?"

"No one knows the student like his master. You can't rely on the coat forever, Simon. You've learned how to use it well, true, but that won't be enough. It's a tool. Think of the knobs as training wheels. You must grow beyond your need of them."

"Why?" I said stubbornly. "You keep saying that, day in and day out, but you never tell me why!"

Hawk looked surprised. "Because, power that can be easily taken from you is not power at all! Do you think that Rone will simply stand idly by and let you find the bloodstones, unite them, and finish Rellik's work?"

"Well, a guy can dream, can't he?"

"And do you think, when you face Rone, with the world hanging in the balance, and all our lives on the line, that he is going to let you *keep* your turncoat? The tool you need to unite the bloodstones? His first order of business will be to deprive you of that which you need most, Simon. Like so."

Hawk moved toward me. And when I say *moved*, I don't mean like a person walking—it was no movement that you could see coming and anticipate. Like I said earlier, he was a Quick, and one of the most powerful wizards in the world. He moved like a bullet fired from a gun you didn't even see in the first place, so fast that the first indication of his movement was the shock wave after he had already passed.

He was standing behind me, holding the turncoat

over his shoulder. "And just like that," he said, "you're on your own." He dropped the turncoat on the ground behind him and flicked his sword out of thin air, stepping slowly toward me.

"Ah, come on now," I said, backing away. "That's not fair!"

"You think Rone will play fair?"

"I can't use the magic without the coat!" I shouted, growing angry. Why didn't he understand?

The Tike stepped from the igloo at the sound of my raised voice, but she did not intervene.[26]

"Defend yourself," Hawk said, and I was forced to lift Kylanthus and ward off an attack.

"What are you trying to prove?" I growled, spinning away from a lunge. "That I've still got a lot to learn?"

"No," he said, striking twice in quick succession.

I blocked the first one, but on the second, my arm wavered, and he knocked my sword aside, kicking me hard in the chest. I fell onto my back, scrambling for position. I slipped on a patch of ice and fell back to the ground. I glanced up just in time to see Hawk's sword burst into flame.

"Defend yourself!" he cried again, and the blade screamed down.

I closed my eyes, but the deathblow never came. There was a clang of metal, and I opened my eyes to see the Tike

---

26 They had some sort of unspoken pact, those two, and were always banding together to make my life difficult. Wise advisers can be such a drag.

crouched over me, her two knives crossed to catch Hawk's sword. She flung it away, and then turned her back on him, bending down to whisper in my ear.

"You are being dense, Simon Fayter. He is only trying to teach you what all warriors must learn. All wizards too, perhaps." As she spoke, the tattoo of the red bird on her neck turned toward me and gave me an encouraging look. The Rimbakka, as the bird was called, was a type of magical blood bond—the details of which I don't really understand—between my mother and the Tike, which, among other things, allowed my mom to see what was going on through the bird's eyes. I know. Creepy, right?

"The power you need isn't in the turncoat, son," Hawk was saying.

The Tike poked me in the chest significantly, then moved away. "Continue, Master Hawk."

Hawk raised his sword again, blade blazing yellow against the dark star system above us. "Defend yourself. Reach for the magic." He swung down, and I rolled to the side, narrowly avoiding the bite of his blade.

"Watch out, you crazy wizard! You're gonna kill me!"

"Your mind does not know how to wield magic," Hawk said. "Your heart does." He swung, and I dodged again. "Your soul does."

Swing. Dodge.

"Let your mind sleep. Let your soul awaken! Danger stills the mind. Wakes the soul. We're never so awake as on the brink of death. Defend yourself!"

I jumped to my feet, trying to let my mind go still, but

there was a lot to think about. I poured out my own attack on him, and he blocked and parried, letting me drive him back. He twisted his blade away and slung it back with jarring force. I faltered, and he cut off my sword hand at the wrist.

"Whoops," he said. "Sorry."

The Tike strode forward and cuffed Hawk on the ear like a misbehaving schoolboy.

I stared down numbly. Kylanthus was still blazing with fire, melting a sword-shaped hole into the frozen ground. There was my hand, gripping the hilt. "Ouch," I croaked. I didn't feel the pain yet, but I knew it was coming. Some things are just dependable, and pain is one of them.[27]

Then the pain did come, but the Tike was already pressing the turncoat into my arms, and the second I touched it, my mind reached for A9 (*Do-Over*).

"Danger stills the mind," Hawk was saying again. "Wakes the soul. We're never so awake as on the brink of death. Defend yourself!"

"Stop!" I said, letting Kylanthus fall. I held up my two intact hands in surrender. "You already tried it, and it didn't work. *And* you chopped off my hand."

---

27 There are two sure things in life: The first is pain. Life just hurts. Sorry. The second is that you will always burp after drinking a carbonated beverage. Always. If you thought that the daily sunrise might make the list, it is a close third. Other honorable mentions include an odd number of socks on laundry day, death (*omnes una manet nox*), milk expiring early, and a lack of parking spaces when you're running late.

"Ah," he said, lowering his sword awkwardly. "Sorry."

The Tike strode forward and cuffed Hawk on the ear like a misbehaving schoolboy.

He grunted. "It was worth a try."

"Easy for you to say," I said, rubbing my newly unstumped hand. I put the turncoat back on and stuffed my hands into the outside pockets. There, I gripped the sorrowstone. I had taken to leaving it there, in easy reach, and here's why: As soon as my fingers wrapped around its smooth surface, my bad feelings vanished. Frustration at being unable to touch the magic, doubt about finding what I was looking for on this frozen moon, worry at how little I knew. All these seeped out of me, replaced by a simple, quiet contentment.

Uncoolness[28] aside, if I made it back to Skelligard in one piece, I was going to give Gladstone a big hug. He had been right, of course. The hardest thing I had faced on this journey was my own emotions—the most dangerous battles, fought inside.

Hawk's eye[29] narrowed. I got the feeling that he knew what I had been doing with the stone, and for some reason he didn't approve, but he had yet to say anything about it. Maybe he didn't want to speak poorly about a gift from the head of the Circle of Eight. If he was about to tell me, I never found out, for at that moment, the ground rumbled.

---

28 Not a word.

29 Not a typo. He only has one. Remember?

The Tike hissed, drawing her knives. She was staring at something behind me, and I felt my ward ring pulse as her heart began to race. The Rimbakka on her neck flew in a tight circle, nervous. Hawk's sword burst into flame again, and Kestra flew down from her perch atop the igloo, soared through the flames of the sword, and caught fire, carrying light into the sky and illuminating the scene as Drake and Tessa ran out. The ground rumbled again, and I turned to see the Lathspell, Fren. He was still missing his left arm, but he was also 200 feet tall now.

"Wow," I said. "That's pretty impressive…"

"Attack!" Hawk shouted. He raised his arms as he bolted toward the giant ice man.[30] One hand held his burning golden sword, and the other pointed at Kestra. The hawk, who was already wreathed in magical fire that matched his sword, now grew in size—I had seen her do this once before—until she was roughly the size of a Volkswagen Bug.[31] She collided with the ice man's chest

---

30 Classic sign of someone who is totally crazy.

31 Volkswagen began in 1930 when Adolf Hitler commissioned Ferdinand Porsche, a now-famous sports car engineer, to design a car that the average Joe (or *Hans*) could afford to buy. Hitler instructed that the car must be cheap, reliable, be able to travel at highway speeds, be oil-cooled, and get at least forty miles to the gallon. World War II kicked off before the factory was finished, so Germany didn't start making the cars until 1949. They have continued making them—in one form or another—for eighty years. The Beetle was the first car to sell twenty million units and was the most sold car in the world for many years. When Henry Ford considered purchasing Volkswagen in 1949, his advisor told him that it would be worthless. Oops.

at high speed,[32] and her burning body blew a hole right though his abdomen.

The giant ice man teetered, surprised, no doubt, at his suddenly empty stomach. At the same time, Hawk reached one of the monster's legs and started hacking at an ankle with his sword. I did the other. I'd like to tell you that we lopped off his limbs and he came down in a cataclysmic[33] ruin, but the truth was, our swords were about three feet long, and his ankles were about fifteen feet thick, so we mostly just made him mad. After that, we had a giant, 100-ton ice monster dancing around. Not good.

"AGGH!" Tessa screamed, retreating from the fight toward which she had been running.

"YEAH," I shouted over the tumult. "THAT WAS A REALLY BAD IDEA."

"Live and learn," Hawk called back, scaling the side of the ice monster's leg with incredible speed.

He was halfway to the monster's hips before I remembered that I could move. I turned E4 (*Size*), thinking to join the ice man in his monstrosity and trade him blow for blow. Unfortunately, I seemed to have misunderstood the exact function of that knob, because instead of rocketing upward, I shrunk to the size of a stick of gum.

---

32 When hunting, peregrine falcons can dive, beak first, at speeds of over 240 mph—which, in case you were wondering, is a pretty effective way to kill a pigeon. Kestra is a hawk, and not a falcon, but there you go.

33 Destruction involving BIG booming sounds.

"Where'd he go?" the Tike demanded, screeching to a stop beside me. "He was just here."

"Did that good-for-nothing hero leave us behind again?" Tessa said, running over.

"No way," Drake said, deep voice booming over the din as he towered over the girls. "No way he did that again."

"I'm down here!" I called at the top of my voice, but they didn't seem to hear me.

"ANYTIME YOU GUYS WANT TO HELP, THAT WOULD BE FINE." Hawk's voice drifted down from above as he dodged the giant ice man's grasping hand, sticking his sword into the monster's side and leaping away toward another slick handhold. He was so high up now, he looked like a LEGO character. He dug his blade into the ice up to the hilt. The monster reached for him, pawing around like a human would smack itself to kill a fly, and Hawk sped away at the last second, causing the giant ice fist to smash into its own body. The ice man groaned and staggered to the side.

The Tike laughed and then glanced around for me again. "I'm sure he'll be back," she said. "I can still feel him through the ward ring. He is okay. Tessa, how much can you bench-press now?"

"Eight? Eight fifty? Why?"

The Tike winked at her. "Toss me up there, would you?"

Tessa shrugged, then rolled her shoulders and planted her feet, engaging her Strong magic. She grabbed the Tike

around the waist and then stepped forward and spun like someone throwing a shot put, launching the Tike upward. The Tike flew about fifty feet and landed on the side of the ice man's thigh, using her knives like ice axes. The monster was slapping at two would-be flies now, slowly beating himself up.

"TESSA! DRAKE!" I was trying again, but it wasn't doing much good.

"Did you hear something?" Drake asked.

"Nope," Tessa said. "Where do you think he went?"

"Dunno," Drake said. He was getting out his sling. He looked sort of silly with it now—a nine-foot, broad-chested beast of a man, holding a little slingshot daintily in his hand. He reached for the belt pouch, which he kept full of stones, and found it empty. "Gah!"

"What happened?"

"Must have opened up somewhere. They've all fallen out." He cast about as if hoping to see them laying in a nice pile nearby.

"Here," Tessa said. She extended her cram cudgel and smashed it against the ground a few times, producing large chips and chunks of ice and rock.

Drake picked up a few pieces, loaded one into his sling, and took aim. I was impressed to see the little chunk of rock glow red hot before he launched it, and realized that he must have been working on his fire skills. The "incendiary arts," as Hawk called them, were a staple in the repertoire of any wizard, regardless of which branches of magic they could touch.

Still, we were relatively new at this. Technically we only got to school about twenty-seven days ago. And nineteen of those days had been spent gallivanting around the universe, not really studying at all. Anyway, he released the chunk of glowing rock, and it shot upward—guided by Drake's now somewhat-polished telepathy skills—right into the mouth of Ice Man.

The monster sneezed and went on smashing at his sides.

"Nice try," Tessa said. "But maybe we need something bigger." She picked up a soccer-ball-sized chunk of rock and bounced it up and down on her palm, leaning casually on one foot. It must have weighed about sixty pounds. "If I chuck this, can you light it on fire and do your missile thing?"

Drake grinned.

As they spoke, I climbed up the hem of Drake's cloak and onto his shoulder. He still hadn't noticed me. Tessa did her shot put dance again and released the rock, which burst into flame and hurtled upward like a rocket. It impacted the ice man's face just above the mouth, forming a third nostril. In response, he staggered backward and moaned, putting a hand to his face.

Drake and Tessa high-fived.

"Dude…" I said into Drake's ear. "You put the rock in *rock*et."

Drake sneezed and jumped backward, while Tessa looked around dumbly for the source of the trouble. I barely held on. A second later Drake ripped me from his

shoulder and nearly stomped me to death before realizing that I was *me*, and not an abnormally articulate insect of some sort.[34]

When they had settled down, I quickly explained what had happened. Meanwhile, the giant was distracted by the new pain in his face, and Hawk took the opportunity to really start working. He began to carve out a tunnel into the ice man's belly. He was moving at super speed now, and there was a *lot* of fire. Twenty-foot-tall golden flames shot backward from the mouth of the ice tunnel as Hawk hacked his way inward, sword moving in the center of the flaming light like a reciprocating saw. The monster screamed and reached for his belly, trying to cram his fingers into the tunnel, but Hawk was too deep to be stopped now.

"Do you think that will do the trick?" Tessa asked, eyeing the ice giant thoughtfully.

"Only if there is a magic spinal cord in there or something," I replied. "Drake, what say you slingshot me up there, eh, buddy?"

"Yeah?" he said skeptically.

"Yeah."

Tessa grinned. "Won't you, you know..." She gestured with her hands. "Just go splat?"

"Nah," I said. "Just do it, Drake." I ran down his arm and hopped into the pocket of his slingshot enthusiastically.

"If you say so," Drake said, "but if I accidentally kill

---

34 A common mistake.

you and doom the whole universe to destruction, it's not my fault."

"Agreed."

He pulled back the slingshot. "Where to?"

"Aim for the shoulder," I said. "The one he's got left."

"Copy that," Drake said, shifting his hands.

"Just to be clear," Tessa said, "do you want Drake to light you on fire?"

"No thanks."

I shot out of the slingshot with the speed of a two-inch-tall boy being shot out of a magic slingshot by a buff minotaur. If you could have seen my face, I'm pretty sure I looked like a naked mole rat in a wind tunnel. I've never, ever moved so fast in my life. Seriously, I think I left part of my lip behind in that flight, because it's never felt the same since, and now I have a bit of a drooling problem at night.

Anyway, it happened so fast that I almost forgot to initiate my secret plan to keep myself from going—to use Tessa's word—*splat.* In a split second, I turned C9 (*Mass*), so that when I impacted, it would be much more powerful, and D6 (*Lightning*) just for good measure, then B6 (*Strength*) in the hopes that it might prevent me from disintegrating on impact if my plan failed, and most importantly, A3 (*Curse*). This was so that the next thing I touched—the ice man's shoulder, in this case—would break.

I held Kylanthus before me all the while, hoping that if I touched his shoulder with my blade, it would both break

and not regrow. It seemed like a good idea. Full disclosure, I may also have turned B5 (*Hair*) and suddenly grown a long gray beard, but whether that was a mental goof or I was feeling Gandalfish[35] right then, I'll let you decide.

I hit the monster's massive shoulder joint like a deadly teenage magic bad-luck bullet. At the exact moment of impact, a bolt of lightning the size of—I kid you not—the Washington Monument struck the monster's shoulder as my sword sliced through it like a flaming razor blade duct-taped to a gumbo pot that had been shot out of a cannon.[36]

Yes. You heard me right. In this metaphor, I am the gumbo pot. This is because I, like a gumbo pot, felt like I was suddenly filled with strangeness and unexplainable discomfortableness.[37] Ouch. I must have passed out for a minute then, because the premonitions began again: The red stone eyes of the lion looking down on that cave filled with water. Kylanthus hanging in the air. Tessa laughing at me from far above. "There are worms in the walls, I am told."

Then, I was awake once more, flying through the air behind the ice giant, watching its detached right arm fall beside me. I turned B1 (*Leap*) and landed gracefully on the frozen ground, shielding my eyes from the projectile

---

35 Not a word.
36 Sorry about all the bad metaphors. I seem to have misplaced my talent today. It must be here somewhere…Ah, here it is! Wait…no, that's just a moldy olive.
37 Not a word.

aftermath of the shattering ice arm that landed beside me.

I turned to see the monster standing there, armless, looking down at the tunnel that now bisected its torso. Hawk had emerged from the back and was giving me a cheery thumbs-up. Apparently he approved of my efforts. The ice man lumbered sideways, shaking the ground and making my knees buckle. Then he turned and bent down so that his face was right above me.

Armless and nearly dead, I thought, it could still probably eat me. Or just fall on me and crush me beneath its frozen bulk.

But it didn't. It just stared at me, thoughtful, and then it melted. It wasn't a gradual melting. It was instantaneous, like a tropical heat wave/laser beam had flash-unfrozen it. Hawk and the Tike plummeted to the ground amid the tsunami-like contents of the ice man's former body. The Tike would have died had Kestra, still magically enlarged, not dived out of the sky to catch her by the shoulders and carry her down.

Hawk, being an insanely awesome wizard, saved himself. If he had been a Strong, like Tessa, he would have simply fallen and landed in a crater of his own that-didn't-hurt-at-all-ness. If he had been a Think, like Drake, he would have telepathically levitated himself to the ground, or perhaps built himself a water staircase using sheer telekinetic might.

But Hawk was a Quick, so he ran, very fast, down the falling water, feet catching and holding in the descending

wet sheets like a water strider.[38]

We all regrouped as the water rolled away and seeped into invisible cracks and crevices in the ground. Soon, there was only a puddle left, and we gathered around it unconsciously.

"Good effort, team," I said, feeling rather proud of the way we had banded together to defeat a monster that would have likely made Superman wet his pants.[39]

"Yeah," Drake said, rubbing his temple with one hairy finger. "Simon, did you forget the part about how we needed to *talk* to him, so that we can meet his master and retrieve the bloodstone that is hidden here?"

"Huh." I chewed my cheek thoughtfully. I *had* sort of forgotten about that part." I jabbed a finger toward Hawk. "He started it," I said. And that was true. He had.

"He didn't seem to be in a conversational mood," Hawk said grumpily.

---

38 The Gerridae family of bugs are usually known as water striders, water skeeters, pond skaters, water skippers, or Jesus bugs. They live and move on the surface of lakes and ponds, walking on the water wherever they go. They are able to do this because water has surface tension, and their specially built legs are designed to distribute their lightweight bodies in a way that doesn't break that surface tension. They also have thousands of hairs per millimeter on their legs, which trap air, so that if they start to sink, they pop right back up, propelled toward the surface by the rising bubbles. They move across the water at speeds of over three feet per second, which, I must point out, is faster than I've ever seen a spider move on land. I know what you're thinking: the hairier your legs are, the easier it must be to walk on water...

39 Lol. That would be super awkward, since he wears his underwear on the outside. Classic rookie mistake...

"Yeah," Drake said, kicking a stray stone into the puddle, "but what now?"

As if the rock striking the puddle had been an invitation, the Lathspell rose out of it, forming ice again and resolving into solid form (normal sized this time, thank goodness). We gasped and stepped back from him. I was disappointed to see that he had his right arm back once more; the left one was still missing. Evidentially, my plan with the lightning and sword and breaking magic wasn't as foolproof as I thought. The ice man had no sooner appeared than he raised that one good arm and clapped it on Hawk's unsuspecting shoulder.

Hawk tried to retreat, but he only got a couple of inches before his entire body was encased in ice. His one gold eye stared out, unmoving, mouth frozen in an expression of mild surprise.

The creature turned toward me, and the Tike roared a battle cry and sprang to my defense. She spun forward and buried her knives in the sides of his frozen skull. He winced at this but simply clapped her on the shoulder as well, leaving behind a second ice sculpture.

"NOOOOO!" I screamed, raising Kylanthus before me. Before I could attack, however, the ice man seized the wrist of my sword arm, and a wall of ice sprang into being between us so that the sword was encased in ice at the hilt. I pulled and pulled, but it wouldn't budge.

Then I noticed that the wall in front of me was now above me and behind me as well. A second later, I was

closed in—not encased like my friends had been, just locked in an icebox. Literally. A little hole appeared in front of my face, and I could see the Lathspell's frozen eyes looking in at me. He was back to two nostrils again, and I was surprised to see breath condensing on the air.[40]

"No more fight," he said.

"Oh yeah?" I cried, attempting—unsuccessfully—to move the sword again. "Let me out of this refrigerator, and I'll show you no fighting!" I turned D5 (*Sidestep*), but instead of reappearing three feet to the left as usual, I slammed into the left side of my cell and rocked back, seeing stars. "Ow," I muttered.

The ice man smiled. "Your magic strong." He touched his chest. "My magic, also strong."

"Yeah, I got that." I rubbed my head, then looked past him to the frozen statues of Hawk and the Tike.

"Do not worry. Your friends are well."

"They don't look very well," I muttered under my breath.

"They were not nice," he said, rubbing his chest thoughtfully, right where the hole had been. "They are better this way."

"I wasn't very nice to you, either," I pointed out.

---

40 You know how you can see your breath when it's really cold outside? That's called *condensation*. It happens because there is water vapor in your breath. The warm water vapor that has been inside your body freezes when it hits the cold air, therefore becoming visible as a cloud of miniscule ice particles. Aka "fog." See? Who said fantasy books aren't educational?

"Mmm," he mused, cocking his head. "But you are the Awaited one."

I nodded. "Sounds about right."

"Simon?" Drake's voice came from outside.

Somewhere close to him, Tessa said, "You okay in there?"

"Little cold," I said. "Not as cold as the Tike."

"Seriously," Tessa responded.

"They're safe?" I asked the ice man, indicating my frozen friends.

"Safe," he agreed.

"They're not in pain?"

"Not in pain," he said.

I sighed. "Fine. You can let me out now."

"No more fighting?"

"No more fighting," I agreed.

The ice walls melted. I shivered and folded my arms across my chest as my friends stepped closer. "So, Frosty, what are we going to do now?"

He smiled and folded his one arm awkwardly across his chest, trying to mimic my action. He frowned, looking down at his missing limb.

"Sorry about that," I said. "But you were kind of unwelcoming."

"No problem," he said. He raised his good arm. "I have spare."

Tessa laughed.

"You called Simon the 'Awaited,'" Drake said.

"Yeah," I said. "Who's awaiting me? And how long have they been a-waiting?"

He spread his arm toward the ground, gesturing in invitation. "Come and see."

"We're going down, I take it?" I said.

He nodded, then tapped his own shoulder. I placed my hand on it. He waited. Tessa put her hand on my shoulder.[41] Drake did the same to her. Then the ice turned to water beneath us, and we fell toward the center of the moon.

---

41 I did NOT feel tingly butterflies in the pit of my stomach. In case you were wondering...

3

THE MAKER'S SON

Wizard's Third Rule: Passion rules reason,
for better or for worse.

—Terry Goodkind

If you've never been on a magically induced water-slide tour to the center of an ice moon with a guide who makes the abominable snowman look lame, I pity you. It was cooler than Disneyland, or sky diving. It was even cooler than Shark Week (and Shark Week is pretty cool).

We rode our slide like a frozen crystal half pipe, and it twisted and rolled through cavernous openings beneath the ice. A remarkable amount of light penetrated from the crusted surface above us, and there were pillars of clear crystalline ice, ten feet in diameter that crisscrossed the caverns and brought light down from the surface like skylight glow sticks. Our slide curved in and around them, deeper and deeper into the moon until we entered a gigantic glittering cave.

"SIMON!" Tessa screamed.

"I see it," I replied, for I just had. The slide apparently terminated about one thousand feet from the bottom of

the cave, dead-ending in midair. "Nothing's ever easy," I muttered.

"WHAT?" Tessa shouted. We were nearing the edge now. Ahead of us, Fren, aka Ice Man, flew off the end of it and disappeared in a cloud of water vapor, reappearing on the cave floor far beneath us.

"I SAID HOLD ON TO ME!" Behind me, Tessa and Drake did just that. We flew off the end of the slide, amid quite a bit of girly screaming from Tessa and Drake (girly screaming sounds odd coming from a deep-bass minotaur voice, by the way). As we did, I turned C10 (*Inflation*) and became a giant, Simon-shaped hot-air balloon. Technically it was just my head that inflated. People forget that, since it can be hard to spot my tiny regular-sized body dangling beneath, but that's how it works.

Drake and Tessa were hanging from my arms, and just as I was trying to figure out how to steer, I realized that we were drifting forward and down already, straight toward the spot where Fren was waiting.

"Drake, are you steering me with your powers?" I asked.

"OUCH!" Tessa shouted. "Simon, not so loud! Remember, your mouth is HUGE!"

"Oh, sorry," I whispered. "Drake, are you—"

"You better believe it, buddy."

"Cool. Try not to impale me on those stalactites."

"Mites."

"What?"

"Stalactites are the ones above us, hanging down.

Stalagmites are the ones on the bottom that are going to impale us."

"Whatever! But I said *don't* impale me, remember?"

"Just kidding, Simon. But you really should know your 'tites from your 'mites…"

As we glided gently down, Drake gave us a short lecture about cave terminology. Then, when we were within a few feet of the ground, my friends disembarked and grabbed hold of my feet, walking me toward Fren like I was some freakish balloon prize they won at the state fair. I was turning C7, but to no avail. My head wouldn't deflate.

"You coming down, Simon?" Drake asked finally as we came up to Fren.

"I'm trying, man! It's not working!"

Tessa cleared her throat. "Didn't you just turn the knob to deflate your big head last time?" Tessa asked.

I scowled down at her—or rather, I tried to, but I couldn't quite see her over my hugenormous[42] cheeks. "Yes, Tessa. Thank you for pointing that out. I'll try that, why don't I? Oh, hey, it's not *working*. What do you suggest I try next, pray tell?"

"Geez," Tessa said. "Whine, whine, whine. Don't worry, Aunty Tessa will take care of it." And she drew Kylanthus from its scabbard at my back.

"Hey, what are you—"

---

42 Not officially a word (*yet*). By the way, please pronounce it "HUGE-normus," not "Hug-E-normus. I don't abide silliness.

Before I could finish, the tip of my own sword punctured the bottom of my chin, releasing what can only be described as a non-digestive facial flatulence of gargantuan proportions. It literally blew me away, by which I mean I flew several yards in several directions at once—exactly the same way a helium balloon does when you untie the bottom[43]—before falling to the ground in a heap. Drake ran to help me up while Tessa chortled with laughter.

"Thanks a lot, Tessa!" I said, nursing what was now a tiny pinprick on my chin. "But I was figuring it out just fine without your help."

"My way was more fun," she said, wiping tears from her eyes. "And faster. Really just better all around."

Fren stepped forward. "You have strange magic," he said.

"And YOU," I said, rounding on him. "How come you didn't extend that slide down here, huh? Too much trouble, I guess?"

He shrugged. "I wanted to double-check that you could command the power of the turncoat. The Maker's son commanded me to bring you to him if you ever appeared, but he did not know what you would look like."

"Uh-huh," I said, stalking over to them. The cave was darker here than it had been in the caverns above. The sparkling stone was gritty beneath my boots. "And are

---

43 Thank goodness she didn't do *THAT!*

there many more of these tests that I need to pass before we get to meet your master?"

"Just one," he said, with a little bow. "Nothing difficult."

"I'm sure. Well, lead the way then, Ice Man."

He led the way, as I asked him to. First into a dark corner of the cavern, then down a sloping tunnel that appeared in the wall there. The tunnel eventually opened onto a scene that I had seen before in my visions: It was another underground cave, but where the others had been light, this one was dark.

We stood somewhere near the ceiling of the cave, and before us, rough stone steps thrust up out of the water below and led down into the darkness toward a familiar scene at the center—two large pillars, rising from the water, and between them, set into the arch, a stone lion with a terrible expression and shining red eyes. Beneath the lion, between the pillars, hung what appeared to be a duplicate of my sword, Kylanthus.

Not knowing what this could be about, but having no other option, I moved onto the sloping stairs, my friends behind me. Fren, for his part, hung back by the entrance.

"I am not permitted below," he said, raising a hand in farewell. "The sword is the key. If it fits, you will enter. If it does not, you will not be able to outrun what lurks below. Do not fall in the water."

And with that, he stepped back into the tunnel, and

the doorway vanished, leaving smooth, seamless stone in its place.

"Well," Drake said, tapping the stone where the tunnel had just been. "That was cryptic."

Tessa was leaning over the edge of the step, gazing into the black water far below. "What do you think is down there?"

"Poisonous frogs?" I guessed. There was a low rumble somewhere below, and the surface of the water began to dance the way water in a glass does when a loud noise strikes it. "Or maybe something bigger…"

"Let's get on with this before we find out," Drake said, and I quite agreed.

The climb down wasn't bad, unless you are afraid of heights (which I am), in which case it was the stuff of nightmares. What I had taken for stairs at first could only be called such by a true giant. The steps were each about eight or nine feet tall. We had to lower ourselves down with each other's help, and the last man on the top step had to hang by himself and drop—a chilling prospect when missing your target means a long drop into icy water and, no doubt, the jaws of a waiting, unseen monster.

I elected to go down last on the first step, but after that it was all Drake. He did better with the heights, and anyway, he was taller. It's not that I was afraid or anything… I can go down the stairs in the dark by myself.

Eventually, we reached the bottom, and I stepped up to the arch. The lion's head that glared down at me was even more frightening in person than it had been in my

dream. Unfortunately, all the fanciful thoughts I'd had about the missing bloodstone being one of the lion's eyes were dashed to pieces when I saw it in person. Its eyes were made of shining white marble, so white it looked wet. But they were on fire, which accounted for the red light and the strange, alive feeling when you looked at them. I tore my eyes away and promised myself that I wouldn't look back. I was afraid that if I looked again, those eyes might actually be looking back at me, as though a second glance might hold the power to awaken a demon from the stone.

The floating version of Kylanthus was identical to the real one sheathed at my back, except that it was just a picture. It was a three dimensional picture, and very realistic to be sure, but it wasn't real. I passed my hand through it, just to make sure.

"Well?" Drake said beside me, following my thoughts.

"Not a thing," I said, because I hadn't felt anything.

"You put the sword in it, I guess?" Tessa said.

I nodded.

"Are you sure this is the right thing to do?" Tessa glanced around the cave, up at the lion, down at the dancing water, and gulped. "Because it's the dumbest thing I've ever done for sure…other than making friends with you."

She punched me playfully on the shoulder, but her eyes were full of the very fear that was reaching for me. I knew I was following the plan—my instructions from Rellik. Find the one who made the turncoat, and he would have the last stone. I was doing everything right.

Still, with that lion glaring down at me, teeth bared, red eyes staring, and the eerie ghost of my own sword hanging before me, and the groans of a hidden demon rising from the black water, I couldn't help feeling like I had stumbled into the fifth circle of hell[44] with my hand poised on the devil's doorknob. I took a steadying breath and reached into my pocket, touching the sorrowstone. Fear drained out of me, replaced by a renewed sense of hope and courage.

Suddenly it seemed like a good time to share my thoughts with my friends.[45] After all, if you are going to drag your best friends along into unknown danger, you might as well tell them what you *do* know about it. I cleared my throat, then quoted Rellik's instructions to me. It was the first time my friends had heard it word for word, since I had elected to follow his orders and keep the recording private:

"Two I have hidden in my past—one with the person who crafted the item that destroyed me, and one with the person who led my brother into evil. The fourth I have hidden in your past and my future. It is in the last place that Rone would ever look for anything." I finished, waiting for Drake to analyze it.

"The stone he hid with the person who led his brother

---

44 This is in reference to the epic poem, *Dante's Inferno*, in which Dante travels through hell with the poet Virgil. The fifth circle consists of a boat ride on the river Styx, which is full of gurgling water and furious dead folks fighting. Spooky stuff.
45 Rule #9 from The Man Code: When all else fails, communicate.

into evil," Drake began. "That's the Tarinea stone, from the dragon's necklace. Broca had it, and he is the one who led Rellik's brother, Rone—Tav—into evil. No doubt they escaped the destruction of Tarinea, and Rone stayed his apprentice for years, maybe even centuries.

"The one hidden in your past and Rellik's future, in the last place Rone would ever look. That's the stone that was hidden in his tomb, which he found before we got there. So, he has that one. The other stone, then, the one he left with the person who crafted the item that destroyed him. You think that's where we are? Since the turncoat—the E6 knob—took you to those other stones? That's exactly what I said earlier!"

"Yes," I agreed. "But what is the object that destroyed Rellik?"

"A sword?" Tessa said. "Or a dagger, maybe? We don't really know how he died, do we?"

I shook my head. "Technically, I don't think anyone has ever seen the body. I'm sure he was killed by a spell. Magic of some kind."

"What about the bloodstone?" Drake said. "It was his destiny to use it, right? But he failed to do so, and, you know…that must have messed with him. *Destroyed* him? Maybe he would call it that…"

"Maybe," I said. "But I think it's something else."

"What?" Tessa said.

I unsheathed Kylanthus and held it up in front of its fake twin. "The turncoat," I said. "I think he depended

on it, and it failed him. Just like it fails me. I think the turncoat got him killed."

I reached forward and set the sword into its floating replica, and the two melded, blending into pure light.

We stepped back, shielding our eyes. Tessa shouted in surprise. The light dimmed slightly, and I squinted through my hands to see that the sword-shaped beam of light was growing—wider, taller, into a doorway.

"Come on," I said, grabbing my friends' hands. "Let's see if I'm right."

We stepped through the doorway of light and were surprised when the light remained. I blinked and shielded my eyes, straining to adjust to the light and take in the scene before me. I tried to think about the fact that my sword had disappeared when creating that light portal and had very much NOT reappeared. I glanced around, hoping to see it lying beside me somewhere, but no such luck.

Beside me, Tessa breathed a sigh of relief. We were in a gorgeous, fertile valley. Above us, the sun shone brightly in a pale-blue sky, and the cool air was crisp and refreshing on my face. Somewhere, a bird twittered happily. A quaint little village was laid out in a semicircle before us, composed of six or seven rock-and-timber houses and workshops, with tails of smoke curling happily out of half a dozen chimneys.

The valley was a small one, and it sloped rapidly upward at the edges of the village on either side, melding with a narrow woodland on one end and a meadow of

wildflowers on the other before terminating at the rocky face of mountains that shot almost straight upward. The mountains were high and fierce—nothing you would want to climb without ropes—white-capped at the top, with a waterfall here and there flowing out of the rock face and cascading down into the valley where small streams pooled into a clear cobalt-blue lake on the far side of the circle of buildings. Far above us to the right, a family of mountain goats stood on a little grassy outcropping on the steep mountainside, looking down at us curiously.

"Well," I said, releasing a breath that I'd been holding, "I definitely wasn't expecting Switzerland."

"Switser what?" Drake said.

"I'm just saying, it looks like something out of *The Sound of Music*…"

"The sound of—"

"Oh, never mind. Come on, let's see if we can find this 'Maker's son' that Fren spoke so highly of."

No sooner had I said this than a youthful man in his early twenties strode out of rightmost workshop and stretched, yawning. He wore a close-trimmed blond beard, a stained leather apron, and the matted, unkempt hair of a blacksmith or woodsman. He stopped short when he saw us and did not move.

The door to the central house sprang open then, and a small boy ran out, crossed the grassy yard at a bound, and clamored at the man's legs, speaking animatedly. The man put a hand over his mouth and pointed at us, whereupon the boy went quiet. Then he pointed back the way the boy

had come, and the child retreated. A woman stepped onto the porch as he neared and scooped him up into her arms, looking out at us warily.

The man stepped back into his workshop and reappeared a second later and walked toward us, a large hammer resting on his shoulder.

"Hello there," he called when he was within speaking distance. "You must be the ones giving Fren so much trouble up on the surface. He says you cut off his arm."

"Uh…" I began awkwardly. "Yes. I didn't want to, of course. But he's not much of a talker."

The man smiled behind his beard, setting the hammer head down and leaning on the shaft like a cane. "Well, heaven knows it isn't the first time. I must have cut him in half at least a dozen times when I was your age, out of sheer spite. Of course, he *usually* grows back." He raised an eyebrow. "This is some sword you have."

To my horror, he extended his hand, and Kylanthus appeared in it, glittering in the sunlight. He twirled it once, then stepped closer and looked straight into my eyes. "Where did you get it?"

In that moment, when I first saw the cold, gray eyes of the Maker's son, my mind slid sideways into another bout of visions: Skelligard burning. Tessa laughing down at me from above. The Tike dying. The turncoat glowing with fifty points of light. Bloody footprints pacing back and forth at the bottom of the Silent Stair in Stores, the labyrinthine tunnel and storage catacomb beneath Skelligard. An upside-down castle tower, hanging over a

bottomless chasm of night, distant screams echoing out of its dark and haunted halls.

"Where did you get it?" the man repeated, and I blinked out of my trance. "It was hanging in the hall at Skelligard. I threw a bloodstone at it and it fell."

The man nodded. Then he brought the tip of my sword up and used it to open the turncoat jacket, peering inside curiously. "And the coat? How did you come by that?"

"It was in a magic trunk that Rellik left behind for me. I opened it by speaking my name."

The man let the tip of the sword drop to the grass. "And what *is* your name?"

"Simon Fayter," I said. "I am the heir of Rellik the Seer. And I have come to claim the bloodstone that he left in your keeping."

He threw back his head and laughed. "Is that all?"

"Actually, no," I said, opening the turncoat to show him the missing pockets. "If you know a good tailor, I was hoping to get some alterations done as well."

He cocked his head at me, considering. Then he grabbed the sword by its blade and offered me the hilt. "Very well, Simon Fayter. I believe you."

I took the sword and sheathed it, relieved.

"I knew you already, of course," he said. "You've seen me before, though I wore a different face last time we met, and I was mostly sure you spoke the truth, but now I know for certain. No one can lie to me in my own house. Welcome, Simon, Tessa, and Drake, to the house of the master makers."

He shook each of our hands in turn and laid the hammer across his shoulder again. He walked back toward the little village. "Come, children. I have much to show you, and you have trials yet to face, and dangerous errands to run, if you would earn my help. Help you, I can, of course. And help you, I will. For a price…"

4

QUID PRO QUO[46]

Beauty is a fading flower,
Truth is but a wizard's tower,
Where a solemn death-bell tolls,
And a forest round it rolls.

—Alfred Noyes

Flint—for, of course, that was the man's name—led us into the house where the woman and child waited, and fed us a hot breakfast of eggs, cheese, fresh bread, and pungent fruit juice. I devoured mine eagerly while Flint's young son looked on with interest. I got the feeling that this valley didn't get many visitors.

As we ate, Flint told us the story that you read in the prologue, about how his father taught him all the skills of his trade, and how they delivered the turncoat to Rellik. The part about his father's death clearly pained him still, and he resented the fact that he had to return to this moon to live in solitude. I, meanwhile, had about ninety-two questions I wanted to ask him, but waited patiently for him to finish.

---

46 A Latin phrase that refers to the granting of one thing in exchange for another. For example, "I'll scratch your back if you scratch mine." The literal translation is "something for something."

"I lived here in solitude for a long time," he said. "I had instructions from my father that I should not leave, that my skills with the turncoat might be required in the future if Rellik needed help, and that in any case it was too dangerous for me to leave after we had thwarted the wishes of Rone and his Shadows.

"I assumed that Rellik would hear of the death of my father, the renowned master maker, and realize my peril. I assumed that he would come to my aid, or perhaps, come to me *for* aid, and he did, but not for over a hundred years. In that time, I came of age and inherited my own power. I was a Muse, like my father had become after the breaking, which made it ever so much easier to continue in the work I had been taught.

"Here on Fordis—for that is the name of this moon—where I was born, and where my father trained me in his arts, I have incredible power. More, perhaps, than any other Muse that has lived. Like Atticus and Shea, I can alter reality with my imagination. But the degree to which I can alter it is much, much greater." He stopped speaking then and stood behind me. He placed a hand on Tessa's shoulder and another on Drake's and said. "Let me show you the reality of this place."

I blinked then, and it was completely dark. Without thinking, I turned C4 (*Headlight*) and opened a corner of my mouth to illuminate the space in which we stood. Tessa gasped. The four of us were crowded inside a small stone chamber. There was a bed—not much more than a cot—on one side and a bookshelf full of manuscripts,

but nothing else. Behind us, a stone staircase rose sharply upward, the steps crusted with ice.

"This is what I came home to when my father was killed. And this is where I lived for many years until I gained the skill to create the place that you have seen."

I blinked again, and we were back in the cheery eat-in kitchen, and Flint's wife was juicing more of the strange berries that we had been drinking.

"Well," Tessa said, while Drake and I were too stunned to speak, "I like your version much better than the real thing."

He gave a little bow. "Make no mistake. What you see here *is* real. After a fashion. In any case, it is real as long as I am here."

"The people?" Drake asked, eyeing Flint's wife and son.

Flint's face fell, and he pushed his plate of food away. "I am afraid they are the least real thing here. One cannot fake a human soul. They are here to keep me company. And of course, to keep me sane. I try to forget, sometimes, but *they* know they are not real individuals. You might think of them as different aspects of my own soul, manifesting in the material world."

"You can call me a figment of your imagination all you want, Flint," his wife said, "but you're going to eat your breakfast before you go back to work. You're not superhuman, and whatever you say, you can't go all day without eating." She pushed his food back toward him and gave him a look that said she meant business.

Flint flashed me grin. "Convincing, right? Ouch!" She'd slapped him on the head with her spoon and was now bending to help the boy with his food.

"So," Tessa said slowly, "you can create all this here, but not if you leave?"

He nodded. "My power diminishes greatly if I leave Fordis. I become much like any other Muse. Outside this moon, I am less powerful, for instance, than Atticus, or any of the Circle of Eight. The greatest way I can take my power out of this place is through my creations. I have made many wizard cloaks, many sets of boots. Many weapons, including that sword you wear, Simon, as well as most of the weapons carried by the Circle of Eight and others who oppose Rone."

"So the Circle knows you're here?" I said. "You've been on our side the whole time?"

"Of course not," he snapped, and I was surprised to hear the bitterness in his voice. He softened then. "I should say, yes and no. They suspect that the master maker who forged the turncoat may have survived. Which, of course, he didn't, really. When the powerful objects I made continued to come forth, sold by various lesser makers claiming them as their own work, they saw through the deception and recognized the likelihood of my existence. Do you think, if I could tell people the truth about myself, that I would have an imaginary family, Simon?"

I looked at the woman and boy, who were gazing— rather sadly, I thought—at Flint now. "I suppose not."

"I swore to my father that I would not leave or tell

anyone where I was. Then, after a hundred years or so, Rellik finally appeared. He had known nothing of my plight and was horrified to learn the truth.

"But I was an old man by then, and on that day there was little time for regrets, for his need was great. He had faced his fate and shrunk before it. Now his brother hunted him, and he had deposited the turncoat at Skelligard for his heir to find one day. He was sure that he was a dead man, and I could not convince him otherwise. He said he had disabled the coat—removed the fabric of most of the pockets so that they could not be used to unite the stones—just in case his brother somehow gained access to the turncoat.

"We both knew that only I could repair it, and as long as my existence remained a secret, Rone would not have access to the power of the coat, even if he were to find it. I told him that only a Fayter, a wizard with access to all six branches of magic, could use the coat anyway, but he was stubborn and paranoid. He said he had seen the future, and that the coat must not be functional when his heir found it. Why, he would not say, though in time the answer became obvious."

"Why?" I said. "What was the reason?"

Flint waved my question away. "You will know in time. Come with me now. I will show you what I have been doing, and then we will fix that coat of yours. I have the fabric ready. It has been ready for a long, long while."

We followed Flint over a well-worn trail through the grassy yard and into one of the other buildings, which was

one part leatherworking studio, one part tailor shop, and one part shoemaker's workbench. Short wooden shelves hung from the ceiling and upper portion of the walls, and these were stuffed with rolls of cloth, leather, yarns, twine, and thread. Drake asked him why a wizard who could create out of thin air needed supplies at all, and Flint gave him a look that made it clear he had no intention of explaining the intricacies of his magic.

He sat down at a bench and gestured for the coat, which I gave to him. He laid it out, inside out, with the sleeves tucked under, and smoothed it flat with a practiced hand. Then he bent and retrieved what looked like a solid silver tackle box from under the bench. He opened it and took out a shiny golden needle as long as my pinky finger. He held it in front of his eyes for inspection and then dropped it in the air there, where it hung, suspended. He then withdrew a spool of shining black thread, a stack of hemmed leather squares, and a bag of brass turn-lock closures like the ones mounted to the bottom five rows of pockets.

He sat back then, scratching an eyebrow as the thread leaped into the air and threaded itself through the end of the needle. The turncoat lifted a few inches off the table, a turn-lock closure and leather square flew over, and the gold needle began stitching the A1 pocket in place. Flint leaned back on his stool, hugging a knee casually.

"It's the nature of the fabric that is the problem," he said, as if we knew what he was talking about. "No other leather would work to make these particular pockets.

Take my word for it. Also, there is a particular intention that the maker must keep in mind and place in the fabric during the construction, and up to now it has been known only to me. You might think the intention is to join the stones, or unite what was broken, or manifest the power of what is inside, but that isn't it at all.

"The coat, you see, is designed to act as an extension of you, Simon. Your skin, your body, your soul. To a bloodstone, being placed in a pocket is the same as being placed inside *you*. When a turn lock is actuated, it does nothing to the stone. It focuses your soul's attention on a particular aspect of the magical field, with which the bloodstone corresponds."

"Uh-huh," I said, feeling my brain going fuzzy.

Flint smiled. "I suppose that is enough information to be getting on with. Let us leave the sewing to itself for a while, and I will show you the rest of my fair town."

He moved toward the door, and behind him, the sewing continued, gold needle flashing to and fro with precision.

"It will be okay on its own?" Tessa asked skeptically.

Flint pointed to his head as he opened the door for us. "Nothing here is on its own, Tessa."

The next building he showed us was a small ironworks, complete with anvil and forge. There, several shining weapons hung on the wall, each one as finely made as Kylanthus. Drake took particular interest in a tall square-shafted staff weapon with a curving scimitar mounted on one end and a diamond-shaped iron cudgel on the other.

"Gunganakel!" he exclaimed, running his fingers over the shaft.

"Gesundheit," I said.

"Ah," Flint said appreciatively. "The traditional minotaurian war staff. My second one, of course, after Bloodweeper."

"What?" Drake whispered. "You made the gunganakel of Godlok Stonehand? Which cut down a thousand foes in the Battle of the Southern Dawn? But that is a famous blade. It was made by a minotaur. Draklar, the master maker of Wyclif. Everyone knows that."

Flint wagged a finger at Drake. "*I* made Bloodweeper. Draklar woke to find it sitting on his workbench with a note tied to the hilt: For Godlok Stonehand. Please claim as your own creation and deliver promptly. Signed, The Maker. Burn this note.

"Many of the renowned makers have received such notes from me, and they honor them promptly. And why not? The hefty, unearned paycheck is enough to assuage whatever negative feelings were invited by my making something better than they could manage, sneaking into their workshops undiscovered and without permission, and using them as my delivery boys. Of course, the craftsmanship of the weapons doesn't hurt their reputation."

Drake was still running a loving hand along the length of the staff when Flint finished, and there was a fire in his eyes that I had not seen before. If I didn't know Drake, I might have thought it was a touch of the bloodlust for

which minotaurs were famous. A second later, he shook his head, as if jostling his thoughts back into their proper order. Then he stepped back and left the room without a word.

The next building he showed us was a library. Drake was even more impressed with this room than he had been with the armory. He ran from one end of the room to the other like a toddler in a toy store, exclaiming things like, "Bingottabottom's *Theories of the Unhinged Sky*! I had no idea any copies were still in existence!" and "Holy gill beards! Muckwuk's *Unlucky Ducky Cluckys and Other Unlikely Curses*! I'd give a barrel of fish to read that one!"

Once Drake was sufficiently beside himself, we moved on to the next building, which was an art studio. There were many sculptures and paintings, some of which were covered with white linen tablecloths. We spent the least amount of time in this one, and though he let us look at the exposed pieces—a sculpture of his imaginary son, an exquisite oil painting of the valley—Flint was a reticent host, slapping Tessa's hand away from the corner of a cloth as she tried to peek beneath it.

At the door to the next building, Flint paused and announced that it would be the last one we got to visit. From the outside, it looked significantly smaller than the others. More of a shed, really. He pushed open the door and let me through first. The room was empty, but there were seven doors, two set into each wall, except for the one we just entered, which stood alone.

Oddly, the doors did not match one another. They

were different sizes, different colors, and made of different materials. Two were simple wooden affairs, relatively plain. A third was of a dark, oiled wood, almost black, while the fourth was huge and rustic and put me in mind of a barn. The last two were brightly colored, one purple, the other brilliant white and ornately carved.

When the others had shuffled into the small room, Flint cleared his throat. "While I have no doubt I've given the impression so far of being something of a recluse, I actually wear several faces in the real world. I am Andramadon, royal tailor of the court of the Sky King of Esereth."

He rubbed his face, and it became longer and thinner. His hair went from blond to black, and his leather apron was transformed into a pretentious suit of blue silk, complete with ruffles. He opened the purple door with a flourish, revealing the inside of a tailor's shop.

A young man, prematurely balding, glanced up from a workbench and gave a sigh of relief. "Master!" he exclaimed. "Excellent! His Majesty has requested a new suit of clothes for the ball tonight, and—"

Flint slammed the door shut. "I am Aekig, a black magic dealer in Ashguld. A dark role, but a useful one for keeping an eye on the world."

He rubbed his face again, and it became gaunt and scarred, his hair long and ragged. His keen blue clothing was replaced by close-fitting leathers covered in dark, suspicious stains. He opened the barnlike door, and a cloud of rancid smoke wafted in.

"Master?" a tentative voice said from the other side. Flint stuck his head into the other room and screamed, "GET BACK TO WORK, SCUM!"

There was frantic shuffling on the other side, and Flint closed the door, wiping spit from the corner of his mouth. "Aekig is a bit of a maniac, I'm afraid."

He cleared his throat and moved to one of the plain-looking wooden doors. He rubbed his face and became a balding old man in shabby leather overalls. He wore three pairs of glasses, and there was a toothpick in the corner of his mouth. "I am Burgess, boot master of Skelligard."

Our jaws dropped open as he pushed the door free of the jamb to reveal the long cobbler's shop where we had all met him together on our first day at Skelligard. He shuffled through the doorway, and we followed. A tingle ran down my spine at being so unexpectedly thrust into familiar surroundings. He settled onto his stool and rapped his knuckles on the long workbench while we walked around to the other side—where students belonged.

Our mouths must have still been hanging open, for he gave us a knowing smile. Then he reached into a pocket of his overalls and pulled out a bloodstone. He slapped it down on the counter between us but did not remove his hand.

"The coat you get for free," he said, "because my father would have wanted it that way." His mouth went into a tight line. "You'll get the bloodstone too, because I gave Rellik my word. *But*, because the long centuries of my life have been a somewhat torturous affair, and because *that* is

the fault of a Fayter, you won't get it for free."

I sighed, sinking onto a stool opposite him. "I suppose that would have been too easy," I said.

"Quite right," he agreed. "I expect you to do as I ask, *exactly* as I ask, remembering that I have two of your friends frozen on the other side of that door."

My heart sank. What with the strange excitement of meeting the Maker's son, I had forgotten about Hawk and the Tike entirely. [47]

"You forgot, didn't you?" Flint said, watching my face.

Tessa sighed. "He's kind of a horrible person."

"He would have remembered eventually," Drake said, gallantly coming to my defense. Good old Drake.

"No doubt," Flint said. "In any case, the three favors with which I will task you with are these: First, go down into Stores and free the prisoner that is bound there, and bring him to me."

Drake jumped up. "There's a prisoner in Stores?"

"Certainly," Flint said. "You've seen him, I think. He leaves bloody footprints wherever he walks."

"Oh dear," I said.

"The Bloody Prince!" Tessa squeaked.

---

47 How could I have forgotten them, you ask? Well…the long answer is that people are very good at accidentally forgetting things. Even important things. I myself frequently forget where my wallet is, or whether or not I am wearing underwear (I have to open my pants and check, which, of course, is a very rude habit). The short answer is that in spite of being incomprehensibly charming, supremely powerful, and critically important to the welfare of mankind, I'm kind of a horrible person.

"Precisely," Flint agreed. "You will need this." He reached beneath the counter and took out a lantern filled with blue flames. I recognized it as the Midnight Blue, a magical fire that wards off evil and devours other enchantments. "And these," he said, taking out a large hammer with a golden head and a matching golden chisel with a sharp point. "It took me many years to construct, but I think it will break the chains that bind him."

I pulled it toward myself and handed Tessa the hammer and chisel.[48]

"Your second task is to go to the Vale of Nightmares, on Ashguld's third moon, and there find the Unright Fortress. It is an evil place. An upside-down castle that hangs over a chasm of never-ending dark. Beneath the castle there is a field of magical coral, sharp at the edges, with remarkable properties. Edge-shale, they call it. You must bring me a piece of that edge-shale, a *red* piece, not black, larger than the size of my hand." He held up his hand to illustrate. "I would get it myself, but I cannot go to that place without being noticed."

"Sounds easy enough," I said, knowing full well that it would probably not be, especially given my track record.

Flint raised an eyebrow and continued without comment. "The third task is to go to Gladstone and collect the remainder of the bloodstones. When that is accomplished, you may return and claim the final stone, and fulfill your destiny."

---

48 What? They were heavy. You think *I* was going to carry them?

"That's it?" Tessa said, breathing a sigh of relief.

Flint gave her a patronizing smile. "It may not be as easy as you think. Now, be gone. Disguise yourselves before you leave this room, though. No one can know that you have returned to Skelligard."

Drake and Tessa both used their *real* magical abilities to disguise themselves, while I turned B5 (*Hair*) and grew a foot-long length of white hair and beard that made me look about two hundred years old. Drake changed only the color of his eyes and the shape of his nose, since he already looked much different post-kulraka than the inhabitants of Skelligard would remember. Tessa gave herself a crew cut and a short beard.

"Simon," Tessa said. "Didn't your mother ever teach you it's not polite to stare at a woman's beard?"

"No," I said, still eyeing it. "No, she did not."

"Well…*I'm* telling you."

"Right. Sorry." I turned back to Flint. "What about Hawk and the Tike?"

He spread his hands in a placating[49] gesture. "They will be fine until your return. I assure you they are in no pain. Just a pleasant, dreamless sleep." He crossed to the door by which we had entered. "You're going to need this," he said, opening it. The turncoat flew inside and came to rest in front of me.

I took it and inspected the lining. It was now filled with fifty pockets, which, though slightly newer looking,

---

49 Trying to calm someone down.

matched exactly the ones on the E row that had already been there. I donned the coat and felt the reassuring presence of the bloodstone in the E6 pocket.

Briefly, I imagined having all fifty pockets full and wondered what it would be like. What would happen when the pockets were filled and I turned the knob, uniting the stones into one again? Would my magic function properly? More importantly, would I suddenly understand how to use it? Would I, perhaps, attain instant god status and be able to change the course of human history at my whim?

Probably too much to wish for.

"Thanks," I said simply. "See you in a few minutes." And I strode out of the boot shop and onto the streets of Skelligard.

4.5

MINGEY'S BINGEYS

If more of us valued food and cheer and song above hoarded
gold, it would be a merrier world.

—J.R.R. Tolkien, *The Hobbit*

We met no one we knew on the streets of Skelligard for the first several minutes. Then, just before we reached the staircase that led down to Stores, Atticus rounded the corner, walking side by side with Finnigan, the great blue dugar.

"I don't care what Gladstone says. However brilliant Hawk may be, he's still a daft old pigeon. They should have let me go along. It's been eleven days[50] since the boy left, and we've had no word from him whatsoever, unless you want to count the report of that fool Montroth from the Wizguard—and I don't."

"Yet we have other reports that corroborate[51] his story,"

---

50 I know I said earlier that we had been gone for longer than this. You have to remember that we spent several of those days on the other side of the universe, where time passes more quickly than on Skelligard. On top of that, we spent several days in the past, during which *no* time passed here. It's confusing, so try not to think about it.

51 To prove something is true or trustworthy.

the dugar said in his deep voice. "The vessel *did* explode."

"Yes, well," Atticus huffed, "half the ships I sail on seem to explode. I won't read too much into it. "You there!" Atticus said, pointing at us. "What are you looking at? Unless you happen to have Simon Fayter hidden under your cloaks, I don't want to see you crowding the streets. Get to class before I ask your names!"

"Yes, sir," Tessa barked, lowering her face and hurrying us on. "Sorry, sir."

We hurried past them, but Atticus's voice trailed after us. "Kids these days…no backbones whatsoever. Why, Finnigan, if a teacher talked that way to me when I was a teenager, I would have been up in arms."

"You must have been punished a lot, sir," the dugar said.

"Yes, yes. That's not the poi—" Atticus stopped walking suddenly.

"What?" Finnigan said.

"There was something familiar about that little bearded man…" Atticus said.

He began to turn slowly on the spot, and I grabbed Tessa and Drake and yanked them backward through a door behind us. I wasn't sure where it went, as I hadn't been paying much attention to where we were, but anything had to be better than here just now.

The dim light and roar of noise and bustle inside came as a shock after the bright quiet street outside. People were everywhere. There was music, the smell of food, and the floor was covered with peanut shells.

Drake gasped. "Mingey's Bingeys!"

"Looks like a good place to hide," I said.

"Looks like a good place to *eat*!" Drake crowed, pumping a fist enthusiastically.

"But you just ate breakfast!" Tessa said.

"But I was living on dirt and spiders before that, remember? Plus, Mingey's is supposed to be the best food in town! It's not fair that we had to go save the world before we had time to try Mingey's!"

"Yeah," I said, feeling my own stomach rumble at the food smells. "We have to hide anyway. Might as well do it at a table."

"*Why* do we have to hide, again?" Tessa said. "I mean, so what if Atticus catches us? Actually, why don't we march right back out and tell Atticus everything? He could help us with the Bloody Prince, and Flint probably wouldn't ever be the wiser."

"I doubt that," I said. "He seems to know just about everything right now. I trust Atticus, but Flint's rules were clear. Until we have that bloodstone and our friends back, I don't think we have much choice but to do as he says."

"Come on, Tessa!" Drake said, dragging her into the crowded restaurant. "Best food in Skelligard! They have a whole minotaur submenu. Fresh-caught grognogler eggs, fever beetle hives, freshly harvested mudmole milk!"

Tessa laughed. "You've got to be joking."

"No," Drake said, looking wounded. "I swear, they have *fresh* mudmole milk here! Dad told me!"

"You guys don't want to hide," said Tessa. "You want to eat!"

"Two birds with one stone," I admitted.

"Unbelievable. You're stopping for *food* when the fate of the world is on the line, and our friends are being held by some crazy powerful wizard?"

"The fate of our *stomachs* is on the line too," Drake pointed out. "Besides, Flint said they weren't in any pain, and how's he to know if we make a quick pit stop on the way to saving the world?"

Tessa rolled her eyes but gave in. Soon she was taking in the sights and sounds of Mingey's Bingeys as eagerly as we were.

If you have ever been in a five-star restaurant where the waiter knows your name and stands behind you in case you should drop your napkin, or in case your glass should become less than two thirds full, and where you know it would be impolite to leave a tip less than the cost of a meal at a *normal* restaurant, then you know the type of place that serves the best food in the world. Food that makes your ancestors drool and moan with envy and haunt you out of spite. Food that is arranged on the plate by an artist, accented by garnishes, and inspected before it leaves the kitchen to be *presented* to you like a gift from the gods themselves. If you have eaten food like that—food that makes you happy on the inside, silent on the outside, and which makes you remember a good childhood memory that you'd forgotten about—well, *that* is the kind of food they serve at Mingey's Bingeys. And the

best part is, it comes without the pomp and circumstance, because Mingey's Bingeys is about the furthest thing from a formal restaurant as you can get.

It's a pub. The room was large and round, with a circular bar at the center, where they served all sorts of drinks—non-alcoholic of course, since this was a wizard school and alcohol interferes with one's ability to touch magic (and one's ability to be a non-idiot). Inside the bar there were a handful of cooks and barmen bustling about, and above it there was a stage, upon which music was played.

That day, the music was provided by something similar to a three-piece jazz band, with an upright bass, a saxophone, and a vocalist, except the music wasn't jazz in the purist sense, and the vocalist was a four-headed alien with green skin singing a four-part harmony with himself.[52] The lighting in the place was dim and reminded me of a barn with the door half open. The floor was inch deep in peanut shells, since Mingey only swept it out once a week, and bowls of peanuts took residence every foot or so wherever you went.

Mingey himself, a pointy-faced Asian wizard of indeterminate age, was the only waiter, as he maintained that no one else could do the job properly. He was always on the move and always had a tray in his hand and a towel in his belt. Luckily, he was also an accomplished Bright

---

52 In case you were wondering, his four heads sung tenor, contra tenor, bass, and baritone, respectively.

and delivered much of the food and drink around the large room using his telepathic powers, or it would have taken forever to be served, no matter how hard he worked.

The bar was high, and the stools had three steps to get seated, so when you sat there, you felt like you were hovering above the rest of the diners, who disappeared into the shadowy lighting of the place anyway. It was the coolest place to sit, and it was our first time, so that's where we sat. I wasn't very worried about us being recognized and didn't see a point in skulking in a corner.

"Three Panza Bonnanzas," Mingey said, sweeping up to us and tapping the counter.

"Cool!" Drake said.

Mingey lifted three drinks from beneath the bar and set them out in front of us. Then he winked and hurried off to care for someone else. "Welcome to Mingey's, kiddos!" he called over his shoulder.

"Gut my fish!" Drake exclaimed, sipping his Panza Bonnanza. "This stuff is to die for."

"He must be a powerful Bright to read our minds about what we want to order," Tessa said.

"I hope that's all he read," I muttered.

Drake finished his drink and belched. "Relax. Mingey's okay. Everyone says you never have to order here, and he just brings you what you want. Still surprised me, though."

Drake set his empty glass down on the bar, and it floated away and began washing itself in a tub. Instantly, another glass, this time with a purple frothy liquid inside,

soared into Drake's hand. "I could get used to this," he said.

We watched the chefs work. The food was real, it seemed, but they used quite a bit of magic in their preparation. Mostly they walked around pointing and talking to the food and cutlery. Rarely did we see them actually hold a knife or lift a spoon, except for taste tests. When they finished a dish, they set it on a huge central table, and from there the plates were either picked up by a bustling Mingey or they soared out to their patrons seemingly of their own accord.

"How does he keep it all straight?" I wondered, realizing that the movement of the plates was all being controlled by one mind.

"Who cares?" Tessa said, smashing a peanut shell open and tossing the leavings onto the floor. She had gotten into the spirit of things quickly after tasting a fizzy brown drink that took her breath away. I informed her it was just root beer, a common commodity where I came from, and she assured me that nothing that good could have originated on Earth.

"I care," Drake said. "He's a Bright, and a successful one to boot. Who knows, maybe *this* is what I'll do for a living someday. I mean, I love food, and I can levitate stuff pretty well…" He tried levitating a peanut into his mouth and shot it into his nose instead. He snorted, spraying mucus across the counter. A rag flew over and wiped the goo up. I clapped him on the back as Tessa laughed her face off.

"Drake," Tessa said, "do you really wonder what you will be doing with your future? You're brilliant. You read a ton. I'm sure you'd make a good writer. You will write down all our adventures, and every wizard alive will buy them."

"Sure," Drake said. "But what about after that? I mean, a guy can't be happy forever just writing books and swimming in money..."

We all laughed at the ridiculousness of the question, and then the food arrived. Three tarnished silver plates flew over from the central table together. Mine held a BLT, chips and guacamole, half a grapefruit, and several slices of thick honey-roasted ham with a sweet-smelling sauce. Tessa had a type of lavender pasta sprinkled with edible flowers, and Drake, whose "plate" suspiciously resembled the ten-gallon tin washtubs that the dishes cleaned themselves in, received thirty pounds of fresh lobster tails, moka heads, and Ruknak gizzards. He explained that this was a traditional minotaurian celebration meal and referred to it affectionately as "surf 'n' turf."

As we ate, I told my friends about the B8 knob, and Tessa got out her chart. "Enemy," she said. And you're sure it lets you hear him? What he's saying?"

"I think so," I said. "I think I've turned that knob a couple times by accident. I didn't know what was happening when I heard the voice, but now I'm pretty sure it's Rone. Here."

I turned the knob and listened. "No voice this time," I said. "But..." I shivered.

"What?" Drake said.

"I can hear him breathing."

"Creepy."

We ate in silence for a while after that, until finally Tessa punctuated it by speaking through a mouthful of noodles. "Thith wath a good idea, guys. Stopping to eat."

"Yeah," Drake agreed, slurping up a lobster butt.

"I thought it would make us feel better," I admitted. "I read this book once about these wizard kids who have to save the world. It always made them feel better when they went and ate at the magical restaurant together."

"You're joking," Drake said. "*You* got a good idea out of a book?"

"Yup," I admitted. "They were even kind of like us. Two boys and a girl, you know. Except the girl was the super smart one."

Drake laughed.

Tessa flung a forkful of pasta at his face.

"Sorry," he muttered, sticking out his big cow tongue and licking his cheek clean. "Hey, that's not bad."

"Did they save the world in the end?" Drake asked.

"Sure," I said.

"You think we will?" Tessa said.

"'Course," I said.

Drake and Tessa looked at each other, then took another bite of their food. "What?" I said. "You guys think we're doomed for failure or something?"

"No," Drake said. "Of course not. It's just, you know..."

"What?"

"You're a bit of a goof, Simon," Tessa said. "I mean, don't get me wrong, you're a genius, and Rellik's heir and all that. But we're just kids, and you're always flying by the seat of your pants. We really don't know what we're doing at all."

I shrugged. "I guess I never really thought about it."

"You're sure he's a genius?" Drake said.

This time, I threw a forkful of food at him.

When we had finished our food, Mingey delivered our dessert himself. I had a root beer float. Tessa had a vubannia split, which looked remarkably like a banana split, except with a delicate pear-like fruit, and Drake had a sheep brain sundae and another five pounds of surf 'n' turf. When we had finished, Drake let out a resonant belch, which was echoed around the room by several other minotaurs.

I must have looked shocked at this, because Drake grinned. "The family that burps together, conquers together." He frowned. "It loses something in the translation."

"No doubt," I said. "You know, we have a saying where I come from too. Friends don't let friends do silly things. Alone."

Drake nodded.

Tessa clapped me on the back. "That's what we're here for," she said. "So that we can rise with you in triumph or go down with you in a blaze of glory."

"That's beautiful, Tessa," I said.

She blushed. "I saw it on an advertisement for socks."

"Speaking of going down," Drake said, taking Rone's jackal mask out of his coat and placing it on the bar between us, "how are we going to take *him* down?"

We huddled around the mask, and Tessa crowded our dessert dishes around it so that casual onlookers would not see.

"We've got a plan for that," I said. "Get the bloodstones, put them in the coat, activate it, and…" I twirled my hands in a magical gesture. "Voilà."

Tessa twirled her hair thoughtfully. "And you really think that's going to work?"

"Sure," I said. "Why wouldn't it? That's what Rellik told me to do, and he certainly knew what he was talking about."

"Yeah, but he *failed* using that plan," Tessa pointed out. "What makes you think it will work for you?"

I shrugged. "I guess because it has to. If it doesn't, we'll all be pretzel."

"Pretzel?"

"Never mind. I'm just saying, I'm no grand wizard guru. Not yet. There's no way I'll ever catch up to Rone in that department, so I'm banking on fate giving me a bit of a handout."

"And if it doesn't work?" Tessa said.

I scraped the last of the ice cream out of my cup and licked the spoon. "Then we all die, I guess. Or get enslaved by Rone. But hey, we've had some pretty cool times, right?"

"That's the spirit!" Drake said, clapping me on the back. "Death and glory! The minotaur way!"

"Sometimes I think the kulraka changed your brain a bit, big guy," Tessa said, pushing the mask back to him. "But I'll take it. Those massive biceps might come in handy when we face off with Rone."

Drake belched again, listening thoughtfully to the echoes around the room as he picked up the mask. "Hey, look," he said, picking something off of it and holding his fingers up to the light.

"What is it?" Tessa said.

"A hair," Drake said. "Has anyone worn this since Rone?"

We shook our heads.

"It looks like his," Drake said, handing it to me. "Might come in useful."

It *was* his. I'd recognize that color anywhere. And it *would* come in useful. I knew that Tessa and Drake were remembering the same thing I was: the time on Daru when I had put one of Drake's hairs in the E7 pocket, and the turncoat had illuminated a path that led me right to my friend. There was another pocket it might be used in as well. One with darker purposes.

I patted him on the back as I tucked the hair into E8 (*Stash*) for safekeeping. "Good find, buddy. It will come in useful for sure."

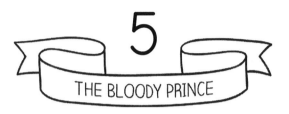

5

THE BLOODY PRINCE

"If you can learn a simple trick, Scout, you'll get along a lot better with all kinds of folks. You never really understand a person until you consider things from his point of view, until you climb inside of his skin and walk around in it."
—Atticus Finch in *To Kill A Mockingbird* by Harper Lee

Eating finished, we left Mingey's Bingeys and made our way to the ugly stinky brown door to Stores. It seemed like a lifetime ago that I had met Hawk here for the first time. As it had been that day, the door was locked.

"Hmm," I said, feeling my pockets. "I don't suppose anyone has a key?"

"I do," Tessa said. She actuated her cram cudgel and swung it at the door like a battering ram. The door shattered into a thousand stinky brown splinters, and Tessa clicked the handle of her cudgel, collapsing it.

"Alrighty then," I said. "Follow me."

Unfortunately, the next locked door was more of a problem. The antechamber of Stores was a sort of staging area, where supplies and artifacts often stopped for a while on their way in or out. It was littered with shelves and cabinets of poorly inventoried items—some of them

thrown haphazardly in places they did not belong by a hasty student, or by Hawk himself. The real entrance to Stores was in this chamber, and it was a portal specifically built to withstand magical tampering. It was made of thick steel, no doubt impregnated with anti-magical mojo, and locked by an intricate mechanism that required seven keys.

Tessa got her cram cudgel out again, but I waved her off. "Don't bother. It would take the whole Circle of Eight to bust through this thing without the keys, and even they might not be up to it."

Tessa sighed and leaned against a wall, folding her arms in disapproval. Drake groaned and cast around himself for food, eventually ripping off the top of a crate and taking a bite out of the corner. He grunted and tossed it away.

"Hawk has the keys, right?" he said irritably. "We could go back and get them."

"Nah. He wouldn't have brought them on a dangerous journey."

"He probably gave them to Gladstone for safekeeping," Tessa said.

"He *definitely* wouldn't have trusted Gladstone with them," I said.

"Really?" Drake said. "He doesn't trust the leader of the Circle of Eight?"

"Hawk doesn't trust *anyone* with the keys to Stores. Especially not since I stole them that one time… He's been uber paranoid ever since. I'm the Fayter. I think he trusts

me more than anyone else in the world—at least enough to run errands for him in Stores. The other day, Gladstone asked to borrow them, and he laughed and said, 'I'd rather jump naked into a volcano with a thousand dancing pigs.'"

"A thousand dancing—"

"It doesn't matter. The point is, he wouldn't trust anyone but himself with the keys. Which means," I said, circling the room slowly, "he probably hid them some place no one would look."

Drake picked up a broom and began searching through the bristles.

"Wow," Tessa said.

"What? No one would look there!"

"Shh!" I said. "I'm trying to think. I ran my hand across the labels of jars, barrels, bins and boxes, then grinned, pulling a large box off the shelf. The label read: "Chamber Pots—Dirty."

"Yuck," Tessa said, stroking her beard in disgust. "Why would anyone keep a box of *dirty* chamber pots?"

"Duh," I said. "They're getting rid of them in Stores. No one will ever see them again, so why bother cleaning them out well?"

Drake nodded in agreement.

"Boys are so gross," she said. "You don't think he'd really—ugh!"

I had removed the lid on the box and opened the first pot. "Nope," I said, slamming the lid back down and turning green. "Not in that one."

"Simon," Tessa said in a squeaky voice, pinching her

nose, "this is the worst idea you've ever—"

"Here they are." I drew the keys out of an empty (and thankfully clean) pot triumphantly.

"Dang," Drake said, clearly impressed. "I can't believe you actually found those."

"No one knows the master like his student," I said smugly. I opened the door quickly using the seven keys, which were of various sizes and shapes ranging from nine inches long to the size of a baby's tooth. I turned them, and the door swung open. "Welcome back to Stores, guys," I said.

"Fantastic," Tessa said. "Coming here worked out so well last time."

"Yeah, but we have permission this time," I said.

"Orders to break in and permission to enter are *not* the same thing," Tessa said.

Drake laughed. "Really? Tessa, Simon is a member of the Circle of Eight, and a *Fayter*. Who does he need permission from?"

The question hung in the air as we stared down the dark, foreboding staircase. I held up the little lantern Flint gave us, and the flickering blue firelight illuminated less of the darkness than I would have preferred.

"This is the silent stair," I said, remembering my first time down it, "where we contemplate the seven horrors contained in the vaults below and pledge our vigilance to keep them contained."

"What are the seven—"

"Shhh," I said. "The *silent* stair, remember?"

Tessa smacked me in the back of the head[53] but didn't say anything more until we were at the bottom. I reached into my pocket and touched the sorrowstone as we descended, so that by the time we were down, I was feeling much more courageous.

"*What*," she said again, "are the seven horrors contained in the vaults below?"

"I dunno," I said, scratching my head. "I mean, one of them was obviously the Horror of Kane, which we already took care of. So I guess that leaves six. In my defense, I did ask Hawk, and he blew me off."

"Uh-huh. And you never thought to ask him again?"

"Yeah, that probably would have been smart, now that I think of it. We'll have to ask him when we—"

"The Horror of Cain," Drake began, counting on his fingers, "the Hive of Nine, the Untouchable Square, the Rope of Akeldama, the Quill of Hukogoth, the Bride in White Silk, and the Bloody Prince."

I blinked at him in the flickering light.

"What?" he said. "Didn't you read *Frequently Asked Questions Concerning Skelligard Castle* by Rudolph Bright? I checked it out for you, remember?"

"I think I fed that one to my hamster."

"You don't *have* a hamster, Simon!"

"Huh. Then I have no idea what could have happened to it."

---

53 Alternate ending: I stumble and fall down a hundred-foot staircase, crack my head at the bottom, and die. The universe is doomed because Tessa just *had* to slap me.

"Anyway," Tessa cut in, "the Bloody Prince is one of the horrors that are bound here! I thought he was pure myth—until we saw his prints, of course—but what did the books say about him?"

"That's just it. They don't say anything. He seems to have been a resident of the island since the time Skelligard was built, or at least, since before anyone can remember. The early wizards maintained that he was dangerous, but as far as I can tell, no one knows anything about him."

We moved through the dank tunnels of Stores in the near darkness, following the flickering blue trail of light cast by our lantern. Low wooden shelves lined the narrow tunnel walls, covered with ancient boxes and bins, often partially decomposed and always covered with a thick layer of dust.

I had learned in my time helping Hawk in Stores that the tunnels had a gradual slope to them, and that this was the secret to finding your way in and out. It was nearly imperceptible, especially if you didn't know what to look for, but the tunnels sloped downhill as you got farther from the entrance. That way, as long as you knew the secret and had a sensitive enough constitution to discern the subtle pitch of the floor,[54] you could never get lost indefinitely. We moved through a small court where

---

54 Or if you were smart enough to carry a bag of marbles in your pocket... Hawk frowns on that practice, though, because of old Milton the Insane, former caretaker of Stores, who lost his marbles and ended up trapped in Stores until he...well...lost his *real* marbles. Poor guy.

eight tunnels intersected, and I picked one at random, continuing downward.

"I'm sure Gladstone knows about the Bloody Prince," I said. "And Hawk. If *I* were in charge of a magical school, I wouldn't just lounge around knowing there was some super evil dude locked in the basement without knowing a bit about him."

"Maybe," Drake said. "But I doubt it. The book said that nobody had ever seen or talked to the spirit that leaves the footprints—or rather, no one had done so and lived to tell about it."

"Great," Tessa said.

I came to a stop and sighed. "My plan isn't working."

"*This* was your plan?" Tessa said incredulously.[55]

"It worked last time, didn't it?" I said defensively.

"That was pure dumb luck!" Tessa said exasperatedly.

"You expected *him* to have a plan?" Drake said amusedly.[56]

Just then, someone knocked on the door to our right.

---

55 Disbelieving, with a slight hint of mockery and/or exasperation.

56 Incredulously, exasperatedly, defensively, and amusedly are all adverbs. That is, they describe *how* a person does or says something. The excessive use of adverbs like this in prose writing is, in the highest circles, considered to be one of the trademarks of inferior writers. Great writers don't need to tell you *how* their characters are saying something, because you know the character well enough to infer this based on *what* they say. I, of course, am not a great writer. I am a great wizard adventurer, and writing is just a side job (as such, I get a free pass with adverbs). But if *you* ever want to become a great writer, avoid adverbs. At the very least, avoid the extra-repellant ones like "amusedly" and "exasperatedly." Yuck.

We all stopped short, looking at it and waiting. The person on the other side knocked again. On our side, the door was locked shut with four shining red dead bolts. A sign on the door read: "No living matter beyond the threshold."

The knock came again. A double tap. Like a heartbeat.

"Okay," Tessa said. "That's creepy."

"Should we open it?" Drake asked.

"It would be rude not to," I said. "You never know. Could be the Bloody Prince."

Before they could object, I had the last of the dead bolts pulled. I opened the door, and to my surprise, there was no one standing there. We were looking into a small clearing in a wood. A woman sat at a little wrought-iron table in a white silk wedding dress, face veiled, dark hair spilling onto her shoulders. A swing hung from the branch of a tilting tree over a bed of wildflowers, and the air was filled with butterflies. It would have been a pleasant enough scene, except that everything was dead. The tree, the grass, the flowers, were all various shades of mottled gray, and the butterflies were black and practically dripping with decay.

"Come," the woman said, her voice sweet and inviting. She patted the chair beside her own. "Sit a while with me."

"Let's not," Drake said, taking a step back.

"No," she said. "Stay."

"Look at the ground," Drake said.

Now that he mentioned it, the ground around the clearing was covered with mounds. Burial mounds, no doubt. All that was left of her previous visitors.

I took a step back as well, and the woman stood. "STAY!" she commanded. She lifted her veil, and I gasped. Drake sneezed. Where her face should have been, there was—[57]

"Okay," Tessa said, slamming the door shut and driving the dead bolts home. "I think that's enough of that. Simon, you are not allowed to open any more locked doors today."

"Agreed," I said.

Drake was halfway through a sigh of relief when a little corner of white silk pushed its way through the door jamb and wrapped itself around the handle of one of the dead bolts, sliding it open.

Tessa screamed and was about to shove it closed again, but I grabbed her wrist. "Don't!" The silk was still wrapped around the bolt, covering it. "I don't think we should touch that fabric."

Tessa nodded, but her eyes were fixed on the door, where another slip of silk was wedging itself through. It grabbed the second bolt and pulled it open.

"What do we do?" Drake asked, backing away slowly. "What do we do? What do we do? We've let out another one!"

"Shh," I said. "I think it's stopped."

We watched for a while, but nothing else happened. The silk was still there, covering the open bolts, but the

---

57 Sorry, that next bit was too scary for a children's book. I'm sure your imagination has thought up something sufficiently scary anyway.

two remaining ones were still locked.

"I don't get it," Tessa said. "Why did it stop?"

"Why did it *start* is what I want to know," I said.

Tessa glanced at the sign. "Nobody crossed the threshold, right? No living matter?"

"I sneezed," Drake said, eyes widening in horror.

"That's right," I said. "Some of his saliva probably flew in there."[58]

"Do you think that constitutes living matter?" Tessa said.

I pointed at the two open bolts. "Apparently."

Drake shivered. "Maybe it wasn't alive enough or big enough to let her all the way out, eh?"

"Looks that way."

"Let's get out of here," Tessa said. "We need to find the prince and get back to Flint as fast as possible. Then we can tell Hawk what happened, and he'll know what to do."

"Right," I said, still eyeing the dead bolts. I didn't like the idea of leaving the situation this way, but what choice did we have? "Okay," I said, moving away from the door. "New plan." I moved farther down the tunnel and cupped my hands around my mouth. "BLOODY PRINCE!" I shouted, at the top of my voice. "BLOODY PRINCE! BLOODY PRI— Oof."

Tessa had tackled me. She had me on the ground now, her knee in my back. "What is *wrong* with you, Simon?

---

58 Fun fact: particulate matter from a sneeze can travel up to 200 feet. You're welcome.

You are the dumbest genius I know."

"What?" I grunted, trying to regain the wind she had knocked out of me.

"What *else* might hear your voice and come out of the shadows? Did you think about *that*?"

"Not really," I admitted.

"Exactly."

"Please get off."

"Not until you promise to—"

"Tessa, get off! I found something."

She let me up, and I brought the lantern closer to the ground where I had fallen. There, just next to where my face had been was...

"Blood?" Drake asked. He dipped his pinky into the corner of the blackish-red stuff and put it in his mouth. Tessa made a gagging sound at this, and I ran through a quick mental checklist to make sure I hadn't noticed any other vampiric[59] tendencies in my best friend.

"No," he said, oblivious to our disgust. "Not blood, but...it sort of reminds me of blood somehow. Could be the stuff from the footprints, but it's not in the shape of a footprint."

"That's because Simon smeared his face all over it," Tessa said, pointing to my cheek.

I wiped it off. "I'm pretty sure *you* can take credit for that, Tessa."

---

59 Not a word. Seriously though, that boy will put *anything* in his mouth. Ick.

"Yes, well, hold up your light, and let's see if we can find some more."

"No need," I said. I dipped my own finger into the blood stuff and then wiped it into the E7 (*Path*) pocket. I closed it, turned the knob, and a bright golden path appeared before me on the ground, winding down the tunnel ahead of us and then branching to the left. The others couldn't see it, but they knew what the knob did.

"Brilliant!" Drake said as I started confidently down the tunnel.

"Hear that, Tessa?" I said. "Drake thinks I'm brilliant."

"Drake is easily impressed," Tessa said, bringing up the rear. "I think you're adequate. Sometimes."

"How romantic," Drake said.

I blushed. Thank goodness no one could see.

The golden path led, as it had done on previous occasions, to the rest of the blood from which it had come. In this case, it led us to a pair of invisible boots pacing back and forth in front of a blank section of wall where the tunnel dead-ended. The boots stopped as we approached and turned to face us.

"Hi," I said. "Uh . . ." Suddenly, I realized that finding the Bloody Prince was as far as my plan went. What to do at this point was a bit fuzzy.

Tessa face-palmed.

Drake cleared his throat. "Hello, Mr. Bloody Prince, sir. We've been sent to help you get out of here. Would you like that?"

The prints didn't move.

"I've got some Midnight Blue here," I said, raising the lantern. "Is it okay to sort of, you know…set you on fire? I think that's what we're supposed to do."

The footprints stayed put.

Tessa spoke next. "Why don't you take a step to the right if it's okay?" Tessa said.

The prints sidestepped to our left, and Tessa jumped slightly. Apparently, she hadn't expected him to actually respond.

I stepped forward with the lantern and opened the glass door on the front.

"Wait!" Drake said. "He took a step to the *left*! That means he doesn't want you to do it."

"He took a step to the right," I corrected.

"No," Drake insisted. "He was there, and now he's there. That's left."

"He took a step to *his* right," I amended.

"Oh. I was looking at it the other way around."

"Fine," I said, lifting the lantern again.

"Wait!" Drake said, grabbing my arm. "How do you know which way *he* was looking at it?"

I sighed. "Tessa, which way did you mean for him to move?"

"I meant for him to move to *his* right, of course. Why do boys always think the world is all about them?"

"There, Drake. You see?"

"Yeah, but he doesn't know that."

"Sure he does."

"I mean," Drake said in a rush, "I know he knows it

now, because he just heard us talking, but he couldn't have known that a minute ago."

"Ugggh," Tessa groaned, stepping forward. "Mr. Bloody Prince, sir, would you please step to *your* right? That way?" She pointed. "If you agree with Simon's plan?"

The prints took another step.

"Okay," Drake said, throwing up his hands. "I was wrong. Call me a worrywart, but I just wanted to make sure before you started lighting people on fire."

"Fair enough," I said, raising the lantern once more. I pushed it through the air toward where the prince's body should have been, right above his boot prints, but nothing happened. I waved it back and forth through the air there, waiting for it to catch something on fire, or at least to touch something. But nothing happened.

"Am I supposed to be doing something else?" I said.

"How should I know?" Tessa said.

"I think this is right," Drake said. "I don't know why it's not working."

The boots turned then and walked away, right through the wall.

"Great," I said, snapping the glass lantern door shut in frustration. "Just great."

Tessa slumped against the wall and put her hands to her face. "This is taking too long."

Drake was thinking hard, staring at the place where the boots had disappeared. Then he pointed. "Look."

The boots had come back through the wall and stood

facing us. Then they turned around and walked back through the wall."

"He wants us to follow him!" I said. Suddenly sure it was the right thing to do, I ran at the wall. My nose hit solid stone, followed by the rest of my face, and my head snapped back as I staggered away from the wall, bleeding.

"Nice," Tessa said, holding a handkerchief out.

"Thanngkss," I muttered, and applied it to my nose.

Drake was running his hands over the wall. "Maybe you had the right idea. I don't think this is a normal wall. I'm not very good with psychic penetration of inanimate objects yet, but this doesn't feel…right. Tessa, why don't you work this wall over a little bit?"

"As you wish, cow boy."

"That's cow *man* now," Drake said.

"Hah!" Tessa extended her cudgel. "As if. That gigantically buff and hairy physique of yours isn't fooling anyone, little man."

Drake laughed good-naturedly but looked slightly crestfallen as Tessa started smashing the wall. At first, not much happened. It was a bit odd, really, when she hit it a few times and no stone chips started to fly. But then she gave it an extra-hard swing, and the wall rippled at the impact like a sheet of Plexiglas.

I placed a hand on Tessa's shoulder, and she stopped swinging. Then I turned A3 (*Curse*) and bumped the wall with my fist. It shattered into a million shards and fell to the ground in big piles, revealing several more feet of

tunnel behind it and an ornate door flanked by two stone statues.

Drake coughed and waved a hand at the dust in the air as he stepped over one of the piles of wall shards and moved down the tunnel. He pointed to the floor, where a trail of bloody boot prints led from the now-shattered wall to the door, and then turned around to face us.

"That wasn't so bad," Drake said, clapping Tessa and me on the back. "Good teamwork, guys."

It was at this point that the statues came alive. They stepped into the center of the tunnel brandishing spears, shaking off the dust that had settled on them over the long years they had lain in wait. In fact, they weren't statues at all. They were people.

"They're just kids," Tessa said, twirling her cudgel in a manner that said she didn't really want to use it. She was right. I had assumed they were soldiers because of the spears, but a more careful inspection revealed short statures and young faces. I drew Kylanthus, and the one on the left—a girl, I thought, though the light was dim—crouched into a fighting stance. As she did, a shining silver medallion tumbled out from the neck of her armor, and I remembered a similar necklace worn by Jake Solomonson.

"They're Fallen," I warned, recognizing them as members of Rone's private army. I realized then that these poor young wizards had probably been enslaved by Rone against their will and then tasked with standing in the dark, haunted tunnels below Skelligard for months, no,

years, in the off chance that someone would... Wait a minute...

"Simon," Drake said, voicing the question I had just arrived at, "why would Rone be guarding something in Stores? What does he have to do with the Bloody Prince?"

Before I could think of an answer, the young guards charged us.

Drake flicked his hands into the air, and the spearheads mimicked his motion, tipping upward and embedding themselves in the ceiling. The young wizards stumbled, letting go of their mutinous weapons in confusion. Tessa, no doubt unwilling to club them, stomped her foot hard, causing the ground to shake. They stumbled again.

"Stop!" I shouted. How could we fight kids? It wasn't like they chose to be here, fighting for Rone. He forced them. He enslaved them. He *stole* their lives! And now *I* was being forced to fight them—possibly to hurt them. It was Mistress Zee all over again. How could we fight them? But if they attacked us, how could we not?

In that moment, I felt a burning hatred for Rone. As if in response, the young wizard closest to us pressed his palms together and made a spinning motion, sending a large pink fireball flying our direction. I turned C3 (*Sponge*), and the fireball sucked into the turncoat and vanished. Unfortunately, that was one of those knobs that only works once a day, and a second wizard had joined the first in the fireball throwing. There were three coming at me now, two pinks and a blue. Not knowing what else to

do, I drew Kylanthus, whispered the sword's name, and cut through their fire with my own.

As my blade cut through their spheres, their fire died, though not all at once. I accidentally sent a pig-sized[60] chunk of fire flying at Drake in my frenzy of swings, and he didn't appreciate it. Tessa stomped the ground again just as the two were preparing another round of fireballs, and they stumbled, tripping over each other. Doing my best to envision what I wanted to happen, I turned D4 (*Giggle*) and E4 (*Size*). As always, I felt the familiar tingle in my gut as the magic flowed out of me.

The wizard closest to us doubled over in an uncontrollable fit of laughter, and the farther one suffered something rather more...extreme. His right foot grew. And when I say grew, I mean that one second it was normal, and the next it was roughly the size of a minivan. He screamed as his toes jammed into the ceiling and his heel rubbed against the floor.

I stepped around the laughing kid and climbed through the little crevice of space between the arch of the other one's foot and the wall, motioning for the others to follow me. Tessa did, and then Drake climbed through last. He had to squeeze a bit, and the poor kid with the humungousized[61] foot made a racket as he did: "Ouch! Stop! Oooh! Whoo, that tickles!"

When Drake was finally through, he clapped me on

---

60 We're talking Pumbaa here, not Wilbur.
61 Not a word.

the back proudly. "That was awesome!"

"Thanks," I said, turning to face the now unguarded door.

The Bloody Prince's boots were standing there, facing us, and as we approached, they retreated behind the door. It was locked, so Tessa broke it down. Then we stepped down into the most horrible room I've ever had the misfortune of entering. Sometimes, I still see it in my nightmares...

6

THE KILLING FLOOR[62]

Murderers are not monsters, they're men.
And that's the most frightening thing about them.
—Alice Sebold

The wide stone chamber into which we stepped was made of polished white marble. It was dimly lit by a skylight far, far above us but bright enough that we could see the color of the liquid that filled the floor. I say *filled* because it was several inches deep, reaching nearly up to my shins.

It was red, by the way. Deep, blood red. For a horrible moment, I thought it *was* blood, and that we had somehow stumbled into a giant cesspit of human gore—but no. It was thick like blood, but it didn't smell at all. Anyone who has ever bit their cheek knows that blood tastes and smells quite metallic, but this did not.

I shot Drake a questioning glance, and he dipped a finger in the stuff, lifting it to his nose. "I thought blood,"

---

62 A killing floor *usually* refers to that place in a slaughterhouse where moo cows take their first step on the road to hamburger. Not a very nice place, really.

he said. "But it isn't. It seems to...*remind* one of blood, though, doesn't it?"

I nodded. It reminded me of other things, too. Dark thoughts. I found myself thinking, suddenly, of all the people Rone must have killed by now. And all those who were alive and suffering under his torturous influence. Jake. Charlie. McKenzie...

I walked on. The Bloody Prince's tracks were obviously no longer visible, but I continued toward the far side of the room, where there was a section of floor that stepped up out of the pool. No one spoke again as we moved across, listening to the sound of the red stuff swishing around our legs. I tried not to think of what the red stuff was, or what might be swimming around in it, or hidden beneath the surface. It was not the type of room that promotes casual conversation.

As I neared the far side, I saw bloodred boot prints step up onto the raised floor, making dark stains on the white marble. A second later, I followed suit. The prints walked out a few steps, and I followed. He stopped, and I did the same, listening to the sounds of Tessa and Drake climbing out behind me. After pausing for a few seconds, the prints moved out further, and again I followed. He stopped again, and I did the same, and behind us I heard a sharp intake of breath.

I turned to see Drake staring at the floor, wide-eyed.

"What?" Tessa said.

Drake pointed at the bloody boot prints—mine and

the prince's, which now lay side by side on the stretch of marble that separated us.

"Oh boy," Tessa whispered.

"What?" I said, and then I understood. Looking at our boot prints, side by side, lying there next to each other on the white marble, I noticed that they were the same. Not just similar. The *same*. They were the same size, the same shape, the same color, now that I had walked through the pool. There was even a gouge out of the corner of the left boot heel that was the same.

"It's you," Drake said, going pale. "From the future, or the past or something. You got trapped down here, and somehow our alternate realities have intersected."

"No," I said, turning back. "It's not me. It's him." I stepped up to the place where the boot prints had stopped and faced the air above them. "Rellik, son of Ronan, son of Rok. We never did look inside your tomb. You're not dead at all, are you?"

There was a loud crack, and a silver chain materialized out of thin air and clattered to the floor in a heap. It was broken on one side. A second later, a figure flickered into existence before us. An old man, with white hair and beard, and a nose that had been broken several times. It was definitely Rellik, though he was significantly older and thinner than he had been in the turncoat recording. His mouth was covered by a metal bracket, which wrapped around his head and was mounted to a steel collar around his neck. Evidently, this kept him from speaking. His hands were bound before him in a thick steel bracelet.

Each binding, collar and bracelet, were locked tight with a lock the same silver color as the pendants of the Fallen.

"Holy anchovies," Drake swore.

"Cut him loose," I said.

Tessa moved toward him with the hammer and chisel, but Rellik held up his hands and pointed at the lantern. It took a while for us to figure out that the chisel had to be placed in the fire. When we did, the fire leaped from the lantern onto the end of the chisel and stayed there. Tessa placed the tip against Rellik's handcuffs, and with the third strike of the hammer, the lock broke and he was free, rubbing his wrists gingerly. The lock around his collar came free on the second strike, freeing his face. He touched his mouth, feeling at the sores around it, no doubt the result of the metal chafing there. He stuck out his tongue a few times experimentally and tried to speak, but nothing came out beyond a hoarse whisper.

He ran to the pool then and jumped in. He drank from the red liquid and then massaged his tongue and lips for a while, finally rising again. He climbed back up slowly and gave us an apologetic smile.

"Been a long time," he said, "since this mouth had the pleasure of speaking." His voice was hoarse, and he had a slight lisp that I did not recall. "For many years, I tried to escape. For many more, I hoped to be rescued. But that hope ended long ago. Yet here we are!" He held out his arms, smiling. "I hope you killed that evil creature that locked me in here."

"Rone?" I said.

"I think so. The one who wears that terrible mask."

"Like this?" Drake said, taking Rone's old mask from the inside pocket of his cloak.

"Yes!" he said, glaring at it. "Yes... You have killed him, then?"

"Uh...not entirely," I admitted. "Listen, you *are* Rellik, aren't you? You're not exactly...um..."

"Ah, yes," he said sadly. "I *am* Rellik, in a manner of speaking, but unfortunately I'm also rather not. Not anymore."

He lifted his shirt to reveal dozens of scars running across his body in specific patterns, as though a rogue acupuncturist had taken a hot poker to his pressure points.

"You can destroy a person's ability to wield magic." He traced the pattern of marks that ran up and down his torso. "It involves manipulation of the magical meridian points along the body to disrupt the proper function of magic through the soul. It is an ancient art with the darkest of origins and requires the most grotesque mangling of body and mind, but it can be done, and my brother was well trained." He lowered his shirt with a groan. "He's not *really* my brother, is he?"

"I'm afraid so," I said.

"Bother," he said. "He has mangled much of my memory of who I was, and while I retain a fair bit of knowledge about the world and the magical arts, I'm fuzzy in some rather important places."

Drake groaned, massaging his temples.

"That's horrible!" Tessa said. "I'm so sorry, Rellik."

"That *is* my real name, then?" Rellik asked. "That's what he called me sometimes. Sometimes he called me Fidget, I think because of how I limp around sometimes. I'm never sure quite what to believe from him."

"It's your real name," I said, thinking of the times I had turned B8 (*Enemy*) and heard Rone's voice. I'd even heard him say "Fidget" a couple times. "You're the most famous wizard who has ever lived!"

"Oh, I doubt that."

"It's true," Drake said. "You basically saved the world… except, it turns out you actually didn't, really…"

Rellik chuckled. "Well, *that* sounds right at least."

"I'm your heir," I said. "I came to finish what you started."

He looked at me for a long time. "That, I believe."

"But you should be able to help me! I need you to tell me what you faced, how you failed, so that I don't make the same mistake. Better yet, you could just try again and do it better this time. If you're not dead, then you don't need an heir yet. Your work isn't done, and you have to do it!"

He was shaking his head. "You're not hearing me, Simon. That is your name, is it not? That is always your name in my dreams… The wizard I was is dead. I am just the man beneath, and that is not such a bad thing. However, my time is done. This is your day."

He laid his hands on my shoulders. "It was always you in my dreams, you know. Coming here to save me. Your name, blazing in starlight across the night sky of

my darkened mind. Simon Fayter. You need no one's leadership today." He pointed at our matching boot prints. "I remember that he made these boots on my feet for me when I was captured, because they look just like my old ones, and he wanted me to appear familiar to him. Now *you* wear the originals. Likewise, the burden is all yours."

Rellik nodded, as if that settled the matter, and then he hopped down into the pool and began wading out of the room. "Come on," he said. "Let's get out of this place before my brother returns." He pointed at a door at the end of the room past the marble floor that we still stood on, and we moved away from it instinctively, following him into the pool.

"How often does he visit you?" Tessa asked.

"Oh, every few days or so. He comes to gloat about his work. 'I've captured another child,' he says. 'I've killed another of your old friends,' he says—as if I could remember them after what he did to me. 'I've enslaved another child. I've set up shop at Skelligard, where they think I cannot come. I've infiltrated the Circle of Eight.' On and on he goes. There is no one so long-winded as a liar or a boaster."

"Wait, he's at Skelligard?" I exclaimed.

"He infiltrated the Circle of Eight?" Tessa said, the horror plain on her face.

"So he says. Though the names have passed far out of my memory. I imagine they are things, places that I cared much for in the past, the way he tries to taunt me with

them. As if this pool were not taunting enough to drown even the tallest hopes in…"

"What do you mean?" I said numbly, looking around at the pool as my mind whirled, coming to terms with this new information. Was it true? Could Rone really be at Skelligard? Could he really have infiltrated the Circle of Eight? What did that mean? Surely he couldn't pose as one of its members, could he?

"This is a killing floor," Rellik said gravely, coming to a stop and indicating the red liquid all around us. "That is what *he* calls it, anyway. It is a foul contraption from the darkest pits of that twisted beast he calls a mind. You noticed, I am sure, how like blood this fluid looks. It is *not* blood, but it reminds a person of it." He trailed off for a moment, then resumed, speaking fast and low, as if the words were heavy things that he didn't like to hold for long. "Every time a person dies because of him, their blood rains down from up above, to fall here and join the growing pool."

"But," I said, "there must be thousands of gallons here."

"Yes," he said gravely. "Thousands. The human body holds almost five liters, you know. Many people have died because of him. He built this symbol to taunt me. To remind me that I failed—that he is strong. That he is out there hurting people, and I can do nothing."

"You remember enough to be sad," I said, "but not enough to help me?"

"I remember that I was a good person. Or tried to be. I know that I do not like what my brother does, and that once I opposed him, and nearly won. The details escape me, but details are of little importance. Our souls are the creation of our past, as a building is the creation of the architect. If the architect dies, the building remains. Thus my soul stands strong, undisturbed by the dissolution of its scaffolding."

I shook my head. "Now that I've met you, I'm pretty sure I'm the wrong guy to be your heir."

Rellik laughed. "I am *old*, Simon. Very old now. How old are you? Five? Six?"

"Thirteen," I said, somewhat insulted.

"Bah." He waved a hand dismissively. "I can't even count that low. Give yourself some time. No one becomes the person they truly want to be in an hour."

Just then, a mist of red liquid fizzled down from above, changing the color of the light. It fell into the pool and covered our hair and arms and faces with a spattering of red.

"Another has gone from this world at his hand," Rellik said sadly. "Let us go now and stop him for good."

"You know how to kill him?" I said.

Rellik chuckled. "No, no. Of course not. That *would* be helpful, wouldn't it? No, Simon. I don't have the answers. Except to this one question, for it has ever been on my mind: Who will save me and the world? Who will right the wrongs that I have made? And the answer comes

in my dreams, in a distant sun's reflection in the red of the killing floor, on the whisper of the still air of these catacombs: Simon Fayter. The Seer Unseen."

7

BIG BIRD'S BROTHER[63]

Soft feathers cannot make a cruel bird kind.

—Munia Khan

Flint opened the door for us when we reached the bootmaker's workshop at Skelligard, then closed it behind us and locked the door. Flint embraced Rellik in a big bear hug.

"How did you know?" I said. "How did you know he was down there?"

"Long have I watched Skelligard," he replied. "Once, long ago, I made the journey into Stores, at great personal risk. Hawk nearly caught me. If he had, my shoemaker identity would have been called into question, and if he had taken me into custody, he may have discovered all. I guessed at the identity of the Bloody Prince, and I am a good guesser. But even after I had made the tools I thought could free him, I dared not risk another trip back."

---

63 "ABCDEFGHIJKLMNOPQRSTUVWXYZ. It's the most remarkable word I've ever seen." —Big Bird, *Sesame Street*

"Will you help him?" I said. "Can you make him remember?"

Flint placed a hand on Rellik's head and closed his eyes, frowning. "With time and great effort, the body is repairable," he said. "But the mind is another matter. Even if he may someday use magic again, he will likely never recover all that has been lost. His memories have been burned away permanently. They will not return."

I slumped onto the stool at Flint's workbench, and he brought four plates of food out from behind the counter. Not conjured food, but real homemade stuff from the Skelligard dining hall. There was spaghetti and meatballs for me, Tessa, and Rellik, and two raw turkeys, feathers and all, for Drake.

"Oh boy!" he said, and gobbled[64] them down with zeal.

When we had finished eating, Flint declared that there was still much to be done and marched us through the door to the back room, which, as I now knew, led into Flint's chamber of doors. Safely inside, he locked the door to Skelligard and bade Drake and Tessa to escort Rellik to the main house.

"He won't leave without you," Flint promised my friends as looks of worry crossed their faces. "Wizard's honor."

They left, and Flint pointed me at the barnlike door. "You must go to Ashguld without delay," he said. "And

---

64 Pun intended.

despite what I said, you must leave without your friends. Ashguld is no place for children."

"But," I objected, "*I'm* a child."

"Yes, indeed, and one child is quite enough to be getting on with."

"So I'm going alone?" I wasn't crazy about the idea.

"Of course not," he said. "You may take an adult with you. I think you will want the warrior on this journey, not the teacher."

I nodded, and an ice chute grew down from the ceiling, depositing the frozen form of the Tike beside us. Flint touched her, and she was instantly freed from the ice, apparently warm as could be. She took a few quick steps in retreat.

"What happened?" she demanded. "Simon, who is this?"

"There is no time for questions," I said. "I'll explain later. For now, we must be going. We have work to do."

Flint opened the barn door, and we stepped into the dank and angry chaos that was the workshop of Aekig, black magic dealer in Ashguld. "Go left on the street outside," Flint instructed. "Look for a man selling tours of Ashguld. His name is Hrog. Tell him Aekig sent you for the special service to the third moon, and give him the bag of coins under the counter. Watch out for Stork."

With that, the door closed behind us, and we were alone.

"What is going on?" the Tike whispered.

"Long story," I replied.

"That's fine," she said, gripping my arm. "I'll wait right here while you tell it."

I looked around at the strange interior of the shop. It was as though Flint had hired Count Dracula as his interior decorator. Black velvet lined the floors, muffling the sound of footsteps. Shrunken heads capped the bannister posts of the stairs leading into the loft above us. In the center of the shop, there was a table and chairs crafted out of human bones and a display of dangerous-looking sharp objects that put me in mind of bear traps. A sales counter of polished black stone stood at the far end, and behind it shelves of transparent jars were filled with what might well have been every internal organ known to man. "Are you sure you want to chat in *here*?"

"Perhaps not," she said, looking around as well.

I made my way carefully to the other side of the room, and the Tike followed close behind. "He said the money was under the counter," I whispered, stepping around it. And it was—a softball-sized leather pouch filled with gold coins. I tucked it into my pocket and moved for what I took to be the exit door. "Who do you suppose Stork is?" I said.

As if in answer to my question, there was a creak in the floorboards overhead. Then footsteps on the stairs. We saw the legs first like long, white knobby sticks, and then we saw the rest of him. He was like Big Bird's emaciated albino little brother, except that there was nothing cute and fluffy about him, unless you counted the plume of blue feathers on the crown of his head. He was all wiry

strength and wretchedness, and I couldn't help imagining him pecking the warm meat off my bones.

I bumped the counter, making a noise, and the birdlike figure spun on the stairs, looking down at us. "Who are you?" it hissed. Its voice was like a snake being strangled.

"Ah," I said. "You must be Stork. Would you believe me if I said we're friends of Aekig, and he gave us permission to be here and told us to take this gold?"

"No." He hopped over the bannister and landed gracefully on the other side of the bar. "Aekig does not have friends, and he does not abide thievery." His wings glistened in the dim light, and his pinions transformed into long, deadly looking spears.

"Whoa," I said, raising my hands in a placating gesture. "Slow down, man. Don't lay an egg or anything."

"WHAT?" he bellowed.

The Tike drew her long knives and leaped, catlike, onto the counter. Stork flicked his spears, and the counter came alive, wriggling and coiling like a snake, so that the Tike nearly fell off.

"Let's go, Tike," I said. I drew Kylanthus and cut the stone serpent in half.

"NO!" Stork screamed when he saw my flaming sword. "The Knights have come!" He took a half step back, and the Tike encouraged his retreat by producing several triangular throwing knives and launching them at him. He raised his wings like shields, backing farther away. A second later, I had the door open, and we were safely out in the street.

It was dusk outside, and the smell of rain hung thick on the air. Underfoot, the cobblestones were wet, so I figured we had just missed it. The street was narrow, with tall, imposing shops crowding in on both sides, their once-brightly painted signs now faded to the same gray color of the stormy sky.

"I hate poultry," the Tike said, taking the street with a casual stride.

"So I've noticed."

She still had two of the strange little throwing triangles in her hands, but after a backward glance at the door to Aekig's shop, she tucked them into the waistband of her leather pants.

I hurried to catch up with her, then had to stop in my tracks as a huge minotaur stepped out of an alleyway to my right. I nearly collided with him, and he spared me a sideways glance and a grunt before passing out of sight into the opposite alleyway. I shivered. I had seen minotaurs before, but this one was wearing armor and obviously led a rough life. His fur was patched and mangy, and one of his eyes was cloudy white, with a long scar traveling through it.

The Tike stepped back toward me and looked into the alley where the minotaur had come from. She was glancing up and down the street and up at the rooflines of the buildings. "This way," she said, grabbing my coat by the lapel and dragging me into the alleyway.

"Wait, Flint said Hrog was left. *Left* on the main road." But she wasn't listening. I followed her into the narrow

alleyway and up a thin iron ladder onto the roof of the building, where she plopped down cross-legged.

"Sit down," she commanded. I complied. She moved closer to the edge of the roof and peered down. From this vantage point, we could see a good chunk of the grubby city. It reminded me of what medieval London must have been like: dirty, gray, damp, tall stone and wooden structures crammed together on narrow streets with a plethora of shadowy alleys and a host of less-than-savory characters. Lovely.

"Now you can tell me what is going on," she said.

"Oh, right." I nodded to myself, thinking that suddenly her behavior made sense. She needed to understand what was going on, she wanted to make her own observations about our new environment, and she needed a defensible position. Suddenly I was glad that I had taken Flint's advice and brought the Tike. Nothing like having an expert fighter beside you when you're heading into… well…whatever we were heading into.

I told her as much as I knew—all about Flint and the turncoat and finding Rellik. For once in my life, I didn't leave anything out, and she seemed satisfied. Upon learning of our current mission, however, she became quite agitated.

"Do you know where we are?" she said.

"Ashguld?" I guessed.

"And did you know that Ashguld is a pirate planet?" she said. "And not the kind of pirates that we have met before. The scum of the universe inhabit this place.

Wanted men. Hunted men. They come here to disappear, and the Wizguard doesn't mind because they know half the people who make it here will be taken down by disease or violence in the streets. You couldn't have picked a worse place to visit. Except, of course, for our destination.

"The Unright Fortress, the chasm of never-ending dark…I know this place. The Vale of Nightmares, we call it on Daru, for that is what Kohman the Foolhardy named it, and *he* went there. No others of my race have been so foolish, until now." As she spoke, the Rimbakka—the bird tattoo on her neck—became increasingly agitated as well, and I knew that somewhere my mother was probably pacing back and forth with worry.

I nodded, trying to show my appreciation for the serious nature of our situation. "Good thing I brought you with me, eh, Tike? Forget this moon we're supposed to get to. That minotaur back there might have had me for lunch!"

"That minotaur back there is probably meeting with his friends right now, telling them about how fresh meat has arrived, and hatching a plan to have us for lunch. Or perhaps sell us to slavers."

"You know, Tike, you're not exactly sunshiney in situations like this."

She scowled. "Sunshiney?"

"Have you ever heard of Eeyore? Well, never mind, then. Are we ready to go looking for Hrog?"

"No looking necessary. That's him there." She pointed at a man two blocks over, who was standing at the corner

of two intersecting streets. He was short, fat, shirtless, and covered in sloppy tattoos. He was smoking a cigar and leaning casually against a building that had three disproportionately large chimneys coming out of the roof.

"How do you know it's him?"

"Every time someone passes, he offers them a pamphlet."

I watched as two women walked past him, and he did as the Tike said he would. A second later, a group of mangy-looking minotaurs huffed past him, and he did it again, but they weren't buying. The next moment, they were out of sight.

"Lovely," I said. "Did you—"

"I saw it. Come. Can you make the jump from this roof to that one?" She pointed at the one across the street. Suddenly I was grateful that the streets were narrow. I nodded. I could definitely make it with B1 (*Leap*), and I was pretty sure I could do it without. "You go first," she said.

I took a running leap and made the jump under my own power, landing gracefully and summersaulting to absorb my extra momentum.[65] A second later, she followed. The next few jumps were easier, since we were crossing alleyways instead of streets as we moved closer to our quarry.

The Tike kept her head on a swivel as we moved, no

---

65 Technically I landed awkwardly on one foot and tumbled head over heels, but it's all how you paint the facts…

doubt checking for signs of our little minotaur hunting party. Then we were making the last jump onto the building against which Hrog was leaning. I went first, and she came next, but as she flew through the air, a big furry hand shot up from the dark of the alley below and grabbed her slender ankle. The hand yanked her downward, and her body smacked against the edge of the roof. I reached for her too late, and she slid over the edge.

I stood there gaping for a second, then dove after her headfirst. I summersaulted in midair, unsheathed Kylanthus, and stuck the flaming blade into the building, which effectively slowed my descent. I landed upright in the center of the alley, flaming sword held before me.

I would like to point out here how awesome that diving-summersault-sword-wallslash[66] move was, especially after the unfortunate incident with the roof-jumping a minuteago. I really *can* be awesome. I just need a good reason. Concern for another person's welfare can inspire heroism in the commonest of souls.[67]

Speaking of my heroism, there I stood, facing nine fully armored minotaurs. Well, okay. *Eight* fully armored minotaurs. One of them had evidently been beaten senseless by the Tike before they got her tied up in the thick rope she now wore. Actually, to be honest, she had broken the arm of a second one and buried her long knives

---

66 Not a word.
67 Not that my soul is common. It just sounded like a really cool and insightful thing to say.

in the horns of a third (terribly painful for them), so they were pretty much out of the picture.

Anyway...there I was facing *six* fully armored, angry, mangy minotaurs, complete with smells.[68] I wasn't sure what to say, so I fell back on my default defense: tasteless humor. "Sorry to cancel the party, boys, but I seem to have forgotten the cake. Let's try this again next week when I'm not here."

When this had no effect on them, I turned E1, and my dumb clone appeared beside me, holding his flaming sword aloft as well. They all took a step back at this.

"That's right," I said. "If I can duplicate myself once, how many times can I do it? I bet you don't want to fight fifty of me! So begone!"

They didn't move. Presently, Dumb Me dropped his sword, sat down on the ground, removed his boots and socks, and began picking lint out from between his toes, humming to himself all the while.

I sighed. The minotaurs took heart and moved forward as one.

I gritted my teeth. "Fine," I said. "If it's death you want, it is death you shall have. I am Simon Fayter, Knight of the Circle of Eight, and you'll not live to remember this night."

Given the dangers that no doubt lay ahead, I had been trying to avoid using up the more powerful turncoat knobs on a street brawl, but enough was enough.

---

68 Man, did they stink!

"Don't kill them!" the Tike called.

"Why?" I said, backing up to keep my distance from them.

"We're not here to start a street war," she said. "And you will accomplish nothing."

"I'll accomplish saving your life," I pointed out.

One of the minotaurs kicked a half-full metal trash can at me, and I sliced it in half, spraying the alley wall with pork fat and rotten lettuce.

"Death begets death begets death,"[69] she insisted. "You'll do more harm than good."

"Argh," I groaned, looking for a way out of the situation. I could certainly fight and win if I used up my powers, but then I would be unprepared for the rest of our mission. I couldn't run. I couldn't talk my way out of it, could I?

"Oh," I said, stopping my retreat and grinning at the minotaurs. "Do you know what we really need? A new beginning!" I winked at the Tike, and she braced herself.

Then I turned E3 (*Daze*)—

---

69 This is a quote from the famous science fiction author, Pierce Brown, and is a recurring theme in his Red Rising series.

8

THE MOST DANGEROUS THING

I am glad you are here with me. Here at the end of all things.
—J.R.R. Tolkien, *The Return of the King*

—And a new chapter started. When I came to, the minotaurs were still unconscious, no doubt dreaming strange, disturbing things. By now, the Tike and I were getting used to this, which was why we were able to recover, cut her free, and run around the corner before the first minotaur began to stir.

"Expert tours of Ashguld," a nasally voice said, waving a pamphlet under my nose. "See the sights with a knowledgeable guide! No better man for the job than Hrog."

"We'll take it," I said. "Just let us inside."

Hrog looked taken aback by our earnest acceptance of his offer. "But…" he said. "I mean, you will?"

"Do you want our business or not?" I demanded, pushing him toward the door of his own establishment.

"I do! I do! Stop pushing. Stop pushing!"

He admitted us into a dank and dusty reception room that bore a striking resemblance to the kind of little travel

agency offices that you'd find in big cities back on Earth. The walls were covered with very bad drawings of what must have been the various sights to be seen on Ashguld. He must have never used it as an actual waiting room, for there was a thick layer of dust on the furniture and floor. A well-worn path led through the grime to a back room.

"Well," he said awkwardly, "have a seat, um…or not." He cast a doubtful glance at the dusty couch and stopped mid sit-down, rising again awkwardly.

Guessing that he was engaged in some sort of back-handed illegal dealings, and the "travel agency" was just a front, I said, "Relax. We're not here to bust you. Aekig sent us. We're looking for the special service to the third moon."

"Oh!" He put a sweaty palm over his chubby cheek and sighed with relief. His other hand went unconsciously to the tattoo on his chest and began tracing the lines of it. It reminded me of how some Catholics would cross themselves while praying. "Thank the gods! Aekig, eh? *Very* serious fellow there. How do you know him?"

"We did not come for the pleasure of your company or conversation," the Tike said, looking him up and down disdainfully. "We came for the—"

"Special service," he cut in. "Of course. Sorry, my lady." He gave a little bow. "I hate to ask, of course, but I must—terribly rude, of course—but do you have—"

I tossed the bag of coins, and he caught it. "Ah!" He hefted the weight and grinned. "Good, then. Follow me."

We followed him through the door at the back, and

the Tike and I made sure to leave some distance between us and him. She would have said it was in case he was planning a trap for us, but for me it was simply due to the smell. When it came to bathing, Hrog was apparently one of those once-a-week types.

The back room was long, narrow, and empty except for what looked like three brick fireplaces. They were not normal fireplaces, however. They had doors rather than regular openings, and the doors were long and tall.

The Tike made a low, growling noise in her throat when she saw them.

"What?" I said.

"Body launchers."

Hrog cleared his throat. "I prefer to call them *Emergency Relocation Devices*."

"I'm sure you do," the Tike said.

"What are they?" I asked.

"Wizards developed body launchers during the minotaurian wars," the Tike explained. "They were used on battlefields, where anti-magic devices prevented wizards from traveling great distances at speed. They were designed to launch warriors like human cannonballs, very high, into fortresses, or very far behind enemy lines. But—"

"But early versions were not very reliable," Hrog said, wringing his hands. "*My* machines, of course, are completely—"

"But they ended up blowing people up as often as launching them," the Tike finished.

Hrog cleared his throat. "I assure you, my lady, *these* ones are completely safe. I have made several modifications myself, and as I'm sure you know, no one has a better reputation than I do when it comes to helping folks in a tight spot disappear quickly."

"Disappearing too…*thoroughly* is what I'm afraid of."

He shrugged. "You don't have to go, but I'm afraid your money is nonrefundable. Look." He opened one of the tall chimney doors and revealed what looked like a shiny launch tube inside. He tossed in the bag of coins and closed the door again, then punched a large button set into the brick wall. There was a thunderous roar, like a fighter jet flying right overhead, and the bag of coins disappeared in a flash of light.

"There," he said. "If it's safe enough for me to trust my money to it, it's safe enough for you."

The Tike turned to me. "Simon, I advise against trusting our lives to this reckless man who, apart from not appreciating the subtle differences between the human body and a bag of coins, also lacks the wits to use a bathtub."

"Hey!" Hrog said. "That's not very nice." He sniffed an armpit and grumbled that he smelled fine.

"We're not trusting him, Tike. We're trusting Flint."

"Whom I do not know," she pointed out, tapping me in the chest. "And who imprisoned me, captured you, and is manipulating us for his own ends while holding our friends hostage."

I scratched my head. "Well, yeah. That's kind of a

glass-half-empty way of looking at it, but okay. He *did* help us find and release Rellik."

"Whom he also now has as a prisoner."

"*Or* whom[70] he is now healing," I said. "*I* trust Flint. *I* talked to him, and while I admit he's a bit wacky, who wouldn't be after living alone for nine hundred years and only going outside to pretend to be other people? I think he is really trying to help us. If not, he wouldn't have waited so long for me to come. Anyway, *I'm* going, so if you want to protect me, you're just going to have to tag along." I slugged her in the shoulder. "Don't worry so much! We're not going to get blown up! We're too important."

The Tike looked skyward and mouthed something to herself in her native tongue. "Fine," she said. "But never hit me again unless I give you permission." She reached out in a casual gesture and flicked my abdomen just above the navel. My legs went numb, my knees buckled, and I fell forward onto my face, squawking.

"We will go together," she was saying to Hrog while I tried to gain my feet again. "In the same tube."

"That is highly irregular," he said. "The tubes are calibrated for only one body, and I cannot guarantee—"

"The boy is small," she said shortly. "And I am slender. Together, we are within ten pounds of your own weight. We go together, or not at all. If you cannot return our payment, I will happily take it from your hide."

---

70 I just want to point out how careful I'm being with the proper use of my whos and whoms here. Kids aint gonna git no bad edumacation readin my books!

Hrog gulped, eyed the knives at her belt, and wisely decided to ignore the fact that she had called him fat. "Of course," he said. "You will go together, of course! Best way to travel, really. Cozy!"

He opened the door to the tube he had placed the money in and reached inside and fiddled with some knobs and levers. "You sure you want to go to the third moon? Whoever's after you, it can't be *that* bad. I can send you anywhere on the planet, you know. Hragantia's nice this time of year. Or the Valley of a Thousand Shipwrecks. No one would find you there!"

"You have our coordinates," I said.

He bumped his head with a hand. "I almost forgot. You'll be needing space rings so that you can breathe out there." He reached into the pocket of his pants, but we waved our hands at him, showing him the ones we still had from our time on the *Calliope*, given to us by Captain Bast.

I stepped past him into the tube. It was narrower than it looked. It smelled of iron, and the sound of my breath echoed back from the curved wall. A hundred feet above me, a little circular patch of gray sky foreshadowed my immediate future.

"I change my mind, Tike," I said. "I think this is a bad idea."

"Calm yourself," she said, stepping in beside me. It was a very tight fit.

"I'm calm," I said, wincing. "Ouch. That's my face."

"Here," she said, wrapping my arms about her waist.

She did the same to me, and I admit we fit much better that way. "How does *he* fit in here?" she wondered aloud.

"I heard that," he said. "I'd think about sending you two somewhere horrible, if there *were* any place more horrible than the one I'm already sending you."

"Relax," the Tike told me, and I realized I was indeed quite tense. "We're only getting fired out of a giant magical rocket."

"I'm relaxed." I said.

But I wasn't. To be truthful, I hadn't even been thinking about the whole human cannonball thing, though now that she mentioned it, that was bothering me as well. What I was really thinking about was the fact that I was a thirteen-year-old boy with about zero experience touching a girl—other than hugging my mom, which was a lot faster than this, and with much less touching—and now I was all wrapped up with the Tike. How did I get myself into these situations? Why did she have her arms around me like that?

"Simon," she said, "you have to relax. If we get launched out of here with you that tense, you might throw off our trajectory."

"I'm relaxed," I insisted. Then I inspected her face. "Hey, *you* relax. What are you, afraid of heights or something?"

"I am afraid of getting blown up by machines that regularly blow people up," she said.

Hrog shut the door and locked it with an ominous, echoing click.

"Tike," I said, "don't your people have a saying… Drake was telling me about it. Something about the most dangerous thing you'll ever do?"

She smiled. "The most dangerous thing you ever do will be the last thing you ever do."

"See?" I said. "This can't be very dangerous, then, because it's not the thing that will kill you. I've got lots more to do, and so do you."

She raised an eyebrow. "Is the little boy comforting the nine-hundred-year-old woman now?"

I blushed. "Shucks, Tike. You don't look a day over eight seventy-five."

She cuffed me on the back of the head. "Hush. I have three hundred and eighty-four great-great-great-great-grandchildren."

"Oh," I said. "Right." And suddenly I felt better about my other problem. Hugging an old lady wasn't a big deal, even if she did sort of look like a ninjafied[71] Queen Amidala…

"You do know what the most dangerous thing I ever did was, don't you?" she whispered, looking up at the sky. I saw the white oval glowing on her cheek, inches from my own, and remembered the day that one of her gods had bound her to me in the most sacred ceremony of her people. I felt her pulse quicken through my ward ring and remembered Gladstone's words when he bound us together as wizard and ward.

---

71 Not a word, technically. That said, it means "having been turned into a ninja."

May these rings bind you, until death finds you.

"I know," I whispered back. "And, Tike, I'm glad you're here."

"As am I, Simon."

Something rumbled deep below us. Then a brief silence, a blinding flash, and we were hurtling through the sky like an intercontinental ballistic missile.

THE VALE OF NIGHTMARES

Hell is empty and all the devils are here.

—William Shakespeare[72]

The Tike and I rocketed through the atmosphere of the third moon of Ashguld, protected by a magical missile-shaped force field as we flew. I had never experienced so much speed, so much light, so much noise as I did upon liftoff, or such deep silence as I heard in deep space.

Things were getting noisy again now, though, and then we plunged into soft orange soil and plowed on for a half mile before we stopped. The force field flickered and vanished, and it was just us, standing in a ten-foot-deep trench, the scar our landing had made upon the face of Ashguld's moon.

We climbed out, and I was struck by the beauty of the place. It looked like what I had always imagined the Sahara might look like. Banks of sand as far as the eye could see.

72 A sixteenth-century Peruvian shepherd most famous for having six thumbs and writing the song, "Lost on High Mountains with Sheep," which can only be played with six thumbs.

Mind you, you'd have to wear some tinted sunglasses to get the Sahara looking quite as red as Ashguld's moon did. Above us, Ashguld itself hung like the belly of an ash-gray whale.

"Peaceful-looking from this distance," the Tike murmured.

"Hopefully we won't have to get closer to it than this ever again," I said. "We've found all of the bloodstones, so I think if I turn the E6 knob again, it should just take us back to Skelligard."

She was scanning the horizon, frowning.

"Do you see something?" I asked.

"No, but I hear it. Don't you?"

"Nope."

At that moment, Leto, the good-for-nothing[73] dragon that lives in my boot poked his head out. "*I* hear it," he said.

The Tike looked alarmed. Leto, of course, was revered by her people as being extremely holy.

He grinned. "It *sounds* like a sleuth of sunbears.[74] You know, I've never actually seen a sunbear."

"RUN!" the Tike screamed. She dashed across the

---

73 Except for that one time when he bonded the Tike and I together. Also the time he fought off a titanically large dragon and saved all our lives.

74 Different animals have different words to describe their groups. These words are called collective nouns, because it describes a collection of the same animal. For example, a herd of cows or a pack of wolves. Any self-respecting geek can rattle off at least twenty or so, so here is a smattering for your perusal: a shrewdness of apes, an

sand as though the hounds of hell[75] were on her heels.

I chased after her, and she slowed down so that we could run together. I began to hear it now as well, a deep thumping rumble somewhere behind us. I risked a glance back and saw a distant sand dune explode with light. It melted away, and a giant golden bear ran through the place where it had been.

"Whoa! Cool!"

"Not cool!" the Tike said. "Very not cool. Faster, Simon. Run faster."

Leto scurried up my leg and back, then latched onto my shoulder, facing backward. "They are magnificent!" he declared in tones of admiration.

"I'm happy that you are impressed, Sacred One," the Tike managed. "How many do your eyes see?"

---

obstinacy of buffalo, a caravan of camels, a swarm of bees, a quiver of cobras, a bask of crocodiles, a murder of crows, a drove of donkeys, an unkindness of ravens, a crash of rhinoceroses, a parade of elephants, a gang of elk, a school of fish, a band of gorillas, a tower of giraffes, a gaggle of geese, an army of frogs, a charm of foxes, a stand of flamingos, a cast of falcons, a business of ferrets, a cackle of hyenas, a shadow of jaguars, a smack of jellyfish (Pro tip: never get smacked by a jellyfish, and you *really* don't want to get smacked by a smack of jellyfish), a conspiracy of lemurs, a pride of lions, a barrel (or troop) of monkeys, a shiver of sharks, a stench of skunks (I wonder how they got that name?), a scurry of squirrels, a fever of stingrays, a game of swans (or a wedge, if they are flying), a streak of tigers, a pod of whales, a sounder of pigs, a zeal of zebras, and of course, a sleuth of bears.

75 In Greek mythology, Hades, god of the underworld, had a three-headed hound named Cerberus who guarded the entrance to the underworld. Other mythical dogs chase you *into* the underworld.

"There are seven, child," he called wistfully. The rumble of the bears running was a roaring noise now. "Truly, they are more magnificent than my race. Alas! I have just lost a bet... On the bright side, the dragon I lost to died four thousand years ago, so even in defeat, I have triumphed!"

I glanced back again and saw that there were indeed seven bears. They were far enough away that it was difficult to judge their size, but I guessed they were each as big as a house. They looked like they were made of liquid gold, with sunlight pouring out at the seams. One in the front roared, and a jet of molten light shot from his mouth, turning several acres of sand into rolling hills of glass.

"Amazing," I said.

"THEY WILL DESTROY US!" the Tike shouted.

"They are born with the energy of a sun inside," Leto was saying reverently. "They never stop running. They leap from one planet to the next and walk on the faces of stars and swim through the depths of space, and wherever they go, there follows beauty, awe, and death."

"Yes, DEATH!" the Tike emphasized. "Can you save us, Great One?"

"Me?" Leto said. "No, no. What would *I* do? Roar at them and get melted by sun fire? They are not beings to be reckoned with. They are a force of nature. They give you life or death, and you simply say thank you."

"Tike," I shouted. "They're gaining on us really fast!" It was true. They had already crossed the majority of the distance that separated us when we first spotted them. At

this rate, they would be on us in seconds.

Seconds…

I turned E2 (*Pause*), and time stopped for a few seconds. Behind us, the sunbears froze midstride, blazing like the radiant, carnivorous centers of seven solar systems. I turned E4 (*Size*) and became a giant. I scooped the Tike up in my arms, turned directly around, and sprinted as fast as I possibly could on my long legs.

"WHAT ARE YOU DOING?" she screamed, but I didn't listen. She would see soon enough…unless time started moving ahead of schedule (in which case we would all die).

In forty strides, we had made it to the sunbears. Leto oohed and ahhed as we passed beneath their gleaming bodies. The heat was almost overwhelming, and though we passed them quickly, I was pretty sure I could smell my hair melting. Leto took to the air and reached out his tiny hands as we passed between two of the sunbears, petting them with a look of ecstasy on his face.

In sixty strides, we were safely behind them, with the sunbears pointed *away* from us, and after seventy-five strides, I stopped and turned around just as time started flowing again. It had only been a few seconds, but it had been enough. The sunbears charged on, oblivious to our narrow escape. I turned E4 again and sunk down to my natural size, depositing the Tike on the sand beside me.

The Tike laughed, the sound high and free, happy to be alive. I grinned and looked down at Leto.

"I thought you were going to cry back there," I said.

He frowned at me. "Dragon tears are a panacea,[76] boy. You wish I'd cried."

"Is this what it takes to get you out of my boot?" I asked. "The promise of near-certain death at the hands of a rare and dangerous creature?"

"This or ice cream," he said.

"I just *had* ice cream! Where were you?"

"You did not *offer* me any," he huffed. "I know when I am not wanted." And with that, he stalked back down my clothes and into my boot.

The Tike and I stood and watched as the sunbears leaped into the sky, soaring from the surface of the moon toward another distant celestial object. I felt relief, for a second. Then I felt a sudden wave of heat spreading over my back.

I turned around and came face-to-face with a sunbear. Its shining head was as large as station wagon, and it rested on the ground so that it could look me in the eyes. Its skin really was like liquid gold this close up, and its eyes were like glittering wet sapphires, big as basketballs. I should have burst into flames being this close to the creature, but I did not, which made me think that it was restraining its heat somehow. The Tike went rigid, and I felt the familiar pinching tickle as Leto dashed up my back and onto my shoulder.

"Well *done,* Simon," he whispered in my ear. "I do believe you have found the mother!"

---

76 A cure-all. A magical substance that heals any ailment.

She exhaled, tousling my hair and emitting a bit of extra light. I felt my skin tighten and knew I was getting an instant first-degree sunburn. Leto purred with delight.

"What do we do now?" I said out of the corner of my mouth.

"Shh!" Leto said. "She is speaking. Can't you— Bah. Here." He pressed a finger to my temple, and I immediately heard a sweet female voice drifting across my mind.

"...place is full of darkness," she was saying. "We cannot banish it, for that is not our work. It is good that you have come, Light Weaver. You have our blessing, Friend of the Sunbear." She touched her nose to my chest then, and there was a little flash of light that felt like butterflies. Then she was drifting up and away, following the path of her gleaming cubs.

"Well, hot diggidy!" I said, rubbing my chest.

The Tike was rubbing her arms as if making sure she was still alive. "Your life is never boring, Simon. I'll give you that."

Leto slapped me on the back of the head, beaming with pride. "I *knew* you would amount to something! Friend of the Sunbear indeed! How about that? Say now, what did it feel like when she touched you? Did it leave a mark? Does it tingle? Let me have a look at it." And he dove through the neck of my shirt.

"LETO!" I squawked, dancing around[77] wildly.

"Ouch!" he exclaimed. "CEASE THAT FLAILING!"

---

77 Like a guy with a dragon down his shirt.

I reached under my shirt and yanked him out. As I held him tightly in my fist, I tried not to think about how big he could get, or how he could breathe fire, or just how fast he could roast me.

The Tike was beside herself. "Put him down, Simon!"

I didn't. "If you want to see it, *I* will show it to you," I said.

He glared at me. "I thought we had a no-touching rule."

"You *live* in my shoe," I said.

"A no-touching-*me* rule," he amended.

"That's fine," I said, "but the deal's off if you jump down my shirt."

"Fair. Now, show me."

I lifted my shirt, but there was nothing there.

"Ah!" he said, as though I had just unveiled a tattoo of the Mona Lisa. "Yes. I see it. Wonderful! This is a great boon."[78]

"Come on," I said. "Stop pulling my leg. There's nothing there."

"There is indeed! Though maybe not to your eyes." He held out his hand and touched my solar plexus. "It is small but quite visible. The face of a sunbear. Creatures of darkness will not want to look at *that*, I can assure you."

"Cool," I said. "Next time Rone comes around, I'll just lift my shirt and flash him."

"This is not a thing to joke about," Leto said sharply.

---

78 A thing that is helpful and good.

"Now. Lower your shirt, and let's get out of this place. I hate deserts."

"Sorry," I said sheepishly.[79]

"That is quite all right," he said, stretching his wings. "Now, in the interest of not traipsing through this bear-forsaken desert all day—knowing as I do how your feet begin to stink in hot weather—I will fly up and see what may be seen."

"Really?" I said. "That sounds an awful lot like helping…"

"I am getting soft in my old age," he said, and fluttered into the sky.

"You should not speak to him so disrespectfully," the Tike said as we watched him do a slow circle high above us. "Even if you do not believe as I believe, he is giving his life for you and your quest."

Her words stung. Not a ton, mind you (I'm a little bit mean at heart), but they stung, and I resolved to do better.

Leto alighted upon my shoulder a second later and pointed to our left. "The sand forms two mountains over there, with a valley between them, leading into a deep canyon."

"That is our way," the Tike said. "Thank you, Great One." She gave me a significant look.

"Uh, yeah," I said. "Thanks for, uh…being useful for once—Great One," I added. I gave the Tike a thumbs-up, and she put her palm to her face. Hey, I was trying.

---

79 I think…I'm not actually sure how sheep apologize.

"And I would thank *you* if you never ate one of those bacon and lettuce sandwiches again, *Light Weaver*," Leto said with a sneer as he climbed back into my boot. "I am *always* downwind."

"Incredible," the Tike said as we began walking in the direction Leto had pointed. "When this is all over, I honestly do not know which will be the stranger fact to me: that an unseasoned[80] youth was chosen to save the world, or that he has one of the Holy Attar commenting on his bodily functions."

"It's all in a day's work, Tike. All in a day's work."

A vale, by definition, is a valley, and this one was full of shadows. Great sandy embankments rose like mountains on either side of it, but the darkness between them was deeper than could be accounted for by shade alone. There was something inside that ate the light. I could feel it. I shivered, then reached into my pocket and touched the sorrowstone. Immediately, my fear left me like water from a sieve, and I felt okay again.

We could see nothing of what lay ahead as we took our first steps into the darkness, and perhaps that is the definition of courage, because I never felt more in need of the stuff before or since.

---

80 By which she means that I lack experience, not that I need garlic salt dumped on me.

"No matter what you see inside," the Tike said, "follow my lead."

"What if you don't know what to do?"

She gave my shoulder a reassuring squeeze. "Then I will follow yours, Master Fayter."

That was the first time she addressed me with what could be called formal respect, and I didn't miss it. I shrugged Kylanthus from my shoulder and held it in both hands.

"Do not ignite the flames," she said as we left the last of the light behind. "But open your mouth and give us just a little light now and then."

I nodded, turning C4 (*Headlight*). I cracked my lips, and a beam of light shot out, piercing the darkness and illuminating a steep downward slope in front of us. I snapped my lips shut just as fast, and the Tike whispered her approval.

Every couple of minutes, she would tell me to light the way once more, and a fleeting flash would help us get our bearings before we were plunged into absolute darkness again. Not that there was anywhere to wander off to.

We were in a tunnel with sloping sides and a high roof. The deeper we got, the colder it became, but we did not encounter anything or anyone. All was silent. If you have never experienced the absolute dark that is found deep underground, it is at once peaceful and oppressive in its totality. Finally, just as I thought that surely we would soon come out on the other side of the moon, I let

out another flash of light at the Tike's signal and nearly stepped into an abyss.[81]

I had one foot out before me, hovering over the chasm, and the Tike's hand shot out and gripped the hem of the turncoat. She pulled me slowly backward until I had both feet safely on solid ground, at which point I lay down and folded my arms, trying not to pass out. Did I mention I don't like heights?

"Thanks," I said.

"My pleasure."

After a minute, I rolled over and stuck my head over the edge, careful to keep the rest of me firmly on the ground. The Tike lay down beside me, and I opened my mouth. The light revealed a long drop that sloped inward at the end, as though the hole curved away from us. I flashed the light out ahead, and there was nothing at all for as far as we could see.

"That is a *long* drop," I said.

"With a blind landing," she added. "Even if you went first and then turned time back, if there turns out to be a pit of lava or some such at the bottom, the fall would take too much time, and I fear you would restart it halfway through."

"Nothing like falling to your death *twice*," I said.

"Indeed. Still, if you wish to risk it, I will follow. I think the inward slope will slow our slide, provided we

---

81 A really deep hole. So deep that you can't measure it.

can manage to slide and not free-fall. It all depends on what lies at the bottom."

"If there is a bottom," I said. "Hey, what if I use C10, Inflation? You could glide down there on my inflatable head."

"Maybe. Though I would hate for you to get punctured on the sharp rocks."

"What sharp rocks?" I looked again and spotted them, a row of stalactites on either side of the tunnel, pointing straight inward. "Ouch," I said. "Okay. *I* can make the drop. I think…I can use B1, Leap, and just jump in. That always gives me a soft landing. If it's a mess down there, I'll turn C10, Inflation, and float back up, stalactites or no stalactites."

"And what if you make a successful descent? How am I to follow?"

"Huh." Hadn't thought of that. "I'll catch you?"

She sighed. "It's not the best plan, but it appears to be our only option. Pity you can't fly."

I started at her words. "That's it!"

She grabbed my wrist in an iron grip. "No, Simon. This is not the time to try learning to fly."

"No, no," I said. "Let me go. I'm not jumping in there. Promise. Give me a few seconds of quiet. I'm going to try doing some actual hard-core wizard stuff for once."

She released me, and I put my fingers to the sides of my head, hoping that the classic wizard-using-mind-power gesture might give me the extra edge. Couldn't hurt, right?

I focused on gravity, where *down* was, and then shifted it in my mind. Not right where *we* were, though. That was important. It would be a pity to suddenly fall down out of the tunnel the way we had come. No, I needed to change gravity just on the other side of the ledge.

When I had it fully envisioned, I turned C7 (*Gravity*). I used my hand for once, not wanting to distract my brain with another task. I felt something shift deep inside, and whether it was a change inside me or the moon itself, I couldn't tell. Until the Tike grunted; she had felt it too.

I felt myself go suddenly weak, and my head burst with pain. The codex[82] that hung around my neck blazed with heat, and I lost consciousness.

I saw the boy with coal-black eyes then, dying to save me. A flash. I saw the Tike dying in my arms, her jacket slick with blood. Flash. She was alive again, fighting a dozen young wizards on a high rampart. Flash. Whispers rising out of the abyss. Flash. A golden chain being cut by a red blade. Flash. Tessa staring down at me from far above, through eyes that were no longer her own. "There are worms in the walls. In case you get hungry."

---

82 The energy from the codex can be used for magic work like this, or to fuel your body and keep you youthful. Or as a sort of magical overdraft account to keep you alive in the event that you, you know, try to change how the laws of nature work or something and end up overextending yourself a bit…

I lurched awake with a shout. The Tike was holding me down. "Shh," she whispered. "You're back now. What did you do?"

"Huh?"

"With the magic. What did you do?"

"Shifted gravity, I think."

"For what?" she said. "For me? For you? I felt something…"

"For the whole moon, I think. At least down here. In retrospect, it might have been a little too complex." I touched the codex, which was stone cold now. Empty, I guessed. Oops. Hopefully I wouldn't need to dip into my nine lives later today.

"THE WHOLE *MOON*? SIMON, ARE YOU STARK RAVING MAD?"

I was taken aback by her vehemence. Not only was she generally silent about the use of magic, she was also generally levelheaded in a crisis. I couldn't see her expression, but I could tell she was livid.

"Uh…"

"You could have killed yourself trying something like that. Don't they teach any safety sense at that school of yours?"

"Probably," I said, "but I think you have to make it past day one."

It occurred to me then that thus far, my tutors had been so focused on teaching me how to use magic at all—specifically to touch it and make *anything* happen—that

there might be some holes in my education regarding practices and procedures.

"Anyway, what's done is done. Did it work?"

She grunted. "Jump over the edge and see."

I peered over and shined my head light. "Everything looks the same," I said. I waved my hand over the edge, as if I could *feel* gravity. But of course, I couldn't. "Let's throw something over and see what happens. Give me one of your knives."

"I will not let you throw my knives into a cavern out of which I may never be able to retrieve them."

I looked around for a stone, a pebble, anything that I could throw, but the floor was bare. "Give me one of your boots, then," I said.

"No, I think not. What if it does not work, and we have to leave this place? Am I to go on bare feet? *Fight* with bare feet?"

"Bah," I said. "Fine. Do you have any better ideas? Should I throw Kylanthus down there? One of the bloodstones, perhaps? That's all I have. I do think we should test it before hopping overboard."

She cleared her throat. "Well, I'm no *genius*, but you could just spit over the side. Or you could turn a knob and throw a fish, or a sheep, or, what, some flowers? I'm not an expert." She gave me a you're-so-*stupid* look, and I flinched.

"Well, of course those are the *obvious* options," I lied. "But when testing the effect of an enchantment, it's best

not to use any living tissue or objects of magical origin."

She squinted at me. "You just made that up."

"Oh, just throw your boot over already. I can't throw *my* boots. They were Rellik's, and they're irreplaceable."

"Boots are very useful things to keep on your feet in the wild, Simon. I'll throw my shirt in."

"Heck no! You have to keep all your clothes on, crazy woman. This is a children's book.[83] Don't your people have any shame?"

"Shame wears off after the first four hundred years or so. But I think the word you are looking for is *modesty*, and I am here to tell you that different cultures have different concepts of modesty."

"Modest is modest," I said stubbornly.

She grunted. You throw *your* shirt, then. Certainly it's not immodest for *you* to take your shirt off, is it?"

"I'd get cold!"

She sighed in exasperation. "You have the turncoat to wear."

"Yeah, and it has all sorts of knobs on the inside, remember?" I rubbed my chest, imagining it without my shirt on. "It's *scratchy*."

"Great serpents above," she said, rolling her eyes. "Throw your pants in, then. Certainly you don't need *them* for any practical purpose."

"And we're back to modesty. Plus, you want me to

---

83 Okay, I didn't say this part, but still…

throw my *pants* into the pit of darkness?"

She said several things in her native language that made Leto chuckle in my boot, then handed me one of her boots.

"Lovely," I said. I peeked over the edge and lobbed it. I turned on the light, and we saw it soar straight down for a while before slowing and landing on the inside of the shaft, as if stuck there by magic…or gravity. "Cool! Give me the other one."

"Perfect," she said dryly, handing it over.

I threw it as far as I could, and the boot went almost twice the distance before it skittered to a halt halfway down the inside wall.

"Good enough for me," I said, and stood up. I walked off the edge, and the world flipped ninety degrees, so that I was walking straight down the shaft. From above, it must have looked like I was walking on walls, but from my perspective, I was still walking on the floor, and everything felt normal.

For her part, the Tike took a more cautious approach, dangling from the ledge so that her torso and her legs were in two different gravitational fields.

"My, this feels strange," she said, then backed fully onto the vertical wall and stood up. I tossed the first boot at her, and she caught it on her foot without thinking. "Thanks," she muttered.

I threw her the other one, and she caught it in like fashion, then we proceeded forward into the pit.

At the bottom of the shaft, we heard the voice for the first time. It was the voice I had heard whispering in my vision. The voice was inhumanly deep and hoarse, like a mountain scraping over a bed of solid steel.

"HUSHhhhh," it said. And twenty seconds later, the same thing, but more insistent. "HUSHhhhh!" It made my skin crawl to hear it, like discovering that there is something alive beneath your house, whispering in the dark.

"I suppose we have to go toward that voice now," I said quietly, and the Tike did not answer, but on we went, for such is the role of heroes. There came into my mind at that moment an old passage of scripture from the Bible, which I had heard a dozen times throughout my life, though I don't ever remember going to church. I had heard my mom recite it, I think, and seen it embroidered on a wall hanging in a pawn shop, and possibly even heard it in a vacuum commercial.

Though I walk through the valley of the shadow of death, I will fear no evil: for thou art with me; thy rod and thy staff they comfort me. I wished I had a rod and a staff right about now. I wondered briefly, as we all do in dark times, whether there really was a god—beyond those mystical Zohar beings that controlled the flow of magic to wizards—and if I was such an important person doing such important things, why we hadn't at least become pen pals.

I said a quick prayer, figuring it couldn't hurt. To

my surprise, I felt my codex glimmer[84] with warmth. I wondered how I was keeping my law by praying. Perhaps it was a part of my best self, or maybe I had given my word to someone long ago that I would pray, and I had just kept it. Perhaps we'll never know.

From a more practical standpoint, I made a pact with myself at this moment that I would do my best to keep my code with precision—at least for the rest of the day—to build up more magical power reserves, since it had recently been depleted.

As we walked on, the floor sloped steeply upward, and the darkness grew brighter, so that I no longer had to open my mouth and flash light on our path. The light was a cold blue color, and it filtered down from somewhere up ahead.

We crested a rise, and there it was before us: the Unright Fortress. The tunnel we walked through became a cave with a wide mouth overlooking a huge expanse of space. Jutting out from the mouth of the cave, like the tongue of some stone lizard, was a narrow bridge with no railings or handholds, which stretched out over an abyss of untold depth and indescribable darkness to connect with the Unright Fortress.

The path corkscrewed halfway up, then joined with the fortress upside down, which was itself built onto the top of the chamber and hung upside down with its towers of glowing blue light dipping into the abyss like some

---

84 Of course, the word "glimmer" usually refers to light, not heat, but we're going to stick with it, because that's what it felt like.

gigantic enchanted stalactite. The points of the towers, the battlements, the ramparts and crenellations, the gates and doors and stairs were all hewn of the same rock that constructed the chamber, and slowly I realized that the whole thing—as in, the chamber itself—must have been *carved* out of the rock of the moon by some magical means, leaving only the castle and the spiraling bridge behind.

"Hushhh," the voice whispered again, and a few seconds later, "Hushhh!"

My skin prickled as I realized that the voice floated up from the unseen depths of the abyss. I wondered if the inhabitants of the fortress—whoever they might be—had ever glimpsed the speaker, or whether the sound of the voice had by now become an invisible nuisance, like the sound of wind or waves, trains or traffic, for people who live near those things.

All of a sudden, the Tike pushed my head down behind an outcropping of stalagmites and crouched down beside me.

"What?" I said.

"Shh," she hissed, then pointed toward the opening of the cave. I peeked around the corner of our hiding place and saw a man sitting there, his chair placed in the center of the narrow entrance to the bridge. His head was lowered to his chest, as though in sleep.

"Rats," I said. "The bridge is guarded?"

"What did you expect?" the Tike said. "An *empty* evil fortress?"

I shrugged. "One can hope."

I took another look but couldn't discern anything useful about the bridge guard. He might not even have been a *he* at all. It was impossible to tell from this distance.

"What do you think?" I said.

"We sneak by. You can use your Chameleon knob, and your boots don't make any noise. I am quite accomplished at moving stealthily. It is bad practice to leave enemies alive behind you in battle, but this isn't battle. It's a heist, right?"

I nodded, peering over the stalagmites again. Below the castle (above it, from my perspective) I could see a glint of red that indicated the gardens of red edge-shale Flint had spoken of.

"That's our target," I said, pointing at them.

"I see it," she said. "We go fast. The more quickly we move, the better chance we have at remaining undetected, especially if we can cover a lot of ground while your camouflage spell lasts. If we get separated, meet here or on the bridge, or on that rampart." She pointed at a long, low rampart on the left side of the fortress. "If you can't find me, leave without me. I will make my way out. No, don't argue."

I shut my mouth, knowing she was right. "Don't worry," she went on. "We will do our best not to be separated. With any luck, we'll be back at Flint's dinner table in less than an hour."

I took a deep breath and then gave the signal. I turned C1 (*Chameleon*) and vanished, my body and clothes

blending seamlessly with my surroundings. The Tike prowled off, low and silent, and I followed.

As we neared the man, I could see that it wasn't a man at all. It was a boy. And he wasn't just any boy. He was one of the Fallen. I could see the silver medallion poking out of the neck of his shirt, and he had the gaunt, worn-out look of one of Rone's indentured servants. I thought of Jake and Charlie—kids I didn't really know but whose faces I could never erase from my mind. But no, it wasn't either of them. On the bright side, he really *was* asleep. Soft snores issued from him, and his chest rose and fell in a steady rhythm.

But that did nothing to assuage[85] the steady flow of disturbing questions that my mind was now posing. Why was one of the Fallen here? Were there more? Did Rone know about this place? He must, if his servants were here. Could he be here as well?

I pointed out the medallion silently to the Tike as we walked past the boy, and she paused, leaning in closer than I would have dared to inspect it. When she righted herself, her expression was drawn, determined. She knew what we might be getting into as well as I did. And it didn't change anything.

She took off at a brisk but relaxed pace, and I did my best to keep up. There was no hiding on the narrow, open bridge. If there were lookouts on the castle ramparts, they would see us. I couldn't see anyone from down here, but

85 To lessen the intensity of an unpleasant feeling. To relieve.

that didn't necessarily mean there weren't eyes up there. Down there, actually, for now.

We came to the corkscrew in the center of the bridge, and the Tike did not slow. We did not fall off or slide, just turned over and began walking upside down. Up became down, and down became up. Now it looked like the fortress was right-side up, and the cave was upside down behind us, with the abyss open above us like an evil sky.

"*Hushhh… Hushhh!*"

We reached the fortress gate without meeting a soul, and now I felt more paranoid than relieved. The Tike was examining the defenses of the fortress. The gate was tall and smooth; the walls were about the same. Far above, on the right, the stone became rougher, and there were little ledges and crevices that could be climbed, but they were a long way off.

"Pity we didn't bring a rope," the Tike said bitterly. "We could go straight up.

"Hold on a second," I said. I reached for D3 (*Summonator*), which had in the past provided me with all kinds of random objects, including a rotary telephone and a broomstick. I turned it, and a Home Depot shopping cart appeared, chock full of someone's home improvement supplies. I thought of a middle-aged guy in line for the checkout, suddenly missing his entire cart, and grinned. I rummaged through the cart and produced a 100-foot industrial-strength extension cord. "Will this work?"

The Tike was staring at the cart with her mouth hanging slightly ajar. She took the extension cord and

nodded, then bent down and picked up two folding utility knives and tucked them into her pants. "I do *not* understand magic," she said, then told me her plan.

I turned B6 (*Strength*) and unsheathed Kylanthus. We tied the extension cord to the cross guard. Then I lit the blade and threw it as hard as I could at the rough stone, twenty feet up. The blade sunk into the stone, right up to the hilt, and I muttered "Kylanthus" under my breath again, so that the fire would go out and prevent the sword from moving. Unfortunately, the extension cord fell off and tumbled back to the ground.

"Cheese and crackers," I swore.

"Watch your language," she chided me.

"I could turn B1 and jump up there."

"No," she said. "You may need that for the way down if there isn't time to climb. We should save the more powerful knobs for possible emergencies." She tied the extension cord around her waist and instructed me to throw her.

"You sure?" I said.

"Yes," she replied, sounding anything but. She was eyeing the abyss above us and no doubt wondering whether, if one got close enough to it, gravity reversed again and drew you in. "Simon," she said, "don't miss."

"Right," I said. "Stiff as a board, Tike."

She held her hands up high and pointed, legs straight, body tense, as if she were trying to impersonate a spear. I picked her up by the waist with both hands and raised her over my head, then I drew her back with just one arm

and threw her exactly like a spear. Good thing she was fairly light. Even with my magically increased strength, that was pushing the limits of what I could do, at least with a body this size.

She hit the wall right above the sword and slid down to grab it. Then she tied the cord around the cross guard again and climbed away, dangling from the rock like a professional climber. I climbed up using the extension cord—a feat I'd like to think I could have done without super strength, but I guess we'll never know. I followed her lead when I reached the sword, wedging my knuckles and toes into the rock and moving away from it. I leaned down to grab the Kylanthus and nearly fell to my death. I righted myself just in time but decided it was too dangerous to try it again.

"Golly gee wizbangers!" I swore. Any other knight of the Circle could have vanished his sword into the mindhold—a place in the primal dimension that was somehow attached to your soul. My silly sword problem wouldn't be a problem for anyone else. I was loath to leave it behind. If only I could vanish it into a holding area of my own and take it with me.

It was at that moment that I realized the behavior of E8 (*Stash*) was very similar to descriptions I had heard of the mindhold.

"Holy smokes," I whispered. I touched E8 with my mind but didn't turn the knob. There was a bloodstone hidden in there, and other things, and I wasn't ready to mess with that just now. I simply wanted to feel. If the

pockets and knobs were designed to help me channel my power across, say, certain wavelengths of magic, maybe E8 corresponded with the powers of the mindhold.

I touched it and tried to imagine the tingling feeling I got in my gut when magic flowed through me. Nothing happened at first, but then I noticed something. A sensation in the pocket. It was a thing that eludes description, like a song almost, a particular song, that I could feel more than hear. I brought my attention to my center again, thinking of Kylanthus vanishing, and the sword disappeared. I felt it resting there, somewhere inside my chest. My soul's chest, that is. It's very hard to explain.

The Tike gave a low whistle. "Simon, you seem to be a hands-on learner."

"No kidding. We need to scale creepy fortresses more often!"

She ascended quickly, and I followed. My magically strengthened fingers and toes felt like iron claws as they gripped the stone. I did my best not to think of how high we must be getting. I kept my eyes on the Tike, and soon we were climbing over one of the middle ramparts. The battlement was wide and empty. Not a soul was on guard.

"Where is everyone?" I said, no longer able to keep it in.

"There are two options," she said, making her way to a staircase leading upward. "The stairway is narrow," she said, changing the subject as we climbed it. The Tike had a thing about explaining battle tactics to me. Sometimes I thought she was secretly trying to turn me into some

sort of warrior. "This is to make it difficult for two men to fight abreast. And it winds clockwise from bottom to top, so that invaders—those going up—cannot easily fight right-handed."

"Good thing we aren't invading," I said. "You were saying? Two options?"

She strode down the highest rampart until she reached a tower with more stairs going up. The door was unlocked. "Either this place is abandoned—which it isn't—or the inhabitants are luring us into a trap. They wait for us to get in deeper and deeper, so that we will be less likely to escape. They know, or suspect, that you have substantial magical power, and they want to make sure their trap springs good and hard."

"Seriously?" I said, coming to a halt. "Are you sure it's not abandoned?"

"Yes. I am sure. There is a smell to the place, and there is a feel to empty places that this fortress lacks. Beyond that, I know when I am being watched."

"And you're just *okay* with walking into a trap?" I said, gesturing my consternation.

She touched a finger to her temple, a sign we had developed during our sparring sessions to remind me that the majority of fighting happens in one's mind. "Springing a trap is not the same thing as being caught in one," she said. "Just be ready. These people fear our strength, which means we are likely a match for them. They are relying on the element of surprise, which they will not have now."

"*Hushhh,*" the abyss said above us. "*Hushhh!*"

"You could sweet-talk a frog into the pot," I said with a shudder, but I gestured for her to lead on.

The last set of stairs wound to a dead end beneath a trapdoor that I punched to smithereens. When we climbed through, we were standing amid chest-high gardens of what looked like razor-sharp coral. Most of it was black, but somewhere toward the center of the garden, I caught a glimpse of red. As we approached it, we saw that there was a little square stone building with one side completely open to the outside.

Here, inside the three walls, the red edge-shale grew. The plants were smaller than the gray ones outside. Sharper, and more deadly looking. Not a bush you would want to fall into. There was a fire pit and a cauldron bubbling over it in one corner of the building, where the shale had been cleared away, and in the center of the far wall was a door.

I peeked in the cauldron and saw bits of edge-shale floating in the hot liquid. Some of the pieces had become semitransparent, reminding me of half-cooked onions. I backed away from it, trying not to wonder about what it was for. I gripped a curved piece of the red edge-shale, about ten inches across, and broke it off, depositing it in the mindhold next to Kylanthus. I grinned. Don't look now, but I was turning into a wizard.

"Simon, look."

I spun around to see thirty or forty teenage wizards walking toward us through the coral garden. Their steps were slow and measured, and they each held a long white knife before them, gripped in one hand and resting on the

open palm of the other. They looked tired and hungry. Their robes were an identical, indistinct gray, and their skin looked oddly pale and white. They did not speak or move their eyes at all, and I had the distinct impression that they were being controlled by someone unseen. Several had silver medallions visible on their persons.

Rone.

As they drew nearer, the daggers began to glow. Then white fire streamed from the tips of the blades closest to us.

"We should make a break for it now," the Tike said. "Straight through their ranks. Stay close behind me."

"Hello?"

The Tike paused. "Did you hear that?" she said.

"HELLO?" the voice called again. It was muffled, coming through the closed door behind us.

"Hello?" I answered, staring at the zombielike army of wizard youth closing in on us.

"*Hushhh,*" the voice called down. "*Hushhh!*"

"I'M HERE!" the voice cried, a little louder. "HELP! HELP ME! OH, PLEASE, PLEASE DON'T LEAVE ME IN HERE!"

"It's a trap," the Tike said. "They want to lure us deeper into the fortress. Block our escape routes. We should go."

I thought of my recent commitment[86] to honor my

---

86 Random writing trivia: the word *commitment* appears only one time in this book. That happens a lot; in a whole book, a certain word will only make one appearance. *Indistinct* only appears once in this book as well. Also, *contrition, tumult, thievery, postulated,*

code. "I will help those I can," I said. "The consequences can figure themselves out later." I made a break for the door, and the Tike cursed, following me. The three wizards closest to us leaped forward, and she was forced

---

superhuman, incendiary, propulsion, inherently, windows, trash, soup, tiger, fascination, and many others. Come to think of it, all of those appear in this book *twice* now that I've written them in this footnote. Dang it… Anyway, other words appear a LOT. What word do you think appears more than any other in this (and every other) book? That's right. *The.* There are over 3,200 instances of the word *the* in this book. Can you imagine? That's 5% of the book! In fact, the words, *the, I, and, of, a, he, it, was, you, to, that, in, my, said, his,* and *me,* make up over 25% of the words in this (and most) books. Now, since I know you probably *can't* imagine what 3,200 instances of the word *the* looks like, I have put together a demonstration for you: The the

to dive and roll to escape the flames from their daggers. I flung the door open, and she flew past me down a stone staircase. I slammed it shut behind me and barred it from the inside.

---

the the the the the the the the the the the the the the the the the the the the the the the the
the the the the the the the the the the the the the the the the the the the the the the the the
the the the the the the the the the the the the the the the the the the the the the the the the
the the the the the the the the the the the the the the the the the the the the the the the the
the the the the the the the the the the the the the the the the the the the the the the the the
the the the the the the the the the the the the the the the the the the the the the the the the
the the the the the the the the the the the the the the the the the the the the the the the the
the the the the the the the the the the the the the the the the the the the the the the the the
the the the the the the the the the the the the the the the the the the the the the the the the
the the the the the the the the the the the the the the the the the the the the the the the the
the the the the the the the the the the the the the the the the the the the the the the the the
the the the the the the the the the the the the the the the the the the the the the the the the
the the the the the the the the the the the the the the the the the the the the the the the the
the the the the the the the the the the the the the the the the the the the the the the the the
the the the the the the the the the the the the the the the the the the the the the the the the
the the the the the the the the the the the the the the the the the the the the the the the the
the the the the the the the the the the the the the the the the the the the the the the the the
the the the the the the the the the the the the the the the the the the the the the the the the
the the the the the the the the the the the the the the the the the the the the the the the the
the the the the the the the the the the the the the the the the the the the the the the the the
the the the the the the the the the the the the the the the the the the the the the the the the
the the the the the the the the the the the the the the the the the the the the the the the the
the the the the the the the the the the the the the the the the the the the the the the the the
the the the the the the the the the the the the the the the the the the the the the the the the
the the the the the the the the the the the the the the the the the the the the the the the the
the the the the the the the the the the the the the the the the the the the the the the the the
the the the the the the the the the the the the the the the the the the the the the the the the
the the the the the the the the the the the the the the the the the the the the the the the the
the the the the the the the the the the the the the the the the the the the the the the the the
the the the the the the the the the the the the the the the the the the the the the the the the
the the the the the the the the the the the the the the the the the the the the the the the the
the the the the the the the the the the the the the the the the the the the the the the the the
the the the the the the the the the the the the the the the the the the the the the the the the

Three white flaming daggers pierced the wood, nearly impaling me. I looked at the wooden door, knowing it would not keep our enemies out for long. Then I drew

the the the the the the the the the the the the the the the the the the the the the
the the the the the the the the the the the the the the the the the the the the the
the the the the the the the the the the the the the the the the the the the the the
the the the the the the the the the the the the the the the the the the the the the
the the the the the the the the the the the the the the the the the the the the the
the the the the the the the the the the the the the the the the the the the the the
the the the the the the the the the the the the the the the the the the the the the
the the the the the the the the the the the the the the the the the the the the the
the the the the the the the the the the the the the the the the the the the the the
the the the the the the the the the the the the the the the the the the the the the
the the the the the the the the the the the the the the the the the the the the the
the the the the the the the the the the the the the the the the the the the the the
the the the the the the the the the the the the the the the the the the the the the
the the the the the the the the the the the the the the the the the the the the the
the the the the the the the the the the the the the the the the the the the the the
the the the the the the the the the the the the the the the the the the the the the
the the the the the the the the the the the the the the the the the the the the the
the the the the the the the the the the the the the the the the the the the the the
the the the the the the the the the the the the the the the the the the the the the
the the the the the the the the the the the the the the the the the the the the the
the the the the the the the the the the the the the the the the the the the the the
the the the the the the the the the the the the the the the the the the the the the
the the the the the the the the the the the the the the the the the the the the the
the the the the the the the the the the the the the the the the the the the the the
the the the the the the the the the the the the the the the the the the the the the
the the the the the the the the the the the the the the the the the the the the the
the the the the the the the the the the the the the the the the the the the the the
the the the the the the the the the the the the the the the the the the the the the
the the the the the the the the the the the the the the the the the the the the the
the the the the the the the the the the the the the the the the the the the the the
the the the the the the the the the the the the the the the the the the the the the
the the the the the the the the the the the the the the the the the the the the the
the the the the the the the the the the the the the the the the the the the the the
the the the the the the the the the the the the the the the the the the the the the

Kylanthus, turned A3 (*Curse*), and broke down the walls as I descended the stairs, causing them to collapse in a cloud of dust.

---

the the the the the the the the the the the the the the the the the the the the the
the the the the the the the the the the the the the the the the the the the the the
the the the the the the the the the the the the the the the the the the the the the
the the the the the the the the the the the the the the the the the the the the the
the the the the the the the the the the the the the the the the the the the the the
the the the the the the the the the the the the the the the the the the the the the
the the the the the the the the the the the the the the the the the the the the the
the the the the the the the the the the the the the the the the the the the the the
the the the the the the the the the the the the the the the the the the the the the
the the the the the the the the the the the the the the the the the the the the the
the the the the the the the the the the the the the the the the the the the the the
the the the the the the the the the the the the the the the the the the the the the
the the the the the the the the the the the the the the the the the the the the the
the the the the the the the the the the the the the the the the the the the the the
the the the the the the the the the the the the the the the the the the the the the
the the the the the the the the the the the the the the the the the the the the the
the the the the the by the way, for the special one percent of you
who noticed this secret message typed all in lowercase, here are a
few spoilers for book five: the the the the the tike dies. the the the the
the very last scene takes place in mingey's bingeys. the the the the
the the bloodstone ends up being more powerful than anyone could
have imagined and changes simon and the the the the the world in
very big ways. the the the rimbakka ends up saving the universe. the
the the the the the the the the the the the the the the the the the the the the the
the the the the the the the the the the the the the the the the the the the the the
the the the the the the the the the the the the the the the the the the the the the
the the the the the the the the the the the the the the the the the the the the the
the the the the the the the the the the the the the the the the the the the the the
the the the the the the the the the the the the the the the the the the the the the
the the the the the the the the the the the the the the the the the the the the the
the the the the the the the the the the the the the the the the the the the the the
the the the the the the the the the the the the the the the the the the the the the
the the the the the the the the the the the the the the the the the the the the the
the the the the the the the the the the the the the the the the the the the the the
the the the the the the the the the the the the the the the the the the the the the
the the the the the the the the the the the the the the the the the the the the the

With my superior strength, I kept the mass of stone from tumbling too far down the stairs and built a thick blockade out of the wreckage. It took less than a minute.

---

the the the the the the the the the the the the the the the the the the the
the the the the the the the the the the the the the the the the the the the the
the the the the the the the the the the the the the the the the the the the the
the the the the the the the the the the the the the the the the the the the the
the the the the the the the the the the the the the the the the the the the the
the the the the the the the the the the the the the the the the the the the the
the the the the the the the the the the the the the the the the the the the the
the the the the the the the the the the the the the the the the the the the the
the the the the the the the the the the the the the the the the the the the the
the the the the the the the the the the the the the the the the the the the the
the the the the the the the the the the the the the the the the the the the the
the the the the the the the the the the the the the the the the the the the the
the the the the the the the the the the the the the the the the the the the the
the the the the the the the the the the the the the the the the the the the the
the the the the the the the the the the the the the the the the the the the the
the the the the the the the the the the the the the the the the the the the the
the the the the the the the the the the the the the the the the the the the the
the the the the the the the the the the the the the the the the the the the the
the the the the the the the the the the the the the the the the the the the the
the the the the the the the the the the the the the the the the the the the the
the the the the the the the the the the the the the the the the the the the the
the the the the the the the the the the the the the the the the the the the the
the the the the the the the the the the the the the the the the the the the the
the the the the the the the the the the the the the the the the the the the the
the the the the the the the the the the the the the the the the the the the the
the the the the the the the the the the the the the the the the the the the the
the the the the the the the the the the the the the the the the the the the the
the the the the the the the the the the the the the the the the the the the the
the the the the the the the the the the the the the the the the the the the the
the the the the the the the the the the the the the the the the the the the the
the the the the the the the the the the the the the the the the the the the the
the the the the the the the the the the the the the the the the the the the the
the the the the the the the the the the the the the the the the the the the the

Then I took the steps three at a time, in search of the Tike.

---

the the the the the the the the the the the the the the the the the the
the the the the the the the the the the the the the the the the the the
the the the the the the the the the the the the the the the the the the
the the the the the the the the the the the the the the the the the the
the the the the the the the the the the the the the the the the the the
the the the the the the the the the the the the the the the the the the
the the the the the the the the the the the the the the the the the the
the the the the the the the the the the the the the the the the the the
the the the the the the the the the the the the the the the the the the
the the the the the the the the the the the the the the the the the the
the the the the the the the the the the the the the the the the the the
the the the the the the the the the the the the the the the the the the
the the the the the the the the the the the the the the the the the the
the the the the the the the the the the the the the the the the the the
the the the the the the the the the the the the the the the the the the
the the the the the the the the the the the the the the the the the the
the the the the the the the the the the the the the the the the the the
the the the the the the the the the the the the the the the the the the
the the the the the the the the the the the the the the the the the the
the the the the the the the the the the the the the the the the the the
the the the the the the the the the the the the the the the the the the
the the the the the the the the the the the the the the the the the the
the the the the the the the the the the the the the the the the the the
the the the the the the the the the the the the the the the the the the
the the the the the the the the the the the the the the the the the the
the the the the the the the the the the the the the the the the the Tike.
the the the the the the the the the the the the the. Of course, there are now
over 6,400 instances of the word the in this book.

10

THE WIZGUARD

When all else fails, try transforming yourself into a giant blimp.
—Simon Fayter, *Life Advice*

Here," the Tike said as my feet hit the stone floor of a circular chamber.

There were cell doors set into the curving wall on all sides and torches burning in brackets. She was fiddling with the lock on the one across from me. I moved to her side and wrenched the door from its hinges with a groan, still brimming with magical strength.

"Thank you," a pitiful voice said. "Oh, thank you."

My codex glimmered.

I grabbed the ragged bundle from inside the cell and nearly fell over in shock.

"Montroth?" I said. He was barely the same person, his blond hair covered in grime, his handsome face lit with cuts and bruises, and he looked like he hadn't eaten in at least a week, but it was him all right.

"We'll take him with us," I said, wrapping my arm around him and grabbing the Tike's hand. I turned E6

(*Travel*), eager to vanish out of this nightmare and stroll the streets of Skelligard once more.

But nothing happened.

"Well?" the Tike said. "Are we going?"

"I'm trying! It's not working."

She swore. "There must be some sort of spell over the fortress."

"Typical."

"Simon Fayter?" Montroth said. He had been following our conversation with a confused look. "But…how are you here?"

"Long story. How are *you* here?"

His eyes closed with the effort of standing on his own as I leaned him against the wall of the central chamber. "The Wizguard heard rumors about activity here," he mumbled.

Somewhere above us, there was the loud thud of something smashing against my makeshift blockade.

"Supposed to be abandoned," Montroth went on. "Sent me to investigate."

His head lolled to one side, and the Tike slapped him. "Wake up, man! Do you know a way out of here?"

He shook himself and nodded. "Secret tunnels," he said. "That's how I got in. Stupid of me. Should have gone back for help when I saw it was inhabited." His eyes snapped open then, and he gripped my collar. "Simon! You can't be here! You have to leave!"

"I'm *trying*."

"Do you know who lives here now?" His eyes were wild, searching my face.

"Judging by our little welcome party, I could take a guess," I said.

"It's *him,* Simon! Rone!" He looked terrified at the thought.

"Well," I said, "I think he is out of the office at the moment. Otherwise we'd already be dead."

He sagged against me in relief, throwing an arm over my shoulder. He was tall, much taller than me, but I still had the B6 strength to help me. "Then let us go. That way," he said, pointing to one of three normal-looking doors in the room.

The Tike snatched a torch from off the wall, and we burst through the door he had indicated, descending the spiral stairs as fast as our legs would take us. I was slower, bracing Montroth. It was cramped, the ceiling low, and I kept accidentally smashing his head against the wall. "Ouch!"

"Sorry."

"No problem," he mumbled. "I am notoriously difficult to kill."

I smiled ruefully. Even half dead and running from his enemies, he was a prideful git.

There was a thunderous noise from above, and I knew they had broken through. We ran on, but seconds later there were sounds on the staircase behind us.

We came to a stone landing with passages going off

to the right and left, and the stairs continuing on down before us.

"Here?" the Tike asked.

"No, no," Montroth breathed. "All the way down. To the bottom."

"We won't make it that far," she said, glancing up the stairs. "They are gaining on us." There were lights and shadows dancing along the walls now, and the distant sound of footsteps. "We cannot get caught on the steps," she told me. I remembered what she said about how the stairs were designed to give advantage to those above. "We should make a stand here."

I nodded my assent.

"Get behind me," she said, moving to the center of the landing and planting her feet.

"You get behind me," I said, stepping up beside her. "And try not to kill anyone."

"How are we going to manage *that*?" the Tike said.

A fair question. I turned A7 (*Epiphany*) and cocked my head as a new idea struck me. I needed to expand my view of what was possible to do with the turncoat. I needed to let go of the idea that certain knobs did certain things and embrace the concept of the knobs as doorways to certain frequencies of magic.

It was only a few seconds until the first wave of wizards rounded the corner. They saw us and screamed, brandishing their eerie white daggers and tripping over one another, mad with the chase. Their eyes were dark and vacant, and I was struck again by the unfairness of

harming them, given that they were clearly being forced against their own will. These were not as Mistress Zee had been, brainwashed and converted to the cause. Their minds and bodies were being manhandled by my enemy.

I raised my hand[87] and turned D5 (*Sidestep*), pointing the focus of my mind at each one of them in rapid succession. With a series of loud pops, the young wizards vanished and reappeared a couple feet to either side, their heads sticking out of the walls of the passage, their bodies encased in stone. Their eyes had lost the dark cast, and several of them were shaking their heads, as if waking from a dream.

"Ouch!" one of them cried. "This hurts!"

There was a clattering sound on the stairs above, and another wave of wizards appeared. If they were disturbed by the sight of their comrades sticking out of the sides of the walls, they didn't show it. They came on in a frenzy, and I spread my arms, embracing all of them at once with my mind as I turned D9 (*Slick*).

At once, the group fell down. They slid over each other like bubbles in oil, pooling onto the landing and coasting gently to a stop here and there against the walls. They tried to get up but simply flopped and flailed. It was odd to watch perfectly normal-looking bodies flail and slide around as though covered with a six-inch-thick layer of grease, and I felt a bit sorry for them, but it was far

---

87 In true Jedi-like fashion, you can be sure.

preferable to killing. I threw Montroth's arm around my shoulder again and grabbed his waist, helping him down the stairs again.

"Wait!" one of the wall-stuck wizards called. "Take us with you!"

"Sorry," I said. "I've helped you all that I can today. I can't risk setting you all free, as I don't know how Rone is controlling you. Here." I pointed at the closest wizard, and he slid free of the stone. "You can work on freeing your friends. That's all I can do."

The Tike was urging me on, and I knew we had to go, but I felt better about helping them—and not killing them, for that matter. My codex glimmered beneath my shirt.

"Hey, Shill," I heard someone's voice called from above, "get me out first."

"No, me!" another voice called. And a third shouted, "Help, Shill! My nose itches!" Poor Shill was going to have his hands full.

We made our way to the bottom of the spiral stairs in relative peace after that, though often as we passed different levels we would hear footsteps running down a passage or shouts echoing through the dark halls.

At the bottom, we found a tub of clear water, which I dunked Montroth's head in. He seemed to perk up after that and didn't have to lean on me as much. He led us through a series of tunnels beneath the fortress. They were full of darkness and the echoing sounds of dripping water, but not much else, until we met our first night-mare.

The Tike barreled around a corner and bounced off something hard and black, which I only avoided hitting because I was moving a bit slower, helping Montroth along. Montroth whimpered when he saw it, and the thing turned. It was covered in scales that glistened in the torchlight, but it was not a dragon or lizard of any kind. It was quite plainly a horse.

That is, a *giant* horse. It stood twenty hands high[88] and towered over us like a baby giraffe. Its black scales glistened in the torchlight like oil, and when it lowered its eyes to us, I saw that they were red. It growled at us, which, apart from the huge size, the red eyes, and the scales, was a strong indication that it was no regular horse. Then it bared a set of ten-inch canines and tried to bite the Tike in half. It sounds bad, but I was really glad the beast targeted her first, because I was so rooted to the spot with shock that my life would have almost certainly ended early—as a midday snack.

The Tike dodged the beast's snapping jaws and spun around, dropping her torch and slashing at its throat with her knives. They sparked against the scales but did not penetrate.

"Simon!" she said, snapping me out of my stupor.

"Oh, yeah. Sorry…" I reached out to touch the horse, turned E4 (*Size*), and it shrunk to the size of a matchbook. The Tike stomped on it without delay.

---

88 That's over six and a half feet at the shoulders (ten feet to the ears), for you city slickers out there.

"So you *are* a wizard," Montroth mumbled. "I was wondering what had become of you since we lost your trail… I guess you've been training."

"Not really," I admitted.

"Are there more of these beasts?" the Tike demanded.

"Yes," he said. "Rone's night-mares. He has been breeding them in the fortress. This one must have wandered into the tunnels somehow."

Following Montroth's directions, we emerged through a grate at the base of the fortress without further incident and climbed a series of narrow switchbacks that led to the gate. It was open now, and we could see into the courtyard, which was filled with rather angry-looking Fallen running to and fro, no doubt looking for us.

"How many Fallen does he have?" I wondered aloud.

"He has been collecting them for a *long* time," the Tike said.

Montroth fidgeted. "Not a good place to stand around," he pointed out.

"Right," I said. I tried the E6 knob again, but it still didn't work. "No luck," I told the Tike. "We'll have to get out of this cave."

She was looking at the long, narrow corkscrew bridge that lay ahead of us, no doubt calculating the odds of our getting across it without being caught or killed.

I closed my eyes and summoned up an image of a Humvee. That would be handy right about now. Or a motorcycle. No, a Humvee would be better, since there were three of us. I turned A8 (*Transportation*)—which had

once created a fully fueled Ferrari for me to escape in—but the turncoat did not create a Humvee, a motorcycle, or a Ferrari. It created a two-seater paddle boat. There, on the rocky foundations of a magical fortress, the boat looked about as out of place as a booger in church. The sound of it hitting the ground caused several of the Fallen to turn and look at us, and that made me feel like a complete imbecile.

"Nice," the Tike said.

"Let's not tell anyone about this," I said.

"*Hushhh,*" the voice from the abyss intoned. "*Hushhh!*"

The Fallen that had seen us shouted, sprinting toward us.

"Time to go!" I said, and tried to throw Montroth over my shoulder. But my magical strength was gone. I hadn't even felt it leave me. "Fairy juice!" I swore.

In desperation, I rounded on the fast-approaching mob of possessed wizards and raised my hands in the best spell caster gesture I could manage, then turned B9 (*Luck*). I had thus far been successful at turning the effects of the turncoat—which before today had only applied to me—upon my enemies, and this instance was no exception. For a second it seemed as though nothing would happen, but then the huge gate snapped free of its chains and came crashing down, locking the Fallen inside.

Almost instantly, the gates began to open.

"Ideas?" I said.

"Use your big idea knob," the Tike said.

"All used up," I said. "Leto! You in the mood to help a fella out?"

"Go away," he muttered. "I'm napping. Interrupt me again and I will roast one of your toes for dinner." He started chewing it experimentally, and I thought better of antagonizing him further. There was a big boom behind us then.

"Run!" the Tike shouted, and she took off once more, but the bridge was long and the gate was rising. Two small side gates opened, and a dozen night-mares galloped out. Running away wasn't going to cut it. This was a disaster, pure and simple.

Just then, I had a brainwave. Thinking of disasters made me think of death and fire, and of course, the *Hindenburg*.[89] This made me think of sleek silver airships and of the C10 knob. Hoping beyond hope that I wasn't an idiot, I turned it. Instead of becoming a big fat-head hot-air balloon, I became a sleek torpedo-shaped airship. My arms dangled below me, and my legs swooped upward like graceful tails. I grinned. *This* was going to be much more maneuverable... Except...

Bummer. I still didn't seem to have any propulsion. So there I was, hovering beneath the dark abyss that whispered hush, hush, while below me, monsters and evil wizards descended upon my friends.

I reached down with one of my big hands and picked up Montroth, who had fallen to the ground when I went airborne. A jumping night-mare just barely missed him as

89 The LZ 129 *Hindenburg* was a passenger airship that blew up in 1937 with ninety-seven souls on board. This catastrophic failure was the end of airships. Too bad. They looked way cool.

I lifted him up. I swatted at it and sent it flying. The Tike, who had stopped as soon as she realized I wasn't following her, was staring up at me in horror.

"What are you doing?" she said. "This is no time to experiment!"

I reached down and grabbed her as well, then pushed off from the ground and sent myself gliding toward the cave through which we had entered. Above us, the abyss repeated its injunction.

"*Hushhh. Hushhh!*"

As I drifted randomly through the massive cavernous space, I wished bitterly that Drake was here. I wasn't sure if he was powerful enough to steer a human airship through telepathy yet, but I would have liked to give him a try. If only I had a Bright here to help me.

I grinned and turned A6 (*Single Person Transport*).

Ioden Bright, dressed in a now slime-sodden lavender bathrobe and looking all the world as if he had been stuck inside a whale for a week eating nothing but fish guts, materialized in the air halfway between me and the bridge below. He fell several feet and landed in a heap. Pushing himself up, he saw a herd of night-mares charging at him, with a hundred angry wizards in tow.

He shrieked and leaped to his feet. Before he ran off, he glanced up and saw my humungous floating blimp head hovering over him, and his jaw dropped open. I snatched him up and set him on my back.

"What in holy blazes is going on?" he cried. "Where

am I? SIMON FAYTER! Why can't you just leave me alone!"

"Yeah," I said. "Sorry about all that. I'll take you back to Skelligard if you can just help me steer this thing. You don't mind, do you?"

"You're lucky I've just eaten!" he said. "I've just eaten a big meal—not that you could call it food—that I have scavenged over the last week, otherwise I wouldn't have had enough strength to escape that blasted whale you left me in, let alone pilot your big head out of this… Where are we?"

"Can we go now?" Montroth called up from below. The Fallen were approaching, and several of them had begun launching fireballs at us. One hit my leg and burned a hole through my pants.

"Ah," Ioden said. "Yes. Where would you like to go?"

"Through the cave!" I said, and we began to fly in the right direction.

Below us, the Fallen were shouting in alarm, sensing our impending escape. They did not disperse in confusion, however. Instead they all suddenly dropped their weapons, joined hands, and began chanting in a strange language. One of them touched the flank of a night-mare, and the beast grew to ten times its normal height.

Sixty feet tall now, it looked down on us, eyes gleaming red.

"FASTER!" I screamed, and Ioden needed no more encouragement. We shot forward, narrowly escaping the snapping jaws of the night-mare.

We flew through the cave where the Tike and I had crept past the sentry only an hour before and banked upward when we reached the vertical shaft. The horse followed us, squeezing through the opening at the back of the cave and lumbering on. Stalactites and stalagmites broke free from their moorings, disturbed by its passing, and the sound of cracking rock filled the air.

We reached the top of the shaft and banked hard, my back bouncing off the roof of the primary tunnel. Daylight was ahead of us, somewhere. Not yet in sight. Behind us, the night-mare, availing itself of the gravitational fields I had created, ran up the side of the vertical shaft and joined us in the main one. We were fast, but so was the night-mare. It ran behind us, man-sized nostrils sucking in air, hooves beating a wild frenzy against the stone floor.

I placed the Tike on my back, next to Ioden, and she attacked. She threw the razorblades that she had picked out of the Home Depot shopping cart, but they missed the night-mare's face, embedding themselves harmlessly in its body. She was about to follow them up with some of her three-pointed knives, but Ioden slipped, and we jostled in the air, causing her to fall down.

"Light!" Ioden shouted. "I see daylight!"

The night-mare gave an extra burst of speed and would have taken off my leg, but the Tike shouted a warning, and I turned D6 (*Lightning*), and the giant animal was blown against the side of the tunnel by a bolt of electricity. It shook itself and came after us again, but we had gained

ground. We were going to reach the mouth of the tunnel before it could catch us.

We burst out,[90] flying high over the moon, and the night-mare followed, but it could not reach us now.

I turned E6 (*Travel*), and at last the knob worked as intended. We vanished from the sky above Ashguld's third moon and reappeared on the bustling cobblestone street outside Mingey's Bingeys in the castle city of Skelligard.

---

90 Picture what that must have looked like to the casual passerby: A peaceful desert. The crack of lightning from within the ground. A giant blimp head flying out of the sand, followed by a sixty-foot predatory dragon-horse. Hopefully, there was no one around to see...

11

FORTY-EIGHT[91]

No good deed goes unpunished.[92]

Lest you think our arrival at Skelligard went unnoticed, let me remind you that I was still shaped like a giant blimp. I filled half the street, and when I say filled, I mean there was one chubby boy who got squished up against the window of Mingey's Bingeys by my huge ear. People noticed.

By the time I managed to set my friends down safely and turn C10 again to deflate myself, there was a small crowd of onlookers. I took one look at the ragged appearance of Ioden and Montroth and then pointed

---

91 I'm so confused! Are we in chapter 11 or chapter 48? Well, maybe neither. Counting prologues, epilogues, and all the other logs, you are in the twelfth chapter of this book, and the ninety-second chapter of this series.

92 This is an old saying that draws attention to the fact that acts of kindness often backfire. They say no one knows where the phrase comes from, but any *Star Trek* fan can tell you it is the 285th statement in the Ferengi Rules of Acquisition.

authoritatively at an older boy in the crowd. "You, boy. Come here."

His eyes went wide. My beard disguise from earlier had now worn off, and with my recent deflation, I looked like myself again. People were whispering my name, and I assumed that I had started to gain something of a reputation, at least around Skelligard. It was well known before I left that I had joined the Circle of Eight and had been accepted—by the Circle at least—as the real Fayter, Rellik's heir. No doubt, news of my adventures abroad would stoke the fire of my legend, if they hadn't already.

"Me?" he said.

I recognized him as Basil, the young man who had acted as our chaperone on the first day of school a few weeks earlier. "Yes!" I barked. "Basil. Do you know who I am?" I said.

He shuffled forward. "Sure, Simon."

"And do you know what this is?" I asked. I pulled my codex out and showed him the image of the tree surrounded by eight swords—the symbol of the Circle of Eight. There weren't many codexes like *that* in the world.

"Of course, uh, *sir.*"

"Excellent," I said. I pointed at the two collapsed men beside me. Montroth had sunk down cross-legged on the cobblestones and begun to doze. Ioden was pale and sickly and looked as though his adrenaline rush was beginning to wear off. "Take these two to the infirmary immediately, and then go tell Gladstone what you have done."

"Yes, sir," he said, and started to help them.

"I don't need *your* help," Ioden snapped.

"You'll do as I say, Master Ioden," I said. "You have been starved and abandoned because of me—mostly on accident, by the way—and I won't have you wandering off and collapsing somewhere. We're going to take care of you."

"Accident, my foot!" he exclaimed, brandishing a wobbly finger at me. "You hated me from the start, young man. I don't care if the whole school thinks you're god's gift to wizardkind, I know the truth!"

"It *was* an accident," I insisted. "I think I focused one of the turncoat knob's magic on you when I was thinking about you really hard. Of course, that *is* what I was trying to do, but I didn't mean to drag you halfway around the universe or make you nearly starve to death. I was just trying to set your pants on fire or something! You can't blame me for that…"

"Can't blame you?" he said, looking a bit crazy now. "Watch me! I am filing an *official* report about your behavior. *And,* if I *ever* suddenly appear beside you while you are fighting demonic bunny rabbits, fleeing from the bowels of evil, falling into a volcano, or anything like that, I will do my utmost best to kill you immediately! You have been warned."

With that, he swept the remains of his purple bathrobe behind him with a flourish and hobbled up the street.

"Wow," I said.

"Surprised that he is angry at you?" the Tike asked.

"Nah. He has the skinniest legs I've ever seen!"

The Tike slapped me on the back of the head.

"Ouch! You've been hanging around Tessa too much."

She grunted, and we set off for the boot shop. I was afraid some of the students were going to follow us—maybe ask for my autograph or something, but they didn't.[93]

When we entered the boot shop, there was an old lady sitting at the workbench, tapping her fingernails nervously. She jumped up when she saw us and rushed over to throw her arms around my neck.

"Thank goodness!" She smacked me on the arm. "I can't *believe* you went off without us like that!"

"Tessa?" I said. "Wow! You changed your disguise again? Even *I* didn't recognize you this time."

She shrugged, and the illusion fell away to reveal my friend beneath.

"Where's Drake?"

She waved a hand. "He's worried sick. He was so stressed, he started freaking *me* out, so I sent him to help Flint play with his chemistry set."

"His what?"

"Oh, he's got some huge cauldron thing boiling right in the middle of that imaginary village of his. Says it has something to do with what you're supposed to bring back. Come on. I'll show you."

Tessa wasn't wrong. Smack dab in the center of Flint's quaint little yard was a boiling black cauldron that

---

93 Kids these days… In their defense, I wasn't actually famous yet.

reminded me of the one we had seen beneath the Unright Fortress, except this one was easily six feet tall. Flint himself stood on a stepladder and stirred the contents with what looked like a wooden canoe oar.

"Simon!" He beamed, hopping down to take my hand. "You made it back alive!"

"Surprised?"

"A bit." He winked at Tessa to indicate that he was joking, but I knew he probably wasn't.

"I can't believe you sent me in there," I said. "I nearly died like six times."

"Ah, yes. Sorry I couldn't go retrieve the ingredients myself, old boy, but I narrowly escaped with my life last time, and I daresay the abyssog has developed a particular dislike of me. Couldn't stand the racket I made last time, you know."

I felt my eyes widen. "You fought the *thing* in the abyss? The thing that says hush?"

Flint looked confused. "You didn't see the abyssog? Goodness, man! You have the luck of ten kings. Of *course* you would show up when it's in the middle of a hush cycle. Only happens for one day every thousand years, you know. That means all you had to contend with were Rone's prepubescent stable boys and a herd of night-mares! A veritable walk in the park!"

"Oh yeah, *real* easy."

Hawk had stepped out of the kitchen. "Did someone say a herd of night-mares?"

"Hawk!" I exclaimed. "You're here!"

"Yes, yes." he snapped. "Our intrepid bootmaker was kind enough to *thaw* me after he was sure of your cooperation. I've just been inside talking to Rellik." His face went slightly pale, and he placed a hand over his gut. "Makes me sick to think of him down there, all these years, following me around like some amnestic[94] puppy. Man still can't remember a thing, but I am hopeful Gladstone will be able to assist him. Memory is a special hobby of his, you know."

I gasped, thinking of the little book I had in the turncoat—or rather, in my mindhold—the one that Gladstone said might be the key to fixing his memory machine. "Why didn't I think of that?"

"I expect, because your wit is inherently inferior to my own. Or perhaps you were simply distracted by a herd of night-mares. Is it true, then, that you saw such beasts? There have long been rumors that Rone has been breeding something fouler than bloodhounds."

"He sure is," I said. "We were there, at his home base, I guess, and— Wait, Hawk! We were *there* at his home base! His lair! I know where to find it! We can gather the circle and…" I trailed off.

Flint was shaking his head. "I'm afraid it won't be that simple," he said. "Rone will have been notified by now that you were there. If you went back, I suspect you would find nothing waiting for you there—except perhaps some trap

---

94 Also, *amnesic*. Suffering from amnesia (an inability to recall the past).

he has left behind. Rone is a very powerful wizard, and it is not beyond him to move his people, or even that castle if he wishes, abyss and all, to a more suitable location. He has done it before. This is the fourth or fifth resting place of the Vale of Nightmares in the last eight hundred years."

I glowered. "So it was all for nothing?"

"On the contrary!" Flint exclaimed. "You have the edge-shale. You do have it, don't you?" He held out his hand. "Give it to me, and I will make you another gift. One that may tip the balance of this war in your favor."

I reached into the mindhold and pulled it out. While Flint inspected it, Hawk inspected me. "Did you just do that without the help of the turncoat?" he demanded.

I sniffed. "No big deal."

"Ha-ha!" He clapped me on the back. "I *knew* you would succeed. Never doubted it! Tell me how it happened."

Flint was sniffing the edge-shale now. Apparently satisfied, he tossed it into the bubbling cauldron and took up his oar once more. I related the tale of my cliffside breakthrough to Hawk, who seemed beside himself at my success.

"Ah! Not the dramatic life-or-death scenario I had anticipated, I'll admit, but who can complain?"

I explained the other things I had done with the coat on our most recent adventure and pointed out that I had yet to successfully channel magic through the other knobs without turning them.

Rather than being disappointed, he seemed even more elated. "You are controlling it now! Quite masterfully, in

some instances. Trapping people in walls, forcing the effects of magic on others rather than yourself. That is *subtle* work!"

With a cry of triumph, Flint lifted the bit of edge-shale out of the cauldron. It had turned a bright silver color and was glistening in the sun. He hopped down from his stool and tossed the shale into the air. At first I thought he was trying to throw it on the ground, but a second before it finished falling, a forge appeared out of nowhere and caught it.

Flint stepped forward and kicked the door shut against the heat. He pulled on a thick pair of leather gloves that he plucked out of thin air, and a large iron anvil appeared before him, along with a rack of tools.

"Pick up those tongs, Drake," he ordered, and Drake pulled on gloves of his own before raising a long pair of heavy tongs. Flint instructed Drake to retrieve the edge-shale from the forge, and as my minotaur pal held it against the anvil, Flint went to work on it with cross pein hammers of various sizes, drawing the now metallic shale out and shaping it while Drake held it steady and rotated it as needed.

Meanwhile, Hawk was still pressing me with questions, and I had to tell him my "music" theory regarding hearing or feeling the location of the E8 knob to keep him satisfied.

"Music!" he said when I had finished. "An interesting comparison. Some scholars have postulated that magic flows out of us like light, in various wavelengths, though there is no known way to measure such things. It's possible

that part of the function of the turncoat is to teach you to distinguish between them consciously. Doubtless, a wizard who could do *that* could wield magical power differently than the rest of us. Gladstone will have a field day with this information..."

He went babbling to himself about magical theory nonsense, and I turned my attention to Flint, who had finished forging. He was now quenching the blade—for that was most certainly what he was making. He took the tongs from Drake and stepped back to the cauldron. Behind him, the forge, anvil, and tools vanished into thin air. He lowered the glowing blade tip down into the mixture, and there was a popping hiss. Then he took the blade in his hands, tossed the tongs away, and sat down at a grinding wheel which, as usual, materialized in front of him at just the right moment.

"If he can conjure all this stuff up," I whispered to Hawk, "why does he have to make the knife at all? Why can't he just think it up?"

"No amount of whispering will prevent me from hearing you while you stand inside my own mind, Simon Fayter," Flint said without taking his eyes from the blade, which was now sparking as he shaped and sharpened it.

"Inside your..." I began, then forgot what I was saying. I remembered being inside the turncoat, inside my mindhold. There, it seemed, I could do anything. Make anything happen. Conjure stuff out of thin air.

"That's right," Flint said. "I hear your thoughts rounding the corner. I may have misled you slightly,

with my earlier display of my creative abilities. I have them, it is true, but nobody could sustain such elaborate manifestations for long. Not in the real world, anyway. You are in my *mindhold*, Simon. Haven't you wondered why Hawk, one of the most powerful wizards alive, has, without complaint, allowed me to hold him captive, send his student on dangerous errands, and more or less do as I please?"

"Uh…no," I admitted. "But yeah. Now that you mention it, that doesn't make sense."

Hawk rolled his eyes.

"It is because he knows he is trapped in my mindhold, a place you cannot leave without express permission, and a place in which I am *god*, so to speak. He could, if he so desired, retreat into his *own* mindhold, at which point our minds, our *souls*, one inside the other, would vie for dominance in a spectacular and—for one of us—no doubt fatal display of willpower and pure magic."

"Killing you all in the process," Hawk added.

"Very likely," Flint agreed.

"Unless I entered *mine* at the same time and joined Hawk in the struggle," I said.

Flint went suddenly pale.

"Whoa," Drake said, swooning with fascination.[95]

Hawk clamped my shoulder in a firm grip. "Don't," he said. "The mind does not function normally in such

---

95 Most people swoon with love, or perhaps nausea. Only *Drake* could manage to swoon with fascination.

a state, and you are not prepared for it. You would very likely kill all of us before you figured out which way is up. Pure magic states are highly volatile[96] and extremely dangerous." He glared at Flint. "Which is why wise old men do not bandy[97] such information about so recklessly."

"Hey, I want to figure out how to use my mindhold!" Drake said. "How come everyone knows but me?"

"*I* don't know either, doofus," Tessa said.

"Don't feel bad, Drakus," Hawk said. "It takes years to master."

"Yeah, Drake," I said. "It takes *years* to master. Don't try to compare yourself to me."

Tessa smacked me.

"It is finished," Flint said. He leaned back from the grinding wheel and tossed the now-gleaming blade into the air. It turned over once, and when he caught it again, the tang of the blade was set into a white bone handle.

He flipped it around and offered it hilt first to Tessa. "This is made from shale-steel," he said. "Forged from the same material that Rone makes his domination codexes from. It will be useful in breaking the chains that bind your foes."

"Wait a minute," Drake said. "Gladstone said codexes are frathenoid objects and can only be destroyed or altered by their creator."

"That is partially true," Flint agreed. "You will not be

---

96 Subject to sudden, unpredictable changes.
97 Give out freely, like it's no big deal.

able to completely destroy their power. Not until Rone is dead, I think, will his codexes completely cease to hold sway over their captives. However, this blade will allow you to *interrupt* them. To damage the codexes and release the captives from the brunt of his influence."

He waved the blade impatiently, and Tessa took it. "Me?" she said.

"Oh, yes, I think so. They will remember you as a liberator, someday. Simon here has more gadgets than he can handle, Hawk has his own sword, and the Tike seems more adept at...other things. Drake, of course, will have his hands full."

He clapped Drake on the shoulder. "There is much fighting to come, I'm afraid, and you will need something more than a slingshot." He twirled his hand and was suddenly holding the long, heavy minotaurian war staff that Drake had drooled over earlier. He held it out to my big friend carefully. "It is smaller than Bloodweeper was," he told Drake, "but then you are no Godlok Stonehand. I think you will find that it suits you."

Drake took it, open-mouthed. "I..." he floundered. "I...I..."

"Yes, yes. You're welcome." He turned to me and reached into the pocket of his overalls again. He drew the bloodstone out and slapped it into my hand. "I've decided I don't want to see what happens next," he said. "I have seen the fall of one Fayter, and I'll not witness a second. I am removing myself from this venture completely. Should you succeed, perhaps my life will not have been such a

waste. Should you fail, I hope never to hear of it. Take it and go."

He made his way slowly back toward the door that led into his kitchen. "Now!" he said over his shoulder. "Get out of my mind."

I glanced at Hawk, who looked uncertain. "But," I said, "maybe you could—"

"I have honored my father's wishes," Flint said. "I have helped Rellik, and you, his heir, as much as I am willing to. The rest of the fight is yours. The last piece of advice I will give you is to not underestimate Gladstone. For a Seer, he is a difficult man to see clearly…"

He paused in the doorway. His son came forward, and Flint lifted the child into his arms. "Goodbye, Simon Fayter, and good luck. I waited a long time to help you, but now that is over. You will never see me again." He nodded respectfully to Tessa and the Tike. "Master Hawk, if your life ever gets back to normal, you will need to find a new bootmaker. I am officially tendering my resignation. Now, get out of my mind!"

He flicked his hand, and the whole valley seemed to ripple with waves. They swept us away from him and then high into the air. There was no fear of falling, for it was the ground—the green earth somehow became liquid—that was moving us. It tossed us into the sky, and I closed my eyes against the light of the sun. When I opened them, I was lying on the floor of the boot shop. Drake, Tessa, Hawk, Rellik, and the Tike lay beside me.

The Tike regained her feet first, scanning the room. I joined her a moment later and couldn't help checking the door at the back. It opened to reveal a long narrow workshop full of storage boxes and dusty tools.

"I guess he's gone for good," Drake said. "Strange that he didn't make you fulfill your third task."

"Get the bloodstones from Gladstone?" I said. "I'm going to do that anyway. What else would I do next?"

Drake shrugged. "I'm just saying. It's weird."

"Yeah," I said, not really listening. I was thinking about the bloodstones. If Gladstone summoned the Circle of Eight and took back the bloodstones they held, I would have forty-eight, missing only the one that Rone had taken from Bartholomew and the one he had recovered from his own tomb. "Forty-eight,"[98] I murmured aloud. If having a bloodstone in the E8 pocket had taught me to use the mindhold, how fast would my power grow with *forty-eight*?

Hawk nodded. "The Circle can search out Rone

---

98 Why on EARTH is 4 spelled *four*, and 48 spelled *forty*-eight? Where did the u go? Why don't we just spell 4 *for* all the time? Y not? Whatever for (4)? By the way, in case you were wondering, the above *is* the correct spelling of the letter you (U), and *you* is the incorrect spelling of the letter u, but the correct spelling of the word *you*. If you ever wondered what the correct names of letters are (you probably haven't, because only crazy, sleep-deprived writers worry about things like that, but I'm going to tell you anyway), here is an alphabet of names: a, bee, cee, dee, e, eff, gee, aitch, I, jay, kay, el, em, en, o, pee (my favorite), cue, ar, ess, tee, u, vee, double-u (how silly is that? I would have gone for *dubbleyew*), ex, wye, and zee (or zed, if you live outside the United States). You're welcome.

together. We will have to take the last two from him by force, I think."

"Maybe," I said. "He does want me to have them, though. He can't use the turncoat himself."

"He wants you to have them on *his* terms," Drake said. "I doubt he'll just hand them over."

"You never know," I said cheerfully. I flung open the door and breathed in the warm summer air.

"You have done well in coming this far, Simon." Hawk said, helping Rellik to his feet.

Drake was counting the bloodstones off on his fingers, quoting Rellik's instructions to us just to make sure. "The one I hid on Daru, you already found. Two I have hidden in my past—one with the person who crafted the item that destroyed me (that's the one we got from Flint), and one with the person who led my brother into evil (that's the one we got in Tarinea). The fourth I have hidden in your past and my future. It is in the last place that Rone would ever look for anything (Rellik's tomb. He found that one first.)."

"High time to reunite the collection, don't you think?" I strode into the cobblestone street, not thinking of Rone frantically moving his secret hideout. Not thinking of the monsters he had made, the wizards he had enslaved, or what he had planned for them. Not thinking about how forty-eight was not the same as fifty. I was thinking only that I had done all that I could, and the rest would figure itself out, as it always did.

"Come on, guys," I said. "Last one to Gladstone's office is a rotten egg."

EYES OF STONE

For we wrestle not against flesh and blood, but against principalities, against powers, against the rulers of the darkness of this world, against spiritual wickedness in high places.

—Ephesians 6:12

Rotten eggs notwithstanding, Gladstone's office was not our first stop. Magical heroes like myself are well served by surrounding themselves with older, wiser advisors—particularly of the female variety—and even weller[99] served when they *take* the advice of said chiquitas.

And so it was that, newly possessed of a tool to break the magical bonds of the Fallen, they made it clear to me that my first priority was to visit the Fallen we had imprisoned right here at Skelligard.

I pushed open the door to McKenzie's cell and entered, calling her name softly. She rose from the chair in which she had been sitting and faced me, one hand resting on the back. As far as cells go, it was a comfortable one, looking more like a cushy one-room cottage than a cell—

---

99 Not a word.

unless you counted the barred windows, locked doors, and magical restraints she wore.

During my previous visits, she had been wearing a long-sleeved sweater, but today she had no sleeves, and I noticed that precautions had been taken against her using magic. The Circle of Eight did not have to resort to drastic measures to restrict her magic use as Rone had done in burning Rellik's body along the meridian points, but now that I was familiar with the concept, I recognized what looked like little brown henna tattoos running up and down her arms, along her throat, and out of sight beneath her shirt. She was imprisoned in more ways than one.

It had been a few weeks since my previous visit, and I was shocked to see how thin she had become. "Haven't you been eating?" I asked. There was food on the table, but it was untouched. Apparently she had been just sitting there staring at it. As always, she looked at me with a sort of tired hatred and said nothing.

I stepped aside, and Tessa entered, followed by Drake and Hawk. The Tike stood guard at the door while Rellik struck up a polite conversation with one of the guards on the subject of the best way to cook eggs.

"Is Rone making you starve yourself to death?" I asked McKenzie bluntly.

Again, she said nothing.

"Go ahead, Tessa," I said.

Tessa drew the silver knife from her belt and stepped forward. McKenzie went pale.

"I'm not going to hurt you," Tessa assured her, but McKenzie was not calmed. She went rigid, knuckles going white on the back of the chair. The little symbols on her skin flashed, but nothing else happened. She closed her eyes as Tessa brought the knife to her neck.

Tessa used the tip of it to lift the delicate gold chain free of McKenzie's shirt. Then she slashed at it, and the chain broke.

McKenzie collapsed and would have fallen to the floor if Hawk hadn't sped forward, Superman style, and caught her. Then she was laughing. Laughing and crying, and laughing again. She threw her arms around Tessa's neck. "You did it!" she said. "How did you ever break that chain?"

"Trade secret," I said, drawing her attention.

Her smile vanished when she looked at me, replaced by something…else. Her eyes went vacant for a second, as if she had temporarily forgotten who she was. She clenched her hands into fists. Then she relaxed again. "Sorry. He's still in my head."

"We suspect Rone's influence will endure until he is destroyed," Hawk said gently.

She nodded, moving to stand in front of a mirror in the corner. She inspected herself as if meeting a stranger, then ran a shaking hand across her face. "He's still in there. But…it's like I don't have to do what he wants anymore. I can choose not to."

"Good," Hawk said, breathing a sigh of relief. "What

about him? Is he still aware of you and your surroundings?"

"Not really," she said. "I think he gets glimpses, but it's not like before." She stood in front of me then, and held out her hand. "Sorry about all that business on Daru. I wasn't myself."

"And are you yourself now?" Drake asked.

All eyes fell on him, and he looked embarrassed. "Sorry. I'm just saying…if I had been forced to do the bidding of an evil master for years, I think it would change me. How do we know she can be trusted now?"

"No," McKenzie said, returning to the mirror. "I don't expect I'll ever be myself again. Not really. Certainly I'll never be the person I was going to be before *this* happened. I can't close my eyes without feeling the hate that drives him. I still feel it as if it is my own. But it's *not* my own. I did horrible things! Some of them he made me do, but some of them I did…because of what he made me into…"

Hawk patted her on the shoulder but said nothing. What *could* you say? Everyone was looking at me again. Looking at me as though *I* would know what to say. Why did they do that? It's not like being the most important and powerful person in the world comes with instant wisdom! Or did it?

I cleared my throat and turned B2 (*Silvertongue*). "Give yourself time," I said. "And be forgiving. Cling to hope, and never think that the bad things inside you will win. The roots of darkness in this world are doomed to fall beneath the ax of fate."

If the others thought my words uncharacteristically wise (or ridiculously pretentious), they said nothing about it during the walk to Gladstone's office. No doubt they knew that I'd simply turned the knob and let the magic do its thing. It really wasn't me at all, if you thought about it.

And yet, I knew that wasn't strictly true. It *was* me. I was beginning to feel that now, as Hawk said I would. The more I used the magic, the more familiar it felt. Even the wisdom of those words had felt like mine, as if they had escaped from some secret, undiscovered chamber of my mind. I was beginning to think that Hawk had been right all along—about the magic being mine, and that my deep mind knew how to use it. That the turncoat was just a shortcut, training wheels until I figured out how to access my power directly.

So lost in thought was I as we walked, that I nearly ran headlong into Gladstone. He was waiting for us at the bottom of the stone steps that led up to his office, arms folded, expression serious. His left eye was light gray. His right one, brilliant white.

"You have finished your task," he said. It wasn't a question, but I nodded anyway. A flicker of fear touched his face and was gone the same instant. He exhaled slowly. "Good…good. Come with me." The others fell in line

behind me, and we followed Gladstone up the long stone steps.

A minute later, I laid the three bloodstones on his desk. It was hard setting them down, and as soon as I did, I felt like I wanted nothing more than to pick them back up again. "Rone got one of them," I admitted. "He got there first somehow. It's a long story…"

Gladstone nodded. "To be expected, I suppose."

"And he still has Bartholomew's," Drake said. "So we only have forty-eight."

"Mmm. You did the right thing in coming anyway," Gladstone said. "We will unite what we have for now, and then we shall see."

"See what?" I asked.

Gladstone laughed. "Why, what comes next, of course! That is what being a Seer is all about." Gladstone opened the secret bookcase and started lining the other stones up on his desk beside my three. Hawk helped him. Pretty soon we had thirty-nine.

"Summon the Circle, Simon," Gladstone said, taking a step back from the desk and easing himself into his chair.

"Me?" I said.

"Certainly. Did you think that *I* remained the leader of the Circle after the return of the Fayter?"

His words stunned me.

"Didn't you tell him, Hawk? Good heavens, man. What have you been teaching him?"

"*Useful* things," Hawk snapped. "His head is big

enough without me putting things like *that* into it before completely necessary."[101]

"Hold your codex," Gladstone instructed. "Tell them to come."

I pulled the medallion out from beneath my shirt and gripped the warm metal. "Come," I whispered self-consciously. Nothing happened. I glanced up at Gladstone. "Do I have to say please or something?"

He smiled.

The air around the room shimmered, and five wizards appeared out of thin air. Five wizards and a dugar, that is. Atticus swore, wiping blood from his gleaming blade, which was still raised before him. Finnigan was crouched in a fighting posture, hair standing straight up along his back.

"I was busy, Gladstone," Atticus grunted. "I hope this interruption is worth the loss of life you just caused."

Gladstone pointed at me, and Atticus's rage dissipated. "Ah."

Tinnay was there. She looked tired but winked at me all the same. Soren looked me up and down with her sad eyes. She was a tall, thin woman with a squeaky voice. By comparison, Martaes was round and happy. She took my hand and shook it, apparently unbothered by my rudely interrupting whatever she had been doing a moment

---

100 I hope you are sensing a pattern here. Geez, Hawk! Get real, man! Remember how when the wise old teacher holds back valuable information from his daring/handsome understudy, it always leads to disaster?! Except, of course, when it prevents disaster…

before. Braccus, tall and dark-skinned, was naked to the waist and dripping wet. Evidently he had been bathing. He pointed at one of Gladstone's curtains, and it flew off the wall, fashioning itself into a fitted tunic, which he donned.

"The time has come, my friends," Gladstone said, addressing the Circle. "The Fayter requires that which you have long kept safe."

Hawk came forward first. He lifted his codex free of his clothing and plucked the black stone out of its setting in the center of the swords and tree. I had seen it, an age ago, it now seemed, and thought nothing of it at the time. When it came free, the stone faded from black to red, and he nodded to me as he set it on Gladstone's desk beside the rest.

Atticus came forward next, then Tinnay, Soren, Martaes, and Braccus. Last of all, Gladstone removed his own bloodstone and laid it on the table. "Forty-eight," he said.

"And the last two?" Atticus asked.

"Rone has them," I said.

"Then the time has come for us to face him together," Tinnay said. "We will hunt him to the edge of the universe if need be, and take what is yours."

"Rone does not have them," Gladstone said. "Not technically." He reached into a pocket and drew out the last two bloodstones. He held them up, then tossed them on the desk.

"Fish gills," Drake swore.

"Heaven's above, Gladstone," Soren squeaked.

"However did you come by those?"

"At great personal cost," Gladstone said. He held up his hands at the outburst of questions and surprise. "We shall leave it at that, for the time being."

My mind was racing. How could he possibly have gotten the stones back from Rone without anyone knowing?

"Now, Simon, put them in the coat, will you? We have all been waiting long enough. Some of us, a very, *very* long time."

I gulped. "I'm not ready," I blurted. "I don't even know how this is supposed to work!"

"Few are ready to face their fate when it comes suddenly upon them," Atticus said. My old teacher gave me a significant look. "One simply does one's best."

I glanced at my friends, who looked almost as shocked as I felt. The Tike was calm as ever. She nodded once. *You can do it,* the look said. *Man up.*

I gritted my teeth and reached into my pocket, touching the sorrowstone one last time. The anxiety left me, draining out like water from sand. I nodded to myself and picked up the stone closest to me. The time had come. Whatever would be, would be. I placed it in the A1 pocket and snapped the closure shut. I did it again and again with the other stones, and as I did, the coat seemed to hum, though the humming wasn't a sound at all. More like a feeling inside me, a rapid heartbeat I had not noticed before. A minute later, all fifty pockets held bloodstones, and the coat was heavy, thrumming with

power. I instinctively wanted to reach for it, but I wasn't sure where to begin.

Drake came up beside me and put a hand on my shoulder. "Well?" he said.

I shrugged, speechless.

"Simon," Gladstone said, "before you do anything else, I would like my sorrowstone back." He held his hand out politely.

"Huh?"

"I'm rather attached to it," he said apologetically. "I'd very much like it back before you release your power and usher in Armageddon. I admit, I don't know what happens next any more than you do. I've never seen beyond this point." He wiggled his hand. "If you please."

"Oh," I said, reaching into my pocket. "Sure. I guess." I held it out, but Drake grabbed my wrist.

"Wait." His eyes flicked back and forth between me and Gladstone, then to the stone in my hand.

I tugged at him. "What?"

"No," Drake whispered. "No, no… How could I be so stupid? Broca's sorrowstone."

"Broca's…" I echoed, and my stomach lurched as everything fell into place. This was Broca's sorrowstone. The *same* stone, he had said. The very same stone. And he had thought *he* was the one who sent me back to the past. Was he? Could Gladstone be Broca? Or had his apprentice inherited the stone? But that would mean—

Gladstone snatched the stone out of my hand, and immediately I felt my mind tip sideways. Of course, you

as the reader can see what I could not. You heard Rellik in the prologue: "He gives a gift, a harmless object. And just by touching it, you become his." But I did not know such things back then; many details of Rone's treachery had been long since forgotten.

"Simon," Hawk said, grabbing my other arm. I flashed with rage at his touch, my mind spinning like a red-hot poker. I pulled power through the humming bloodstones. B6 and C9 (*Strength* and *Mass*), and planted a double-fisted punch in Hawk's gut with all my might. He flew across the room and smashed against the bookcase, breaking several shelves. He fell in a heap on the floor and didn't even twitch as books cascaded down on him.

I looked in horror at what I had done. I knew *I* had done it, but I couldn't remember choosing to. Is this what it was like to be controlled by Rone?

Something massive shifted in my mind, drawing my attention to the turncoat, which was still humming with magical energy. *Potential* energy, I realized. That's what it really was. A thought slipped into my mind, an idea about how to activate all the stones at once. What would happen if I did? I forgot about my friends then, the danger of the present situation. All I felt was curiosity.

The Tike stepped up beside me then, and in one fluid motion, she placed two fingers at the edge of my jaw and bumped my temple with her opposite palm.

My nervous system spiked lightning from my heels to the crown of my head, and I blacked out. What happened next, I only know from secondhand accounts, since I was

drooling on the floor after that, completely unconscious.

Tessa screamed and leaped at Gladstone, actuating her cram cudgel and aiming for his head. Drake charged as well, horns lowered for the kill.

Gladstone got Drake first, hit him with a blast of light that dropped him like a bag of bones next to Hawk. He wasn't dead, but he was pretty close. Gladstone sidestepped Tessa's attack. He picked her up with both hands and lifted her high, then slammed her down, back first, onto the top of his desk, breaking all four legs and shoving her right to the floor. Blood leaked from her nose, and her head lolled to one side. He patted her on the head and took the codex from around his neck and placed it carefully over hers.

Finnigan bellowed in rage and charged, but Gladstone raised his hand, and the dugar's fur burst into flames. He screamed and ran straight through the door, lurching down the steps two at a time.

Nobody noticed the Tike disappear into the shadows. She later told me that the way forward was unclear, and when wizards fight, it is best for more normal folks to wait for the appropriate moment to strike.

"How long has he owned you, Gladstone? I would not have thought he was powerful enough to control a mind such as yours." Atticus summoned his swords, and they flamed white and red in his hands. His face was a mask of anger, no doubt worried for Finnigan, as well as the rest of us. The other knights followed suit, drawing their own blades. The knights were surrounding Gladstone now, the tips of their flaming swords pointed at the man who had

been their leader moments before.

"From the beginning. He *is* powerful, Atticus," Gladstone sounded almost as if he were pleading for a moment, then recovered. "And he doesn't just own me. *I* made the codexes, remember? Those long years ago, when we re-formed the Circle?"

Atticus glanced down at the silver medallion hanging from his neck and paled, no doubt thinking of the similar objects worn by those who had been enslaved by Rone.

"He owns you already," Gladstone spat. "He's just never made you feel it. But now he will, Atticus. Now he will." He closed his eyes and looked heavenward, spreading his arms as if in complete surrender. When he opened his eyes again, they no longer belonged to him.

The knights brought their swords back to strike. It was Rone's voice they heard next. That terrible, haunting blend of a myriad voices. "You are *mine.*"

The knights all froze mid-thrust. The medallions around their necks had begun to glow with a pale light. Their swords trembled. Some inched toward Gladstone. Others dipped to the floor.

"Fight!" Drake cried. "Fight him! Don't give in!"

"You," Atticus said with great difficulty, "have... made...a...m-mistake, Rone."

"Yes," Braccus spoke up. He seemed to be speaking his own mind with less difficulty, though he still couldn't move; his was one of the swords that had dipped to the floor. "You cannot hold the five of us at once."

"You're right," Rone said through Gladstone's mouth.

Gladstone twisted, summoning his own flaming sword. Before he could strike, Tinnay leaped forward and cut off his sword hand. Then she shivered, screamed, and plunged her sword through Soren's chest. To execute their own will, they had to let down their guard, and Rone was making them pay for it.

Atticus and Braccus ran Gladstone through the heart from either side. Before he could crumple to the ground, Tinnay was on her feet again. Her eyes were wide and vacant. She dropped her sword and opened both palms. Strands of black fire burst out of them, seething, writhing around her forearms like snakes, until her whole body was covered.

"NO!" Atticus cried, but it was too late.

She flung herself at Martaes, tackling the other woman in a full-body hug, and soon they were both covered in the devouring black fire. They ran toward the stone wall of the tower, still clinging to each other. Flames dripped off them as they went, turning a chair to ash, burning a hole through the floor. When they reached the stone wall, the black fire ate that too, and they tumbled into the night.

Atticus and Braccus faced each other. Neither moved. Neither spoke. Their swords neat at their sides. The controlling will that had been spread across six wizards before, now bore down on the two of them alone.

Tessa stirred on the desktop, rising to her feet with un-Tessa-like[101] grace. She caressed the codex that she now

---

101 Not a word.

wore, cracked her neck, and picked up her cudgel. A dark, silent form dropped from the rafters and landed behind her. The Tike wrapped her legs around Tessa's and twisted her whole body, moving like a crocodile in a death roll, with Tessa as her prey.

Tessa toppled to the floor, and the Tike sprang onto her. She laid two fingers across Tessa's jaw, bumped her forehead with the other palm, and Tessa went limp. The Tike lifted Flint's knife from Tessa's belt and walked to the two men. She cut the chain around Atticus's neck. Then she freed Braccus. The two men shuddered. Atticus ran to the hole in the wall that Tinnay and Martaes had passed through, and Braccus dropped to one knee, checking Soren's pulse.

"She is gone," he said. "What of the others?"

Atticus returned from the wall, shaking his head. "In their right minds, they could have saved themselves from such a fall, but I believe the nightflame consumed them even as they passed from our sight.

"Igninoctis," Braccus spat. "I didn't know Tinnay was even capable of summoning such a thing."

"Capable, yes," Atticus said wearily. "Willing, no."

"But Rone was willing," Braccus said.

"And now we will see what else he is willing to do," Atticus said, nodding to me.

Just then, I stirred. I blinked my eyes, trying to remember

where I was. Even as I opened my eyes, the weight of Rone's mind came crashing into my own. He barreled through my thoughts, my feelings, my desires, like a bear through a glass forest, shattering as he went. In one breath, he absorbed all of my memories of the past week. All my plans, my power, my knowledge of the turncoat.

Then he was gone.

I got to my feet and shook my head. It was pounding. The turncoat was covered with dust. I brushed it off and felt the hum of power roll over me like a renewing wave. I froze at the shock of it, waiting for Rone to invade my mind, to force me to use it, but he didn't. I saw Hawk and Drake on the floor to my left. They were breathing. Not dead, then...

I closed my eyes in a prayer of thanks, then opened them to assess the rest of the damage. Soren *was* dead. And Gladstone. Tinnay and Martaes weren't in the room. There had been fighting. The Tike was okay. She was standing between Atticus and Braccus, and all three of them were looking at me as though I might kill them at any moment. I forced down a laugh. Imagine that. *Them* afraid of me. It was—

Tessa was on the floor. She wasn't moving.

I ran to her side. I picked her up in my arms.

"She's okay," the Tike told me. "I had to knock her out. She was going to kill Atticus. Here, Simon. Give her to me."

"Rone," I corrected coldly. "*Rone* was going to kill Atticus."

"Simon?" Atticus said carefully. They were all still watching me warily.

"Yeah," I said. "It's okay. It's me. He's gone."

"He will return," Braccus said.

"You have to take off the turncoat," Atticus said.

My temper flared at that. What a stupid idea. How would I fight Rone without the turncoat?

"Quickly," Atticus said. "Take it off and give it to me."

"Do what he says, Simon." The Tike raised her hand, and I saw Flint's knife. My temper flared again, and I did not see the codex around Tessa's neck. I didn't see that the Tike was trying to free her. All I saw was my friend, my closest ally, the *Tike*, afraid of *me*, and raising a weapon.

And it was all *his* fault.

My teacher and my best friend lay unconscious on the floor behind me—partially my own doing. And it was all *his* fault.

Gladstone and Soren and Martaes and Tinnay were all dead, and it was all *his* fault.

Tessa was unconscious, bleeding, and it was all *his* fault.

"Rone," I whispered. His name tasted like poison. My heart contracted. I saw red. My mind screamed in fury, consuming all thought until it broke, searching for vengeance, for fire, for fuel to burn. The turncoat hummed with power, a noisy, throbbing portal to my magic, and I devoured it with the fervor of a starving lion. I pulled at the power, wrenched it through the fifty little openings

that the bloodstones showed me, and set my hatred free. The stone beneath my feet melted. Books burst into flame on the shelves beside me. My face blazed with the light of the sun, and the Tike stumbled backward.

"NO, SIMON!" Atticus screamed, but I could not hear him. I could hear only the throb of hot blood in my ears, the throb of Rone's heart, ten million miles away.

I knew where to find him. I could see the path, a straight line from my brain to the place where he sat, waiting for my arrival. He knew I was coming for him. He was foolish not to run. I raised my hands and blew the top of the tower away in a pillar of light, opening my path to the sky.

Atticus was pulling the others toward the edge of the room. The walls were melting away. He jumped out with them, soaring down beyond my sight. But my eyes were fixed on my path. I flew upward at the speed of light. I *was* light. I was something more. I burned out of the atmosphere, and then out of the galaxy.

Later, when people told stories about it, they would say the sound was like the earth cracking in half. They would say women screamed, and grown men wept for fear, and the grass withered in the heat. They would say that one day, long ago, without warning, Skelligard gave birth to a star that nearly destroyed everything in its violent climb toward heaven.

I had gone a million miles in a breath. Then two million. Three. Four. But it was far too slow, so I opened a portal and stepped into the room where Rone sat waiting.

I didn't know how I worked such magic. Hows[102] were far beneath me. I was pure power. Pure creation.

I stepped into Atticus's old living room, across the street from the house where I grew up. An odd choice, but sort of poetic, if you liked irony. This would end where it began. The man who smiled at me from Atticus's chair was not Atticus, though. He was thin and old. The wheat-blond hair that had graced him in boyhood was an empty field now, long since laid bare by the reaper's blade. Time had cut sharp lines into his face too. His heavy eyelids drooped, but the eyes behind them looked much the same as they had ages before, when the boy Tav wore them.

"Hello, Simon," Rone said, and for once his voice was the single, raspy note of an old man. "I see you've brought Tessa. How thoughtful."

I glanced down and was shocked to see her still in my arms. "Oh no," I said.

"Oh yes," he said. "Lay her down on the couch."

I did as he commanded.

Now come back, his voice was in my mind, and again I did as prompted. *Good,* he thought in my head. *You came here to fight me, I know. But you won't fight me, will you, Simon?*

"No," I said. I knew it was true. How could I fight him here? He wasn't just in my mind, like he had been before. This was something much more imposing. There was no resisting him. I was a part of him now.

---

102 Technically not a word.

Do you know where we are?

"We're in your mindhold," I said.

That's right. You should be more careful about where you choose to step. We're in this little house that looks just like Atticus's house, where your journey started. And that house is inside the Vale of Nightmares, which, due to your little stunt, I have had to move to a more secure location for the time being. The most secure location there is. My mindhold. As we speak, I am walking along a pleasant country lane, and I am also here with you. You and I have a lot of work to do, Simon. I couldn't be happier with how things turned out. You used that sorrowstone so much. I had bonded my consciousness with the stone quite completely, of course, before my puppet gave it to you. Every time you let it eat your emotions and feed your soul, you were opening doors to me and binding us together. This really couldn't have turned out any better. We're in my mindhold, Simon. And in here, I am god.

I nodded. I felt pleased that he was happy.

He stood and put an arm around my shoulder. "Why don't we get started?"

"Of course," I said. I reached through the bloodstones for my power and pulled it out in one united flow, weaving the bloodstones back together in the rush. It was as easy as tying my shoes.

The entire universe condensed before me in the form of a glowing, golden-red orb—a single bloodstone, unified once more.

"Go on in," Rone whispered in my ear. "We need to make some changes."

I cocked my head, and the orb lengthened, forming itself into a door of light. I smiled at it and stepped through.

Men should never be given the power of gods. Not before they are ready. That is what I learned upon entering the bloodstone. It was a portal into the beating heart of all that is. The place where changes are made. It was the mindhold of the universe itself, and when I entered, I was god. I knew everything, I saw all ends. I could change anything, create anything, anywhere, any time—past, present, or future. It was all before me.

I stood on a golden walkway, suspended in the midst of space, all the galaxies of the universe sparkling beneath me like lightning bugs on the water of creation. I touched one—the Milky Way galaxy. The Solar System. Earth. They expanded before me like a holographic pop-up book, and then I was in everything. All life on Earth was part of one big invisible hive mind, with me at the center, and the moment-to-moment experience of each person, each ant, each leaf on each tree, was as real to me as my own right hand. I could change anything, if I wanted. It would be as easy as flexing my fingers. The bloodstone had become my portal to power, my eyes of stone to see all that was.

I closed the celestial pop-up book and turned. Rone

was standing beside me. He stood in darkness, I knew. He could not see what I saw. Not through his own eyes, at least. And yet his influence remained in my mind.

"Change it," he said. "Give me the power to touch all five branches of magic. Make me a god among men."

As he said it, I felt myself wanting to do it. It felt like my own idea. My own desire. But it wasn't. That much was clear in here. He had influence, and he *might* be able to force me to do his will, but *here* I could put up a fight.

"Sure," I said. "*Or*, I could do this…" I pointed my finger at him, thumb upraised in the universal gun symbol used by children, and shot ten thousand comets at his face. His head exploded, and his body toppled into the universal soup, but unfortunately he reappeared a second later, looking livid.

He gripped my face in both of his hands and screamed at me, overwhelming my mind by brute force. My own thoughts faded away. My wants. My memories. My identity. I felt his lust for power, his deep need to be above everything and everyone. To have what they did not. To make the universe his plaything. I felt the power within me to make that happen, and I reached for it.

The golden path upon which I stood split into six bands of light. The six branches of magic, I knew. I wove them into one and folded it up into a ball. If I handed him this, shoved it inside his chest, he would become what I was. I would become like everyone else. He would be happy.

I was halfway to doing it when something deep inside me awakened. This wasn't right. I wasn't the pawn of some

old, mentally deranged, megalomaniacal[103] wizard.

The *something* deep inside spoke my name like a clarion call.

Simon Fayter.

Yes. I was the Fayter. This was the moment where I stood up and triumphed. That was the task that no one else could do. And I did it.

I dropped the light, and it became the path beneath our feet again. I smiled at Rone. "Nice try."

He screamed again and reached for my face, but I was too quick for him. I couldn't risk coming under his power like that again. Not here, here where I might undo everything. I reached through the turncoat for the only means of escape available to me. There was only one place to run. Hawk had said it was dangerous to enter your mindhold when you were inside someone else's mindhold. He warned that it was dangerous to enter pure magic states—whatever those were—and that it would likely kill me. But what choice did I have?

I channeled my power through the E8 knob and entered my mindhold. But I did not appear in the old clearing on Fluff as I had done when entering with Tessa last time. Hawk had been right. Something very strange happened when one mindhold opened inside of another. I didn't go anywhere. Or rather, I went to nowhere.

I was in a place of pure light. Or maybe pure darkness. Complete nothingness. All there was, was me.

---

103 Obsessed with one's own power.

And then something else appeared. Something that wanted to devour me. Rone, of course. We weren't people there, we were *forces*. Pure energies. I was love and friendship, hope and ignorance, childish whimsy, humor, and regular old-fashioned humanity. He was hate and envy, jealousy and rage, loneliness, lies and oppression. Violence manifested in pure form.

Our warring body-minds raged against each other in waves, our hands crashing together in a froth of fire and water, our legs were a thousand incomprehensible monsters. Nothing existed but us, and we could *not* coexist. One of us had to lose. One of us had to yield to the power of the other or die. I had fate on my side, of course, and youthful vigor. Not to mention good luck, good looks, and good reasons.

But Rone had a thousand years of bottled rage, a mind honed by centuries of study and practice, and an iron will the likes of which I had simply not lived long enough to develop. I know this is the part of the story where the hero is supposed to come through with a clever win, where everything is supposed to turn out good and end on a high note, but the plain fact is, I lost.

I lost big time.

13

PRISONER

Despair is only for those who see the end beyond all doubt.
We do not.
—J.R.R. Tolkien, *The Fellowship of the Ring*

I woke up on the floor of Atticus's house. Rone was sitting in the easy chair. The bloodstone, now a single semitransparent orb the size of a basketball, sat in his lap. Tessa, with the gleaming silver codex around her neck, was serving him lunch on one of Atticus's silver tea trays.

I got to my feet.

"Sandwich?" Rone said, offering me a triangle.

"No thanks."

"You sure?" he said. "It's the last chance you'll get to eat in...well, *ever*."

I put my hands in my pockets.

"Suit yourself."

"What are we going to do now?" I asked.

"Well," he said, "we've proved that I can't control you when you are acting as the Fayter." He gave me a polite nod. "We have also proved that you are no match for my will and power in a pure magic state, so we know you can't escape my mindhold."

He paused, considering. "I will strip you of your power, I think." He raised a claw-shaped hand and slashed downward in my general direction. Beams of light shot from his fingers and slashed the turncoat to shreds. He slashed again and ripped the shreds off of me. It felt like getting stabbed by fifty hot knives. I felt each place where the magic had touched my soul, each doorway, just recently opened, slam shut.

I collapsed to all fours, gasping for air. The pain was unbelievable, but more than that, I felt…wrong. Broken, suddenly, as if some essential part of my soul had dropped dead.

"There we go," Rone said. "That should give you some…perspective. I can restore your power, of course. And I assure you that's the only way you will be getting it back. But I will not do so without certain promises on your part. I'm sure you can imagine what the promises will be. There *are* ways, of course, for wizards to make promises to each other that they cannot break. Binding contracts. Those will do, when the time comes. You can restore me to power, and I will set you free to live like anyone else in my kingdom, provided you play nice. Of course, such contracts cannot be forced. You must enter into them of your own free will. So, it will be up to you when your imprisonment ends."

"My imprisonment?" I said.

"Of course. Oldest tool of persuasion there is. Stick a tiger in a hole alone, with nothing to eat, and eventually

he will be nothing more than a hungry kitten. He'll do anything you want."

"I'll never do what you want," I said.

Rone shrugged. "We'll see."

He drew a circle in the air with his finger, and a hole opened up in the living room floor. There was a long dirt-walled shaft beneath, going straight down.

"You're going to get quite hungry, you know," Rone said. "But you won't die. I won't allow it. I'm god in here, remember? You'll be thirsty too. And lonely, I expect, though you never know what dark things might appear out of my imagination in the middle of the night to play with you. Tessa, put your friend in his hole."

Tessa flashed me a wicked smile, devoid of her natural warmth. "There are worms in the walls, I am told. If you dig a little. We wouldn't want you to get *too* hungry."

Then she shoved me backward.

My prison is a pit three feet by five feet, thirty feet high. There is no light. There is no sound. There is no food or water. There is hunger and thirst, but death will not come. All my yelling is of little use. There is no food besides the worms that Tessa mentioned.

She was right about those. Sometimes you have to dig for them, and sometimes they seem to come up for air, resting on the surface of the dirt-packed wall for a while— ripe fruit waiting to be plucked and eaten. They are so

large that sometimes I fear that if I did not eat them, they might eat me. They don't taste that bad, as long as you don't think about what the crunchy bits are.

My friends are gone. Dead or lost or enslaved. My turncoat has been taken. The Circle of Eight is no more, though I hope Atticus, Hawk, and Braccus might have survived. There is no purpose for me now, beyond waiting upon the whims of a maniac. I failed my test, it seems, as my predecessor did before me. I can only think of how he knew he had failed and saw an heir in his future.

I have had no such vision. My failure has ended not with a promise of redemption, but with a cold and lonely silence. I am not bound. The soul points on my body are not guarded. They don't need to be. Rone knows as well as I do that in tearing the turncoat from me as he did, it injured me in some way. Ripped something out of me. Something that I cannot put back in. Something without which my magic is gone.

I'm not being a baby about this, I promise. I *have* tried. I have reached for the mindhold. It just isn't there anymore. I can't even conjure a fish or grow my beard out. I certainly cannot leap thirty feet or call down lightning. Someday, perhaps, my captor will get bored of waiting. He will pull me out of my pit and put the coat on me again. Likely, after years in this place—a decade or two of worms and water, silence and dirt—I will no longer possess the will to refuse him what he wants. If the turncoat works once more, he will eventually get his way, and all will be

lost. I do not look forward to the nightmares he promised to send me.

My prison is a pit three feet by five feet, thirty feet high. There is no light. There is no sound. There is no food or water.

There is no hope.

EPILOGUE

When I despair, I remember that all through history the ways of truth and love have always won. There have been tyrants and murderers, and for a time, they can seem invincible, but in the end, they always fall. Think of it—always.

—Mahatma Gandhi

"What happens now?"

Drake's voice rang out through the still night air, unheard by all but the distant stars, the singing crickets, and his three companions. Atticus, Finnigan, and Rellik huddled closer to the small snapping fire. The four of them constituted one half of a new Circle of Eight. A band of wizards with one purpose. The world had changed in a single day. Everywhere, Rone's forces were mobilizing. Taking over worlds, toppling governments, enslaving wizards by the household. But those were problems for other wizards tonight. Their only purpose was to find Simon.

"You mean how do we find him?" Atticus asked.

"I mean where do we even start looking?"

Atticus nodded. "The task is a daunting one."

"Impossible's more like it," Rellik chimed in. "Hopeless. Unreasonable. Insurmountable. Unviable. Outrageous.

Absurd. Ludicrous. My kind of mission."

"You can think of eight synonyms for *impossible*," Drake said, "but you can't remember Baum's basic principles of subatomic thermo-acceleration?"

"I can't remember how to build a fire with magic, if that's what you're trying to say, fuzzball. Ain't that a rub?"[104]

Drake glowered. "This isn't going to work."

"I said it was impossible. I didn't say it wouldn't work. Honestly, I wouldn't have agreed to be a part of your posse if I knew you were going to ignore all my advice." Rellik sniffed, considering. "Young man, if you live long enough, you will learn as I have, that when the impossible meets the indefatigable,[105] the result is often implausible."[106]

Finnigan rolled his massive shoulders thoughtfully. "Are you sure it was a good idea to bring him, Atticus?"

Rellik snapped a stick in half. "I'm right here, you know! I'm not dead, I just don't remember who I am."

"Same difference," Drake mumbled.

Atticus cleared his throat. "Where do *you* think we should begin our search, Drakus?"

Drake shrugged.

---

104 A significant difficulty. The phrase was made famous by Hamlet in his classic soliloquy (a soliloquy is a fancy word for a one-person conversation): "To be, or not to be"…blah blah blah…"To die, to sleep, perchance to Dream; aye, there's the rub, For in that sleep of death, what dreams may come…"
105 Tireless persistence.
106 Incredibly unlikely.

"No idea? Fine. How about you, Finnigan? No ideas either? The most powerful wizard alive has gone to ground, holding our friend—and the fate of the world—hostage. He might be in a hotel room in Paris, Earth, the Milky Way galaxy, or he might be hiding inside this pine nut!" He plucked a tiny nut from the collar of his robes and held it up for our inspection.

Rellik leaned forward and plucked the pine nut out of Atticus's hand. He tossed it into his mouth and swallowed. "Well, if he's in there, he's going to have a really weird day."

Atticus blinked and Finnigan burst into laughter.

Rellik still seemed to be thinking. "If my brother is as powerful and brilliant as you make him out to be, I would look somewhere beautiful. If he's smart, he has taken his whole kingdom and placed it in his mindhold. He is mobile. He is in disguise. He is an old man playing cards at the local tavern, or a young milkmaid working for a farmer. He is walking down a country lane somewhere, picking flowers for the old lady who lives in the cottage next door."

Atticus nodded. "Are there any previous known residences of Rone in the countryside or some other idyllic setting?"

"Little is known for sure about his whereabouts for much of his life. He is rumored to have lived in Avensheer for a time after he left Broca, but such rumors are plentiful and hard to substantiate."

"Perfect," Atticus said. "That is where we will begin our search." Atticus smiled at Drake and stoked the fire.

"*That* is why we brought him along."

Rellik grumbled. "Nonsense. You brought me along because you are secretly hoping that it takes a Fayter to find a Fayter. In that, I'm afraid, you are mistaken. I am telling you that whatever I was, long ago, I am not anymore. If this boy is found, it will be because he finds himself. It is his own power, not ours, that will free him." He gave a long, world-weary sigh. "That is how it always happens. People are their own worst enemies. Their own heroes."

Drake and Finnigan traded uneasy glances. Words like that, words that ring true and made your heart sing at the same time, were not welcome companions on a cold night.

Something snapped in the fire, sending a shower of sparks into the air, and Drake grinned. "Still," he said, "we have fate on our side. I mean, we're trying to save the *Fayter*, the executor of Fate's own will, correct? So fate itself should be on our side. I think we can expect some pretty good luck."

Atticus clapped him on the back. "That is a hopeful thought, Drakus. And well-reasoned." He looked up at the stars and wondered if his old pupil was somewhere, looking back. "A hopeful thought indeed."

ACKNOWLEDGEMENTS

Thank you to…

…My beta readers: Spencer Bowen, Spencer Bagshaw, and Hailey Walton.

…To God.

…And to my launch team, upon whom I depend:

Patti Anderson

April Angel

Sonia Arroyos

Terri Arturi

Candice Aucamp

Katie Babbit

Angel Barraza

Lydia Barron

Julie Bennett

Karen Bennett

Melanie Bessas

Jeanine Bevacqua

Bry Boler

Melissa Bonaparte

Rachel Bonnichsen

Randall Booth

Sofia Bostrom

Daniele Bourhis

Alisha Bowen

Riche Boyce

John Chasteen

Suzanne Christensen

Rachel Church

Amanda Comrie

Emma Curtis

Brandy Dalton

Janice David

Tom Davidson

Maureen Davlin

Bryan Deal

Brandy Emmert

Charlie Evans

Roger Fauble

Jennifer Firestone

Sarah Flint
Shannon Forslund
Danielle Foster
Jamie Francke
Sierra Furrow
Jennifer Fury
Bradley Gartin
Kisara Gibbons
Carmen Gomez
Daniel Grala
Mike Grant
Charlene Greene
Phil Gulbrandsen
Elva Guzman
Linda Hansen
Riley Harlan
Bruce Hastie
Shirley Holten
Claudia Howard
Jody Huffman
Sara Ingles
Krista Jasper
Bonnie Keck
Richard Kellerman
Manie Kilian
Emily Killgo
Keith Klayh
Jennifer Lapachian
Tiffany Lawrence

Georganne Lynch
Khyla Malone
Arisleny Martinez
John Maxim
Marilee McQuarrie
Veronica Meidus-Heilpern
Joyce Michelmore
Candace Miller
Michael Minkove
Becky Modderman
Mary Moffatt
James Morrow
Cathy Mulcahey
Shirlee Nicol
Debbie Nix
Anna Olsen
Daria Peterson
Eva Pontious
Isaac Reyes
Nicky Robinson
Angela Ross
Kari Schick
Britton Schwartz
Shelly Sessions
Crystal Shapiro
Michelle Shelton
Leena Smith
Lauren Smith
Eileen Smith

Jim Stavast

David Thorp

Aiden Tombuelt

Cheryl Torricer

Chelsea Tracy

Lana Turner

Stacey Valdez

Maria Wetherbee

Kelly Williams

Deidre Williams

Liz Wilson

Ron

Jeanine

Shari

Anna

Tanya

Robin

Karen

Made in the USA
Monee, IL
20 September 2023

43015790R00164